"SO YOU GOT THE MONEY?"

"Yes, Jamie," Sorrel nodded.

Just for once I was moved by genuine feeling towards her. Whether it was from gratitude, or from the brandy, I did not know, but I felt, not passionate, but warm and kind. So I put my arm round her shoulders and drew her even closer, and bent my head and kissed, first her forehead and then each of the eyelids which had closed as soon as I touched her. I would have released her then; but she gave a little cry and clung to me. And her body was like a closely coiled spring in my arms, and her mouth, hot and avid, sought mine.

But all I could think of was the money. The money that was now mine. . . .

Fawcett Crest Books
by Norah Lofts:

The
Brittle Glass

NORAH LOFTS

A FAWCETT CREST BOOK

Fawcett Publications, Inc., Greenwich, Connecticut

THE BRITTLE GLASS

THIS BOOK CONTAINS THE COMPLETE TEXT OF
THE ORIGINAL HARDCOVER EDITION.

A Fawcett Crest Book reprinted by arrangement with
Doubleday and Company, Inc.

ISBN 0-449-23037-6

Printed in the United States of America

10 9 8 7 6 5 4 3 2 1

The
Brittle Glass

PART ONE

Clear Glass of Affection

FOR nearly fifty years I had performed the tasks and carried out the duties which fall to the lot of the unmarried and not-quite-independent members of a large family. I had been present at births, and deathbeds, tended numerous cases of sickness, and been often entrusted with the tactful breaking of bad news. But I do not think I ever had a task less to my liking than that of telling my cousin Josiah that his first-born was a daughter.

Chlorinda herself asked me to do it, and as one cannot argue with a woman who still hovers upon the boundary between life and death, there was nothing for me to do but to go downstairs and get it over as quickly as possible.

I had thought to find Josiah in the little dark room we called the study. He had ordered a fire there, announcing that he would not go to the office that morning. But although the fire was burning and the paper lay untidily on the table beside the salver that bore a bottle of wine and two glasses, the room was empty. However the side door was open and I could hear Josiah pacing, heavily and impatiently, up and down the tiled floor of the long glass-roofed passage which led to the office and which he had made into a hothouse for his collection of orchids and tropical plants.

It was a cold morning; outside on the lawn and the flowerbeds the rime frost glittered, unmelting in the sunshine; but in the long passage, where the little stoves burned day and night, the air was warm and fragrant. Josiah had paused by a plant that bore a livid speckled bloom and was examining an opening bud with the determined and yet detached air of a man who would avoid his own thoughts. He whirled round as I approached him and said, "Well, Louisa?"

"It's over," I said. "A girl."

In the harsh bright overhead light I saw his face contract and his big body stiffen as though he had been struck. For a moment I stood prepared for an outburst of fury; for few men are reasonable about such matters, and of all men Josiah was the least reasonable ever born. But after a moment's silence he said, quite quietly,

"How's Chlorinda?"

"Doing nicely," I lied, since there was nothing to be gained by upsetting him.

"Ah, well," he said, "what's a wench more or less? It's only the first trip, after all."

He walked down the passage and into the study beside me. I paused for a moment to rake the logs together and put on fresh ones, and while I was doing so I saw him stoop to the sideboard and put away the bottle that had stood on the table and bring out another. The new bottle was of a much inferior wine. Dr Burnett was not one to notice what he was drinking, I knew. But I noticed. And I thought how strange men were. *My* father had not welcomed me; yet it was I who stayed with him to the end and nursed him through two apoplectic strokes and closed his eyes at the last. Men were indeed very strange.

Still, on this occasion Josiah had, I thought, behaved far better than could have been expected after all the betraying signs which had shown his ardent longing for a son. But Josiah was like that, unpredictable, unaccountable. And no man could be more jovial, more generous, sweeter-tempered in a good mood, or more savagely intimidating in a bad. It was with the utmost relief that I stole upstairs and told Chlorinda of the kindly way in which he had taken the news. I think that turned the tide in her favour; she cheered up and began to get better.

It was rather amusing to me, during the next few months, to watch Josiah's rather furtive interest in this, his first legitimate child. That may sound an extraordinarily frank statement, coming from a spinster who has been delicately reared; I believe that old maids are not supposed to know that there are other than legitimate children, except among the poor. But although I have always been kept busy my mind has never been so much occupied that I could not notice what went on around me. And maybe because my own life has not been very eventful, I have tended to take a great interest in other people's more exciting ones. (Sometimes I thought that if I had had more time and more privacy when I was young I could have written a book like Mrs Radcliffe or Miss Fanny Burney.)

And of all the people I had known and watched my cousin Josiah Kingaby was one of the most exciting, although hardly anyone else in the family approved of him or thought his pranks amusing. I've heard him called "rip" and "rake-hell" many a time. Even his father deplored his ways. But *my* father, whom I suspect of having been much the same make of young man, had a soft spot for him; and since we lived at Bury St Edmund's in Suffolk, which was a very gay town, with a Fair each year which brought the frivolous and fashionable elements from four counties, Josiah was always pleased to be invited to stay in our house which overlooked the noble open space called the Abbey Hill. For some years, when we were both young, he would invite me to accompany him to the various gatherings which marked that festive season; but I was always plain; my father did not approve of the fashions which were in vogue when I was a girl, the panniers and hoops and "plastic ornaments"; and between consciousness of my plain face and unfashionable attire and diffidence before my gay dashing young cousin, I was much afflicted by shyness, and thus unable to make up by wit or vivacity what I lacked in other respects. I usually ended the evenings in some secluded corner while Josiah carried on a violent flirtation with some newly found charmer. Nevertheless, I looked forward to his visits and to the change which his cheerful boisterous presence wrought in our quiet house. I loved him sincerely and quite without hope.

His father and mine died within a few weeks of one another; the only difference was that my uncle died suddenly, whereas my father had borne a long, painful and most distressing illness. Josiah was abroad at the time, doing some business in Jamaica or Havana. Everyone said that upon his return he would marry and settle down. We were both then in our middle thirties, and although Josiah was still an eminently eligible bachelor, I, of course, had been an accepted old maid for many years. He came over to see me soon after his arrival home and most kindly helped me in settling my father's affairs, and in disposing of our big house and then purchasing one more suitable to my reduced means.

He settled down, so far as attention to business was

concerned; but he did not, for some years, marry, though his name was connected with those of several young women, eligible and otherwise. And although, watching his career, I suppose I had often cause for shocked disapproval, I could somehow never muster much sincere feeling, save perhaps an envy for the women whom he found attractive. After all, he was generous and pretty well-to-do; and if they had wanted more than an *affaire* and a subsequent allowance they should have behaved differently.

At last, when he was not far short of fifty, Josiah married, all in a hurry, the pretty, pale, delicate daughter of an impoverished gentleman who for the greater part of her life had been dragged round the health resorts of Europe where her parent tried cures and took waters. One of Josiah's ships, on the Mediterranean voyage, had given them passage, since the old gentleman, dying and penniless, was obsessed with the notion that he must die and be buried in England.

Josiah, with the casual open-handedness which was one of his better qualities, took them into his big house at Bywater, surrounded the parent with comfort during his last weeks on earth and a month after the funeral married his daughter. Poor Chlorinda who had never had a home of her own was as capable of ruling East House as she would have been of governing England. Josiah, after three weeks, during which, he declared, Chlorinda cried every day, sent for me; and for three months I tried, patiently and persistently, to initiate her into the mysteries which the average well-brought-up English girl absorbs with her daily food. She was a willing, if inapt pupil, and together we made jams and jellies, salted down meat for the winter, cured hams, made rushdips for the servants' quarters and pot-pourri for the parlour. "Unless you know how things should be done," I told her, "the servants will take advantage of you." And she would say "Yes," and "Yes," and be little the wiser.

However, at the end of three months, great-aunt Claribel, at Woodford, was taken with what proved to be her last illness, and I was sent for. And after that my youngest Braintree nieces, twins, were to be married, and I must go to stay to help with their preparations. My sister-in-law, a woman I detested, had just made me what was obviously a "parting" present, and I was wondering, since my Bury house was let, what exactly to do next, when Josiah in person swooped down on the Braintree establishment, gave me half an hour in which to pack and bore me off, back to Bywater where Chlorinda, newly pregnant, welcomed me like a frantic puppy.

I loved Bywater, which was small and old-fashioned and homely; it was more congenial to me than my home town where the county families had their big town houses, and where to be poor, old-fashioned and elderly was to be lonely and out of things. And although East House had never been "improved" by having its beamed front plastered or its gables hidden behind parapets, in the modern manner, it was warm and solid and comfortable. Too many households at that time were closing in the wide open fireplaces, and having moulded frescoes and "water-closets" installed, and then stinting upon fuel and food to meet the expenses. There was none of that in Josiah's household. And to a person like myself, occupying a peculiar status between guest and servant, such things are im-

portant. I have noticed so often that, when one arrives
to help with a crisis, one is pressed to second helpings,
the fire in one's room burns brightly, the water in one's
can is hot. But when the crisis is past food grows
scarcer, the chimney in one's room takes to smoking,
the can under its flannel hood is tepid. One grows
sensitive to such changes.

At East House these subtle reminders that I had
outstayed my usefulness were not forthcoming. Chlorinda, very happy in her pregnancy, showed no signs
of wishing to retain the reins of the household in her
own hands. The most cursory visit to the kitchen had
showed me that the servants had had things all their
own way, and I spent most of the time between my
arrival back at Bywater and the baby's birth in clearing and cleaning and making up arrears.

Once the baby was born I was even busier, sewing
for Chlorinda and the child, supervising the nursery
as well as the kitchen, making preparations for Christmas and minding Josiah's linen. He always swore that
no one could do up a shirt as I could.

It was a happy, comfortable time; only marred for
me by the thought that sooner or later I must go away
again. Once or twice I mentioned the matter and each
time Chlorinda refused to listen.

"Stay until after Easter," she said. And when Easter
had gone by, "Oh, Lou. If you go what shall I do
about the jam?" When the jam was safely made the
question arose about reletting my little house, and
when I was discussing the matter, this time with
Josiah, he said firmly, "Look here, Lou. Don't be
forever on the fidget. We need you here. Chlorinda is
no housekeeper, and sooner or later there'll be another

baby, I hope. You know it isn't a case of being welcome here, you're the peg the whole damn thing hangs on."

So I stayed, and came to regard East House as my home, and Josiah, Chlorinda and their child as my special family.

Josiah's hope of another child was not very soon fulfilled. And as the time sped away I began to be anxious for his sake. He had now, belatedly, settled down, and part of that process is always a looking towards the future, which in men, I think, often takes the form of interest in their successor. I was especially anxious that Josiah should have a son, because he had taken the birth of his daughter in so kindly and philosophical a spirit. If he had regrets he never voiced them either to Chlorinda or me. And his first, slightly shame-faced interest in the little girl had changed to something much warmer and nearer pride.

He even condescended to choose a name for the little one. I think it was on account of her hair which, with great rapidity, changed from a colourless down to a crop of rusty red.

"What's the name of that stuff in meadows that comes with the bull daisies and grows a bit higher?" Josiah asked one day. "Ah, I have it, sorrel. That's what we'll call her."

"But dearest," protested Chlorinda, "that's not a name for a little girl. It sounds somehow like a horse." This question of the name had been the subject of several chats between Chlorinda and me, and we had picked upon Felicity, because the baby was happy by nature and had had such a fortunate reception. But neither of us dared mention it now.

"A horse. That's so, and what could be better," demanded Josiah, who rated horses high. "Sorrel. My little sorrel filly," he added jovially, raking the little red pow with one huge forefinger. And so the child was named. We grew accustomed to the outlandish name in the course of time and ceased to mourn the Felicity.

From the first there seemed to be a strange affinity between the two of them, father and child. As soon as she could distinguish one person from another she showed a preference for him in a hundred ways, and this although his mood and his treatment of her varied just as violently as his behaviour did in other respects. There were stretches of days when he never approached her without cramming into her small hands some offering, often highly unsuitable; there were other days when he would ignore her completely. But these latter days grew fewer after she grew to an interesting age; for, at an astonishingly early period she would make real efforts to engage his attention, working away in the face of indifference or discouragement until he smiled and swung her on to his shoulders, or stood, patiently, while she swarmed up one of his enormous legs as though it were a tree she was climbing.

When Sorrel was five Chlorinda was brought to bed again. The new baby was another girl. After the long delay Josiah took the second disappointment hard and the sky darkened. There were no more jovial, present-bearing visits to the nursery; there was no name specially chosen for the new child. I suggested the old Felicity, but Chlorinda, with her hurt, gentle smile turned back to the little book of English Names and Their Meanings, and murmured:

"No. This is not a lucky baby. We'll call her Dinah; it means 'judged.'"

People differ very much in their estimates of the amount which children know and understand and feel; and, indeed, it varies with individual children; but I will vouch for the fact that the gloom which succeeded Dinah's birth fell as heavily upon, and was noticed as sharply by Sorrel as by anyone else in the house. It gave me a stab every time I entered the nursery or the parlour to see the little tawny head lift or turn, hopeful, expectant. In the nursery she was doomed to disappointment; her father never climbed the stairs in that direction; but sometimes he did come into the parlour at an hour when both children were there, and then it was pathetic to see her pleasure, the efforts she would make to engage his attention, and her disappointment and bewilderment when she found herself repulsed and tactfully swept off to the upper regions again.

However, in rather less than a year after Dinah's birth Chlorinda knew her moment of triumph and produced a son. The change in Josiah was ludicrous, though not one of us would have dared show the slightest sign of amusement. He began to talk about Kingaby and Son; about the boy's education and how he should make the Grand Tour, all before the child, a fragile, over-beautiful little boy, was out of diapers.

My own hearty reaction to the new state of things —so much had I already fallen under Sorrel's spell— was joy to know that Josiah could once more regard his daughters with an unjaundiced eye. Dinah was too young to know or care that the nursery was once more visited and beamed upon, but it was easy to see that for Sorrel the sun had come out after the rain.

She was, perhaps inevitably, jealous of Little Joe, as we called the baby; and this jealousy had unfortunate results upon her nature, despite everything we could do to mitigate it. Worst of all, she very soon discovered that Josiah's attention could be drawn from the infant and riveted for a while upon herself by the report or the sight of some naughty, high-spirited piece of behaviour. She developed into a very troublesome child indeed. Chlorinda and I—and Chlorinda had, oddly enough, a marked preference for her first-born —would plead and argue with her; Ada, the nurse, had no scruples about smacking her; either treatment was vain. Josiah liked naughty little girls, so Sorrel in the face of argument and punishment was bound to be naughty.

She grew very fast, a sturdy, hearty child with a square face, a stubborn chin and eyes which, though too small for real beauty, had a startling green brilliance between the thick lashes that were much darker than her hair. Dinah and Joe were both prettier children, but there was something about Sorrel: her straight little shoulders, her capacity for abandonment to the mood of the moment, the way her wide mouth curved into a smile over her square sound teeth, which was irresistible. She was a lovely little girl.

And Josiah, now that his grudge against her was removed, gave way to her charms. He was certainly the last man on earth to take pleasure in a child's company or chatter, yet, on increasingly frequent occasions, he would say, "Put on her things, she can come with me for an hour," and carry her off to the warehouse. On such a morning the radiance on the child's face was quite dazzling; and from each excursion she would return full on unquenchable talk and self-importance. Once or twice he took her farther afield; and I never saw them depart in the high gig without a sense of foreboding which more than once was justified, for Josiah was careless even at his best. Once on a very cold day he left her for five hours; the mare was tethered and rugged, and he had forgotten that his daughter sat exposed in the high vehicle, cold and hungry. When he returned and found her she had crouched down on the floor of the gig and dragged back a corner of the horse-rug; but for all that she was still so cold that we dreaded a fatal chill. The fact that she rose next morning as merry and lusty as ever was as much a matter of pride to her father as of relief to her mother and me. He recounted how she had smiled up at him when he found her, and never let out a whimper; but he failed to realize that to have behaved like a child, like a little girl, would have resulted in the cessation of such excursions; he underestimated the attachment which his daughter felt for him.

On another occasion, returning home rather the worse for drink, he refused to give the mare her head, and pulled too sharply on a rein at a corner. The gig overturned. Sorrel, weighing so little, was cast some distance, over a hedge and into the middle of a blackberry bush. Josiah, suddenly sobered, dragged her out, scratched but undaunted, and had a new story for his cronies next day. According to him Sorrel had looked up and said, "That was like flying; Daddy, I felt like a bird." Chlorinda, who had wept over the scratches, disbelieved the story, but I saw no reason for incredulity. Alas! I knew that on the few occasions when

Josiah had chosen my company no mere accident, no scratches would have seemed a heavy price to pay for the honour. I had been in love with this cousin of mine ever since I was a plain awkward girl of sixteen, and the passing years, although they had accustomed me to hopelessness, just as they had accustomed me to being plain and awkward, had not made me either blind or insensible. Josiah, sweeping through his life, careless, selfish, moody and unreliable, exercised a strong, uncalculated charm. I at least could see in his young daughter a fellow victim.

In the spring, when Sorrel was seven, Dinah two, and Little Joe just over a year old, another relative of Josiah's, his mother's youngest sister, Caroline, was widowed for the third time and left penniless. I heard Josiah discussing her situation in his bluff way, and suggesting that she should be asked to make East House her home. Chlorinda, who was again pregnant, just smiled and said:

"If this goes on we shall have to enlarge the house."

I took that as a hint for dismissal; and as soon as I could decently do so, suggested to Chlorinda that with Mrs Fennigard in the house my presence would be neither necessary nor desirable. To my surprise and no little delight, Chlorinda began to cry and hold on to me.

"But Carrie is no good at all. She is a dreadful old lady. We visited her when we were married. Lou, darling, you mustn't think of going away now of all times. I couldn't do without you."

So I stayed; and Mrs Fennigard arrived. Josiah always called her "Aunt Carrie," and we all fell into the habit, though it never seemed natural or proper to me to use the homely, familiar term.

She was, I suppose, almost seventy years old then; and at one time she had been pretty. She was tiny, with a great pile of hair which, despite the threatened tax, she still powdered in the old-fashioned style. The flesh had gone from her face, leaving a bony mask which was always meticulously painted; she had big black eyes which noticed everything, and one of the sharpest tongues ever found in a woman's head. The atmosphere of a gay and fashionable life still hung about her. And although she was now a poor old woman, widowed, dependent upon a nephew's charity, racked with rheumatism, she still behaved, and demanded to be treated, as though she were a young belle. In the presence of Josiah, or any male creature, however young or old, she behaved coyly, flirting her head, making play with her eyelids, gesticulating with her little ringed hands. But left alone with Chlorinda and me she was acid, sarcastic and spiteful. Especially she could never forget or forebear to mention that whereas she had found three men to marry her I had not found one.

She made me very miserable, and I was determined that as soon as Chlorinda was well again I would leave Bywater. I was not quite penniless. I had my little house and about twenty pounds a year. The house was let to good tenants for ten pounds a year and I hated the thought of living alone. But rather than bear Carrie Fennigard's tongue I contemplated returning to my house and finding some way of eking out a livelihood.

However, Chlorinda never did get well. After the birth of Lydia she settled down to a state of semi-invalidism; and with the nursery full of children, the

quarrels between Carrie and the maids, the care which
Chlorinda demanded and the comfort and attention
which Josiah expected, I was so busy that I had little
time to think of myself. Three years passed rapidly.

One bright summer morning Sorrel had gone down
to the warehouse with Josiah, and when he brought
her back for midday dinner her clean muslin frock
was wet and muddy, her shoes soaked, her face and
hands filthy. From the door of the warehouse which
opened onto the wharf she had seen some dirty barefoot children playing on the foreshore which the reced-
ing tide had left bare. They were setting up bottles on
the river wall and shying them down with pebbles. She
had strayed out to join them. Josiah had roared at her
from the doorway as soon as he missed her, but she
had only laughed and invited him to admire her skill.

"Don't scold her too much, Lou," he said to me
privately. "Damme, she'd be a riot in a skittles alley.
Eight of nine shots told, and the little urchins who've
been playing all their blasted lives standing there open-
mouthed." He gave a short sigh and added, "I hope
the boy'll make half the man she is," as though to
himself."

"Of course he will," I said confidently. "Remember
there are six years between them." But privately I
knew that the delicate, nervous little boy would have
a hard task to measure up to the standard which Josiah
would expect from his son. Poor child! At least he
never disappointed his father, for during the next fortnight first Sorrel and then, one after the other, all the
children were stricken down by fever, which, we
learned, had been decimating the child population in
Fendyke Street and the lower parts of the town, and

which, no doubt, was already at work amongst the little ones with whom Sorrel had played that summer morning. Finally Chlorinda, who had insisted upon taking a share in the nursing, sickened herself, and succumbed with the rapidity which testified to her lack of reserve strength. She was spared the knowledge that little Joe had died two days before her. They buried them in the same grave.

The three girls recovered.

Those were terrible days. Josiah was not the man to bear bereavement patiently; and the irony of losing his wife and his son while retaining three daughters warped his nature completely. Never an abstemious man, he took to drinking heavily and slouched about the house, unshaven, half-dressed, and so morose that it took real courage to go near him or address him.

Once, in a burst of drunken fury he announced that he would never set eyes on the girls again. They could all be packed off to school as soon as their state permitted.

"But, Josiah," I protested, jerked out of caution by my feelings, "they are so young. Dinah is barely five and Lyddy but three." I had once, for three most wretched years, been at school myself, and I could not endure the thought that such infants should be exposed to the treatment that had been meted out to me, or anything like it.

"Then they can be boarded out," he said. "I tell you I won't have them here. As for . . . the little bitch who brought the damned fever into the house, she shall go to school, and I hope they tame her."

I said no more, trusting that time would alter his state of mind. I took scrupulous care to ensure that no sound or sign of the little girls' presence reached him. But my care was wasted. In a few days he announced that he had fixed for the little ones to go to Halstead, where the widow of one of his ship's captains would take charge of them. For Sorrel arrangements had also been made; she was to go to Miss Gould's Academy for Young Ladies in Baildon as soon as I could get her clothes together.

"It'll break her heart," I said.

"And a good thing, too. I'd have broken her neck long ago if I'd guessed where her pranks were leading."

And she, poor child, had been worrying me to fiddlestrings with inquiries as to when her father would visit her, asking anxious questions about his health, listening for the distant roar of his voice, and always turning those expectant eyes upon the opening door.

She had lost her looks. Illness and long days in a darkened room had made her skin pallid; she had grown lanky and thin; we had cut off her curls and her hair was at an awkward stage of re-growth, tufty, like a chicken's first feathers. It went to my heart to have to break bad news to so frail and pathetic a shadow of Sorrel. But the thing could not be delayed for ever, so one afternoon, armed with a plate of apples, I went and sat beside her at the open window of her room. While I was peeling an apple and cutting it into slices she gave me an opening by asking, fretfully:

"Cousin Lou, what is it about Father? Why does he never come to see us?"

I said, "Sorrel, I know that you are a brave little girl and will try to bear courageously what I have to tell you. Your father is so much upset, so distraught by the death of your little brother and your dear mother, that he doesn't feel able to see any of you yet."

"He sees you."

"Yes, dear. But that is rather different." She turned a face which, between the ravages of illness and an unhappy precocity of wisdom, had lost all traces of childishness.

"Cousin Lou, is it because Dinah and Lydia and I *lived* and Little Joe died, that he can't bear to see us?"

"He would be reminded," I said weakly.

"And really Little Joe mattered most, didn't he?"

"He was your father's only son."

"And he would have learned the business; and even if he got married would still be called Kingaby. Is that why?"

"I suppose that has some part in it," I admitted, growing more and more uncomfortable.

"I see. Well, you know, Cousin Lou, I could learn to look after the business. And if I didn't marry I could be called Kingaby."

"But, darling," I said. "That wouldn't do at all. One day you'll want to be married and have a husband and a home and some children of your own. Then you wouldn't have time to think about the business. There is the difference between boys and girls, you see; and that is why your father is so much disappointed. And that is why . . ." She interrupted me again.

"Cousin Lou," she said gravely, "I'd be like you. *You* would have time to look after the business if you wanted to. I promised I'd live here for ever, and I would be as good as Little Joe. Shall I tell Father that? Would that make him feel any better?"

"No, Sorrel, it wouldn't. There are so many things that you couldn't understand. I hardly do myself. But you have to accept this, dear, that your father is in a peculiar state of mind and can't bear to see any of you children for a time."

"Have we to stay upstairs always then?" she asked with a look of horror.

"No. That wouldn't be possible. Dinah and Lyddy are going to Halstead to stay with Mrs Benson. And you are going to school."

I should have thought that her face was already as white as a face could be, but it now turned so ghastly that I dashed to the table and snatched the smelling salts. She pushed them aside.

"What school?"

"At Baildon. It is called an Academy for Young Ladies, and you will learn many interesting things there." I did my best to make it sound attractive and full of promise.

"I won't go. Even *he* can't make me; not unless he picks me up and carries me. And then I'd scream all the way."

I had, I think been prepared for tears, but not for this cold white rebellion. I felt helpless before it. I could only say:

"Sorrel, I do beg you at this moment not to cross your father's will. Rebellion will only make things harder for all of us. I don't think anything could alter his mind; certainly defiance upon your part would only worsen matters. Be a good girl. Go to school and learn all you can and then we'll see. Time may heal his heart and he will be pleased to have home his clever little girl who gave him no trouble at a time when he was very unhappy." And then inspiration came to me. "After all, your brother, if he had lived, would have gone to school, you know."

Her face thawed a little and became thoughtful. "I suppose he would," she said slowly.

In this unenthusiastic but resigned way she helped me to complete her packing and made her departure. I went with her to Baildon and saw Miss Gould—a massive, pink-faced lady with an affable manner which was, I am convinced, more a matter of habit than sincerity. She inquired after "your dear father," and I gathered that Josiah had impressed her favourably. I saw Sorrel blench and bite her lip. She had been obliged to leave home, despite ruses and entreaties, without seeing him.

He had paid the fees and given me permission to do any shopping that was needed, but he had not mentioned pocket money or made the child any parting gift. I gave her ten shillings from my own purse when I left her and urged her to write to me often. I hardly realized until I went back to East House without her how firmly, in ten years, she had entrenched herself in my heart. It had always been my secret dream to be the mother of Josiah's child, and if Sorrel, who was so emphatically his daughter, had been mine as well I could hardly have loved her better. I missed her more than I could say, and that autumn, with only Josiah, moody and unapproachable, and Carrie Fennigard, spiteful and carping, for company, was a dull and unhappy time for me.

I had taught Sorrel to write a little, and soon her letters began to arrive, letters written with insight and passion which accorded ill with the round childish

writing. She hated the Academy; she learned nothing
that was useful; she was always hungry, she reported.
And did I think that Father could bear to have her
home for Christmas? When that season drew nearer
I broached the subject to Josiah who repudiated the
notion with oaths. There would be no more Christ-
mases in *that* house, he said. I had to write and break
this sorry tidings to the child, softening the blow as
well as I could by sending two presents, one from me
and one purporting to come from her father.

Despite the decree about not keeping Christmas,
Josiah ordered special food, and on Christmas Eve
entertained Dr Burnett, Mr Raikes, the notary, and
Mr Groatan, to supper. It was a horrible day of East
wind and sleet, the kind which comes so often in our
corner of Essex. Carrie and I were not to be present
at the supper which was to be a men's affair; and I
had gone in, at seven o'clock, to take a last look at the
table and see if one more log could be crowded on to
the fire. As I came into the hall the front door opened,
slowly, and there was Sorrel, her drenched hat brim
cascading water down her small purple-nosed face,
and a bursting paper parcel of night wear under her
arm. She dropped the parcel, ran across the hall in her
squelching boots and seized me about the waist in a
convulsive grip. "Oh, Cousin Lou. I got here! I'm
home!"

"How did you come?" I asked, as soon as I could
speak.

"A man gave me a ride in a cart as far as Steeple
Rising. I walked the rest of the way." It was all of eight
miles from Bywater to Steeple Rising.

"We must get these wet things off, and your feet in

a mustard bath," I said, drawing her towards the stairs. "I don't know what your father will say to this."

She stopped still and went stiff. "I thought he was better," she said in a small voice. "He sent me a present." What had I done—all with the best intentions. "And no one stayed at school except Marie, whose father is in India, and the Staple twins who are orphans."

"Well, we won't talk about it now. You'll catch your death," I said.

If only I had thought of the back stairs. But I was so impatient to get the child between blankets with a brick to her feet and something hot inside her that I forgot Josiah, changing his clothes before supper in his room at the head of the stairs. The door of it swung open just as we gained the landing and Josiah came out, settling the seals and fobs of his watch. It was the first time father and daughter had met since that day in the summer.

He had been drinking. Later I tried to remember that and to think that at some other time . . . if he had been sober . . . if Sorrel hadn't looked like a tramp's child . . . Would things have been different? I don't know. Who does? Josiah stopped as though there had been a snake in his path.

"What the devil is the meaning of this?" he demanded.

"I've come home for Christmas, Daddy." Josiah turned his heavy pouched eyes on me.

"Is this your doing?" Before I could say anything Sorrel said, "It's nobody's doing. I just came."

"Then you can just go back again. And please understand, once and for all, that I don't want you here."

His voice was cold and hard, and he was doing that cruellest thing, addressing a child as though it were grown up. He brushed past us towards the stair head. As he passed Sorrel swung round, rather as though she had been drawn by a magnet. "Please, Daddy . . ." she said, in the most pleading voice. But he did not turn his head. The curve of the stairs hid him and a second later we could hear his voice greeting Dr Burnett in the hall.

Sorrel was crying as I led her away. I got her into bed and applied every remedy against a chill I could think of; and soon, from sheer exhaustion, she grew calm and peaceful. Just before I left her she looked up from the pillow and said:

"He didn't send me that book, did he?"

"No," I answered. "I'm sorry, my dear. I was trying to give you a happier Christmas."

"It's all right," she said, turning her face to the pillow. "I don't mind any more."

I took the words to mean that peace and comfort were stealing over her. It was not until later on that I realized that the sad little sentence had another, deeper, meaning—that she was free of the fascination her father had held for her. Yet I might have understood; for in me a similar change had taken place. When, on the next morning, Christmas morning, Josiah said ruthlessly and relentlessly that the child was to return to school on the next day, I also was set free from the allegiance of a lifetime. I could love a man who did not love me, a changeable, moody tyrant, a drunkard; but the man who could push past that child on the stairs as he had done could never more have a place in my affection.

Seven years passed, with the dreadful rapidity which the years assume in their passing as one grows older. In the second of them Josiah married again. Everyone professed surprise, but I had been prepared for the change for some time. The new wife was a farmer's daughter, a pretty black-haired creature with a milk and roses skin, the build of a brood mare and the mind of a sheep. If ever a woman were born to be the mother of healthy children Lucia was that woman, and I am sure that Josiah had chosen her with that thought in his mind.

She was overwhelmed by her sudden advance in the world from a seventy acre farm where she was one of a family of ten, to the chatelaineship of East House, and her airs and graces would have been amusing if they had not been pathetic. She quarrelled fiercely, with the concentration which such a very feminine creature can bring to a quarrel, with Carrie Fennigard, and I can remember the day when Carrie, with a spiteful smile on her painted mouth, said:

"My good young woman, *when* you have given my nephew the son whose birth is the sole object of this marriage, you may possibly have the power to turn me out, which seems to be your wish. But until then I should advise you to remember that with the Kingabys family means something and that blood is thicker than Florida water. Go on, tell your husband that I have insulted you unbearably and see what happens."

I did not quarrel with Lucia, nor did I wait to be turned out. By some means, which I did not understand, though Mr Raikes once tried to explain it to me, my twenty pounds a year had been growing less

and less, until, in the year of Josiah's marriage I had
received only four pounds. Since this made my return
to my own house completely impracticable and I felt
I was no longer needed at East House, I began to look
about for a post which would provide me with a home
and a little money without shaming my name. And
after a little time I was lucky enough to be engaged as
housekeeper by a pleasant old gentleman with a large
house not five miles from Baildon.

I was very happy there; and I could see Sorrel every
week. Dinah and Lydia had joined her by that time,
and in winter they had permission to meet me at the
cake shop, in summer in the park, and while the little
ones employed themselves with cakes or play, Sorrel
and I could talk.

I learned so much, on those Wednesday afternoons,
about the Academy for Young Ladies. Schools had
not changed a bit since my day. There was still the insistence upon deportment, embroidery, back-board
drill, the cultivation of a pretty warbling voice. The
underlying idea was still that a girl went to school in
order to learn arts which enable her to snare a husband; it had been the same in my youth, when a mistress had told me bluntly that with my face and figure
I had special need to cultivate a pleasing manner, and
a modest demeanour, and that a sweet smile and a
blush could often redeem the most homely face.

It was Miss Gould's object in life to turn out mar-
riageable young ladies; and although sometimes on
Wednesday afternoons I agreed with the discontented
Sorrel in deploring the methods, the deceitfulness, the
spying system, the unhealthy insistence upon triviali-
ties, at the same time I could not help thinking that to

marry quickly and successfully was my dear girl's one hope in life. What else was there for her?

If Lucia had borne a son it was possible that Josiah's natural feelings would have asserted themselves, and he would have received his daughters again. But after four years the new marriage had produced only one child, another girl. A peculiar look had crossed Sorrel's face when I conveyed the news to her, almost as though something long hoped-and-worked-for had come to pass.

"I can't pretend to be sorry," she said.

"I am, a little. It might have altered things . . ."

"For me and the girls? I wouldn't go back, Lou, much as I long to see Bywater again." Her chin came out stubbornly exactly like Josiah's.

"But what is going to happen to you?" I demanded. "You have no idea how hard the world is for a woman without a home and either a father, or a husband. . . ."

"Next year I shall be eighteen, and then I shall try to obtain a post as governess. I'd have done it before, but they like you to be at least eighteen. And it isn't much use my pretending, is it?"

I said, "A governess's life is sheer drudgery," almost without thinking, for I was looking at her in the light of that last sentence. Miss Gould's beliefs had given her a straight back and a neat, tight waist, and since she held her head well her lack of height did not matter. Her face was not young in repose, it was too sharply planed and too pale; but it broke up easily into a childish look, uncertain, insecure; and her figure, her neck and arms were still very immature. And she was badly dressed; so were Dinah and Lydia.

For that Josiah was partly to blame, though Sorrel's

obstinacy had a hand in it. Having paid their fees, and given me leave to buy necessary clothes, Josiah considered his responsibility to his daughters finished. He did not know that Miss Gould's catering was of a kind to keep you, as Sorrel expressed it, "just full enough not to bite one another, and hungry enough to spend a shilling a day at the cake shop over the road." There were gossipmongers who swore that the cake shop was kept by a poor relation of the schoolmistress. The staff, Sorrel said, were always young and as hungry as the girls, and one could bribe good marks or cancel bad ones by treating a mistress at the mid-morning break. So comfort and promotion at the Academy depended, as it does in the wider world, upon financial status.

I took pleasure in giving the children what I could; but when Sorrel was old enough to know about money she objected to taking anything from me. So we evolved a system of juggling. Josiah paid for good clothes, but we bought inferior ones. To get subscriptions for Miss Gould's birthday Sorrel wore, all through one winter, a pair of leaky shoes. It was the same winter when the Assembly Rooms at Baildon were subscribed for and Josiah had given fifty guineas.

"No wonder they call us the 'close Kingabys,'" said Sorrel with a wry smile, "knowing he has all this money and then looking at us."

"I think," I said, for the hundredth time, "that he should be told. I'm sure it was an oversight. Men don't often realize that women need anything more than enough to eat and some clothes. Besides, Lydia is getting on now, she would appreciate some pretty clothes."

"It wasn't oversight," retorted Sorrel, unjustly, I am sure, "it was petty spite. I wouldn't ask him for a penny extra, and I forbid you to."

It was the end of October and within three weeks of Sorrel's eighteenth birthday when they sent for me from East House. I remember very clearly because I was making her a dress for a birthday present—a warm dark brown woollen, it was, with some lime-green braid on it. I put it out of my lap when the maid said that there was a man to see me, with a note that he wouldn't give to anyone else.

The man was Josiah's head stable-boy, Sam; and the note was written by Carrie Fennigard in her cramped hand. Josiah had been taken ill, Lucia was behaving like a Bedlam case, she herself was too stiff to move and the house was in confusion. Could I come back, at once, with Sam?

It was with the thought of those three girls, and, of course, of Sorrel especially, that I prepared to uproot myself and return to the place I thought I had left for ever. Josiah might die; Lucia and her child might inherit everything—but not if I could help it.

"Confusion" was too mild a word for the state of the house which in Chlorinda's time and mine had been a model of cleanliness and old-fashioned comfort. Josiah had apparently been in bed for a fortnight; Carrie was quite rigid with one of her periodical attacks of stiffness; Lucia, sluttish at the best of times, had no control of the maids, and had done little except weep about the house. Even her own little girl, Phœbe, looked dirty and neglected.

In the midst of the discomfort and disorder Josiah lay like a great tree which in its fall had smashed the undergrowth and brought down the moss, the ivy and the nestlings which it had sheltered. His bulk made a vast mound under the bedclothes, his face was drained of its colour except for a few purplish veins which marked its suety surface. I realized with a pang as I looked down upon him that he was sixty-six and that I was a year older. We had been young together; I had entertained most romantic and sentimental feelings for him; and now here we were, a sick old man on a bed and a sad old woman staring at him. But the last words between us had not yet been spoken.

I had told Dr Burnett that I had a matter of extreme importance to discuss with my cousin, and asked his advice about a timely moment. At first he had counselled postponement, but when I had been at East House a week he told me gravely that Josiah would never be better, and that anything I had to discuss had best be broached without delay.

Josiah opened the interview upon a kindly note:

"It's good to have you back, Lou. I've noticed the difference. You mustn't go away again."

It seemed so strange to hear that low, weak voice issuing from his mouth. That and the dim light of the candles upon a sidetable, the shadow of the old-fashioned canopy on Josiah's bed, and my own feeling of looking backwards and forwards at the same moment, gave the interview an unreal air as though he and I were ghosts already, discussing a matter which had no more concern with us. Yet we were practical enough.

I said, "Josiah, have you made your will?"

"Once. Long ago. All useless now."

"I think," I faltered, "that you . . ." But it is not easy, I found, to suggest to a man's face that his time is short and that he should arrange for the disposition of his goods.

"Should do it again," Josiah finished the sentence. "That's all right, Louisa, my dear. I know it: I'm for the high jump. I'll see Raikes to-morrow." Such heart-breaking meekness. Then he added, with a trace of his old manner, "Shove another pillow behind me and take off a quilt, Lou. I'm stifling." I raised him a little and turned back the quilt.

"You know," he said, "I've made a hell of a mess, Lou. Look at Lucia. What'll she be like with nobody to look after her? And old Carrie, four girls and you, Louisa. A clutter of women I've always had about me."

"It was about the girls I wanted to speak, Josiah, Chlorinda's girls. You will remember them? I know to mention them is to remind you of old unhappiness— but they are as much your children as Phœbe."

"Phœbe? You mean that squalling brat with the dirty face?" he said contemptuously. "Lou, you've seen Sorrel lately. What is she like?"

"You," I said. "Not in feature or build; and she has learned, what you never did, to curb her temper. But for all that she is your daughter, exactly." I realized as I spoke the intense, inner truth of that statement, and knew that there lay the secret of my feeling for Sorrel. And I thought how illogical we are—he had treated Dinah and Lydia equally ill, with less reason, yet it was on account of Sorrel that I had cherished a grudge against him. Because, in wronging her he was what they speak of in the Bible, the house divided against itself; it was Josiah wronging Josiah.

Suddenly, without knowing quite how I started, or
what possible purpose I hoped to serve, I found myself telling him all about the petty shifts for money,
the financial jugglings and small economies to which
the child had been reduced, and her stubbornness in
refusing my help.

"I can see you there, Josiah," I ended, "and also in
her almost fierce protectiveness towards the two little
girls. That's you again: you'd have taken in the whole
family if they were in need and were prepared to accept your dictates. So—when you make your will, remember Sorrel."

"You've always been her partisan," he said sulkily.
"I suppose no woman could understand what she did
that day."

I was not prepared to argue with him then. I had
done what I could. Next day Mr Raikes came along
and was closeted with Josiah for an hour. At the end
of that week, during which the patient seemed to be
making progress, he had another attack, and although
he lingered for another eight days it was only as an
insensible log. I did not send Sorrel's birthday present,
for it was only too plain that she would shortly need a
mourning dress, and two days after her birthday Josiah
died.

I sent Sam off, early in the morning, with a letter
for Sorrel, and that evening the children were home
after rather more than seven years of exile.

Until the coffin had been negotiated around the
bend of the stairs and out of the door I was not
strangely aware of the temerity of my action and of

Sorrel's presence in the house. I cannot explain it, but I felt as though at any moment Josiah might rise in his wrath and demand to know what she was doing there. And although he had lain quiet enough for nearly a month, now that the end had really come it was very difficult to realize that here in his house his loud voice would never be heard again, his frown cause no one to tremble, his laughter never again set the chandelier a-tinkle.

The two little girls were, of course, strangers in the house. Uncertain whether to cry, because Lucia was crying, or to rejoice, as children will, over the break in their routine, they were sent off to share Phœbe's nursery, while Sorrel and I, aided by Miss Phillimore and two 'prentice girls, made mourning dresses for us all.

There seemed to be a suspension in time. There were no meals, no normal pattern to the days. Of the whole period between the death and the funeral I only remember clearly the moment when the girls arrived, and another moment when I came along the passage towards the stairs and saw Sorrel, who had just mounted them, pause for a breathing space outside the white-painted door of the bedroom where Josiah lay. It was the very spot where he had met her on that Christmas Eve, and I knew by the look on her face that she remembered it as clearly as I did. The expression on her face was not pleasant; it was bitterly reminiscent and faintly triumphant. I thought how strange it was that you have only to outlive one who has wronged you in order to taste vengeance and triumph of a kind, which is perhaps why it is easy to pardon a dead enemy. And I was sorry that there was no sign of softening or forgiveness on Sorrel's face.

And so, on a day of leaden sky and slanting rain, Josiah went, meekly as any clerk, out of the wide front door and through the town and was buried, as lesser men had been, in the shadow of the old church, whose tower, they say, was old when the Armada's coming was signalled from its top.

Mr Raikes, the notary, came back to the house after the funeral and acquainted us all with the contents of Josiah's will. It was, I should imagine, one of the briefest ever made. It left everything of which Josiah died possessed to his "beloved daughter, Sorrel," and it expressed the hope that she would do her best to care for his dependents. That was all.

My first thought, I am afraid, was self-congratulatory. I had not chosen ill when I decided to come back to my anonymous post in Bywater; this was my doing. My second was, how like Josiah! In a belated endeavour to compensate Sorrel he must needs be unfair to the rest of them, especially to Lucia, who was after all his legal relict. And, thirdly, I thought of his words to me about the clutter of women. We were Sorrel's responsibility now—Carrie, Lucia, three little girls, and, yes, I must admit it, myself. For I had lost my post by my cavalier departure, and it is not easy to find employment when one is nearing seventy, although one may still be active and sensible. People are so afraid of a collapse, and that they must either be long-suffering or callous in their behaviour to the wreck. And in the kitchen there were Agatha and Janet, both aged, in much my own position. Eight women at least. Of the responsibility that lay outside the walls of the house I did not, at that moment, think. So little did I understand.

So very little did I understand that, as the significance of the lawyer's announcement bore home I looked at Sorrel anxiously. Now, I thought, she will see that her father did, at the end, remember her kindly and try to atone; now perhaps the tears will come, the more bitter for having been withheld so long. But there was no change in her face or demeanour. She had been looking straight out at the leafless sycamore in the middle of the lawn, and she might not have heard the momentous words. But when Mr Raikes had taken his leave I saw her hurrying towards the kitchen, and almost at once it seemed there stole about the house the scent of cooking such as was usually associated with one of Josiah's supper parties. When I first smelled it I was helping Lucia into bed. Between grief and fury she was almost insensible. She asked me to ask Sorrel kindly to spare a bowl of bread and milk for Phœbe as she didn't wish the child to starve. And at that Phœbe, who was a greedy child and had also smelled the cooking, set up a wailing, through which I tried to tell Lucia that of course the will was unfortunately expressed, but that she could trust Sorrel to carry out the spirit not the letter of it.

"She's his daughter, and he was a hard, cruel man," moaned Lucia. Earlier in the day he had been a paragon among husbands. I was beginning to lose patience with her, so I thrust her nightgown at her and left her. Phœbe came away with me, clinging to my hand. I took her to the other children, and myself went in search of Sorrel.

The door of Josiah's room stood open, and its

painted panels reflected the leaping flames of a stick-fed, newly lighted fire and the steadier glow of several candles. Wondering, I poked my head inside and surprised Sorrel, who was moving about from chest to table making a collection of oddments which she was piling on the foot of the stripped bed. The cupboard doors which flanked the fire stood open and all Josiah's heavy clothes hung there like shadows.

Sorrel gave a little nervous start, and then said, "Oh, it's you, Lou. Come in. How long d'you think it would take to clear this room?"

"You needn't do that," I replied. "Some time during the week we'll go through the clothes. I expect Cousin Alicia's husband would be glad of the linen; the other things would be too big. Some poor man perhaps. . . ." I looked at the collection of small things, the heavy gold watch, the pocket tinder box, a silver cigar case, a pearl-headed stock pin and studs. "I daresay," I mused, "that some of those ought to be given as mementoes. There was no mention of mourning rings, was there? And there's old Cobbitt, and Mr Bagworthy, and several more who were attached to your father." I thought as I spoke how pitiable it was to see things which had outlasted their owner. Attributing some of my own feelings to Sorrel, I added, "But, dear, all this can wait. Come away now. I'll see to it all."

Sorrel was letting a slim, snaky chain with several keys attached to the rings at its end slip from one hand to another. She eyed the collection on the bed indifferently, still moving her hands like a juggler.

"I don't care what happens to the things. Lucia can deal with them. But I want this room cleared, now."

"But why?" I asked.

"I'm going to use it," she said, looking at me with surprise.

"Not immediately, Sorrel?"

"Yes. To-night. Why not?" Before I could make any sensible objection there was a sound of bumping and scuffling on the landing, and Agatha, helped by the little boy who chopped sticks, cleaned boots, and did other odd jobs, appeared in the doorway with two large linen baskets.

"Put the boots at the bottom and the clothes on top," directed Sorrel, "and take it all away into the attic. Then make the bed, Agatha, and put on fresh covers. Come along, Lou, we'll have supper. You must all be starving."

I was, in truth, neither very hungry nor in very good spirits, yet I could not help seeing something at once comic and pathetic in that meal, the first ever ordered by Sorrel in East House. It was the kind of feast which schoolgirls, full of porridge and bread and potatoes would dream of and perhaps describe to one another. Sorrel had evidently been indiscriminately through the storeroom. There were pheasants, still hissing from the spit, a vast cold ham, three-quarters of a pork pie, and a succulent pink sirloin which, from the way in which it was hacked about, showed that the kitchen had not shared the scanty meals of our last few days. There were dishes of oranges and dried French plums, and candied fruits and preserved ginger in little blue-flowered jars. There were cheeses and raisins, mince pies and a large plum pudding.

Carrie, leaning heavily on her ebony cane, hobbled to her chair, surveyed the table and asked, "Do you want to make all these children ill, Sorrel?"

And Sorrel, unostentatiously taking Josiah's place at the head of the table, looked at the little girls with affection and said:

"It would do them good for once. Set to, my dears. It's Thursday night. Potato pie and We Thank Thee for This Food." To which Dinah and Lydia, wriggling into their places, responded, "And For All Thy Other Blessings."

I had forgotten the capacity for food which children have. They ate prodigiously, Sorrel keeping pace with them; and the talk turned upon food, so that soon they were giggling together over some dishes served at Miss Gould's table—the tea made in the coffee urns, the coffee in the tea, so that though there was always "choice of beverages" the substance and taste was the same whichever one chose—the sausage pie, the recipe for which ran, said Sorrel, "Take one sausage, bury it deeply under eight pounds of potato, preferably black" —the rabbit pie, from which, they all three solemnly swore, large patches of fur were often extracted.

In the middle of the chatter and laughter Dinah, who at thirteen was old enough to see beyond the moment, turned grave and said solemnly:

"It's all very well to laugh *now*. It won't seem funny next Thursday."

"Next . . ." said Sorrel, momentarily puzzled, "but darling, you're not going back there."

"What! Not ever, Sorrel? Do you mean it? Do you promise?"

"Across my heart."

They left their chairs and flung themselves upon her, exclaiming and laughing. She emerged from their embraces, begging them not to strangle her, laughing, her hair disarranged and her face more nearly flushed than I had ever seen it.

"*Dear* Sorrel," said Dinah, with emotion, "we were so afraid we might have to go back without you. You see," she added, turning to me and Carrie, "Sorrel always stuck up for us. It would have been *unbearable* without her."

And I remembered the little girl, younger than Dinah, as young as Lydia at that moment, who had found no one to stick up for her, who had found it unbearable and had come home, only to be sent back again. And as I remembered I found it easier to understand the apparent callousness with which she had said, "I want this room cleared," and ordered the removal of Josiah's clothes to the attic. I thought how careful one should be in meting out any kind of judgment; poor human people are so much what they have been made, and in regretting this and that foible about them one should ask what their mould has been.

Carrie was half-somnolently sipping a glass of port wine and the girls were challenging one another to eat just one more raisin, one last nut, and I was contemplating carrying Phœbe back to her mother when the dining-room door opened and Lucia stood there, her bed gown trailing from a fur-edged purple wrapper. Her black hair tumbled in glossy disorder upon her shoulders and weeping had merely given her a heavy-lidded, voluptuous look. She might have been a tragedienne, just come to take the stage. She wept, in silence, down the room to where Phœbe with half a crystallized pear still clenched in her little paw leaned drowsily against my arm. She gathered the child into

her arms as though saving her unmentionable con-
tamination. Then, turning to Sorrel, she said, in a
voice like spitting,

"P'raps this seems to you a time for making merry;
but I'd like *my* child to remember that her father isn't
yet cold in his grave."

There was a moment's rather horrified silence. I
looked at Sorrel and saw her eyes running over the
table, untidy now, crammed with dishes, empty, half-
empty, untouched. There was a wry expression on
her face, and some sharp retort, I'll warrant, in her
mind. But before she could utter it, Carrie Fennigard
rapped out, "And must we all starve on that account?
If you had known a little more about the man who
was your husband, you'd know that he would have
preferred us to sit down to table in an orderly fashion
than to run about the house like hysterical trollops!"

"That's right," said Lucia in a high, vindictive voice,
"take her part now! And yesterday, when it looked
like being *my* house, who came sucking round lending
me some snotty jet earrings."

A purple flag of mortification and embarrassment
ran up under the red paint of Carrie's face. "And why
not?" she cried. "I knew you had nothing suitable to
wear. For all you make such a fuss about the child's
father did he ever give you ought but a wedding ring?
Did you ever see his first wife's jewellery? Did you
ever . . ."

"Aunt Carrie, please!" Sorrel had risen from the big
chair and now stood at the head of the table, one hand
on either arm. "Lucia, I should think this kind of thing
does Phœbe more harm than a good supper. Dinah,

take Lydia and the rest of the fruit, if you want it, and get along upstairs."

Lucia, breathing hard, and clutching Phœbe in a fierce, uncomfortable grasp, stood aside for the little girls to scamper past her and then swung back, not towards Carrie who had jibed at her but towards Sorrel, who had, in a fashion, taken her part.

"Every cock," she said, with rustic spite, "crows on its own dunghill."

"But every cock doesn't have a dunghill," retorted Carrie. "Get along with you and your farmyard jargon."

Sorrel came along the side of the table and took the old woman's elbow. "We'll have tea in the parlour," she said, and began to help her along. Lucia swept away upstairs, her dignity rather marred by the fact that Phœbe had somehow managed to entangle the sticky remains of the sweetmeat in one of the thick tresses of her mother's hair. Carrie, Sorrel and I went into the parlour where Agatha had just set the tray of tea before the fire.

"A common, vulgar, envious woman," gasped Carrie, lowering herself inch by inch into the chair nearest the fire.

"She is upset—and disappointed, Aunt Carrie. You shouldn't bicker with her."

"Bicker? One of these days she'll provoke me to lay this stick about her backside," said Carrie, who had retained, besides the fashion, a good deal of the coarse-tonguedness of an earlier generation.

Sorrel said simply, "But if we are all going to live here together we must come to terms, otherwise life will be unbearable."

I saw Carrie Fennigard's beady eyes brighten.

"And do you intend that we should go on living here together, Sorrel, my dear?"

"Naturally. I thought that was understood."

I said, "It's too early to talk about that. You'd be very unwise, Sorrel, to commit yourself at this stage to any promise that you might regret."

"Ha! Listen to Lou! I've no doubt, my dear, she has something to suggest that would much outweigh your dear father's wishes."

"I have several things to suggest," I admitted. "And I don't for a moment believe that Josiah intended Sorrel to keep up an establishment of this size. And caring for dependents doesn't necessarily mean keeping them all under one roof, eating their heads off and making life hideous with their differences."

"You never eat anything, of course! You're not a dependent. You're not trying to quarrel with me now, I suppose. Oh, no!" She glared at me venomously. "I know what you're going to suggest, Lou Kingaby, that you stay here and show Sorrel how to keep house, and do it so successfully that she'll be like her mother, unable to stir hand or foot without you. And the rest of us are to be sent packing. That's the kind of plan you would put forward."

"Nothing of the kind," I said, trying to keep my voice under control. "I happen to have a house of my own, and I think it would be very pleasant if Sorrel, having fulfilled certain obligations, should come with me to Bury and enjoy a little gaiety."

"With you as chaperon, of course. Like all old maids, Sorrel, your Cousin Lou is an inveterate matchmaker."

"Must you always throw . . ." I began. But Sorrel's thin warm hand shot out and her fingers clasped mine.

"It *was* a very pleasant idea, Lou, and I'm grateful to you for planning some gaiety for me. But you know it's impossible, don't you? I must stay here with the business."

Carrie and I jerked out, "The business?" simultaneously.

"But, of course. Didn't you realize, when Mr Raikes was talking to us, that apart from the business there isn't very much? And we're a big family. I shall have to work quite hard, Lou, learning things, and shall have very little time for frivolity."

"Do you mean," I asked incredulously, "that you intend to go down to the office, and walk about in the warehouse, and buy things and sell things . . . as if you were a man?"

"Exactly that, Lou. After all it's what I always wanted to do. You knew that."

"But years ago, my dear, when you were a child. You can't, at your age, seriously suggest such a thing."

"Of course not, it's preposterous," said Carrie. "What on earth would people say? I'm sure that was the very last thing your dear father intended."

Sorrel's manner changed suddenly.

"Don't, for God's sake," she snapped, "keep talking about my dear father. You know just how dear we were to one another. And I am not concerned at all with what he would have wished. He pleased himself and I shall please myself. And I may as well tell you exactly what I mean to do, so that we are spared any further scenes like this. Lou, you may not remember, but you got me peaceably out of this house once by saying that if Joe had lived *he* would have gone to school. So I went. If Joe had lived he would have stayed in Bywater and looked after the business and held the family together. So shall I. To talk about it any more is a waste of breath."

"But you will be insulted, laughed at," said Carrie.

"I'm accustomed to that. Lou knows all about it, and why." She turned to me. "Can you imagine that after the seven years I've been through, I'm going to throw away my chance of being a rich woman some day, take my miserable portion and invest it, as yours was invested, so that it melts, like pond ice?"

"But you could stay here. We could all live here—" (Carrie's one concern seemed to be to keep a roof over her own head.) "The business could be looked after for you. There is no need for you to take part in it."

"There is need." She made, I think, the only dramatic gesture I had ever known her make. She smote her own forehead, quite heavily with her hand. "The need is here," she said.

I felt that further argument was useless and might lead to hysteria. I was more disappointed than I could say over her rejection of my plan for our living together. To have gone back to Bury with sufficient money, to have entertained for her, watched her enjoying herself and at last seen her married to some worthy gentleman would have meant so much to me. It would have been like having my own daughter. It would have compensated me for all I had missed in my youth. Besides, the idea of her going down to the office appalled me. . . . And I felt that if that vixen Carrie Fennigard had not forced my hand I could have

led up to my proposal in a better way; I really hated
the old woman. However, all such speculations and
regrets were useless. Hadn't I myself said to Josiah,
"Like you." And when had anyone turned him from
his own way?

So now I said, "This is going to be very cold tea."

"I think I'll leave it to you then," said Sorrel, moving to the door. I hurried after her.

"Where are you going? Not to sit alone in that
room, dear?"

"No. Down to the warehouse. I just want to smell it
again."

"I'll come with you. It'll be dark there, and lonely."
And what a perverse taste in smells, I thought—tea
and coffee and molasses and whale oil.

"I'd like to go alone. You stay by the fire, Lou." Her
hands were already busy with the little lantern and the
means of lighting it which always stood on a table near
the door of the orchid-passage. When it was burning
she drew out the chain of keys that I had noticed
earlier in the evening, frowned over them for a moment, and then selected one. With her head slightly
on one side and an inquiring look on her face she
turned the key and the heavy door, lined with baize on
both sides, swung open. She turned to me, as pleased
and triumphant as a child.

"I remember which one," she said.

The long passage ran straight ahead, past the side
door of the study through which I had gone tremu-
lously upon another November day to tell Josiah of this
girl's birth. The orchid plants in their tubs and vases
and boxes were invisible in the darkness, though one
or two made their presence known by their fragrance.

Sorrel held her lantern low, so that its light fell upon the floor, laid with large square tiles, black and white.

"I always wanted to play Hop-scotch in here," she said ruminatively, "but I always had to walk straight through in front of him so that he could see that I didn't touch anything. Less than an orchid at my best, you see! And now that I'm too old to hop I could do it. Isn't it funny? I could even pick an orchid. Sacrilegious thought! I shan't be long, Lou. Don't wait about."

I watched the lantern glow diminish along the passage. Then I fetched one of the branched candlesticks from the chest in the hall. I set it on a shelf, and using the tiny embroidery scissors which hung with my thimble, my salts and spectacle case at my waist, I cut, with great deliberation, half a dozen of the choicest blooms I could find.

The maids, under Agatha's eyes, had worked hard at the room upstairs; there was a different scent about it now, turpentine and beeswax polish, clean linen fragrant with lavender, the piny smell of burning wood. The heavy masculine flavour which had been there, composed of leather and hair oil and good cloth, had vanished. The big bed was mounded high under a clean flowered quilt. On the dressing chest where Josiah's big brushes and bottles had been, Sorrel's pathetic belongings were displayed: a small ivory hairbrush that had gone to Baildon with her, its ivory yellow, its bristles worn almost to the root; a common comb with several teeth missing; a handkerchief sachet which I myself had worked for her. No more.

But I stood the glass in which I had set the orchids near the mirror, and moved one of the heavy silver candlesticks forward so that the light would catch the flowers as soon as it was kindled. Their sharp elegant curves and bright colourings struck a strange note in the room, which, for all its recent cleaning, was, by nature of its heavy furniture, old-fashioned bed and worn sombre carpet, a gloomy apartment for a young girl.

And as soon as they were placed I realized that I had performed a highly significant action. Josiah was dead. His house, his worldly goods, his clutter of women, everything, down to his very orchids, now appertained to Sorrel. And with these things went the allegiance of an old woman's heart: shifted once by a scene outside that same door, and now, by the placing of a few flowers, made certain and manifest for ever.

The future did not look much like the peaceful happy time I had planned when I tackled Josiah about remembering Sorrel in his will, but there was one thing I knew about it. It would find me on Sorrel's side and by her side, whatever happened.

I took a last look round the room and then went slowly and thoughtfully downstairs.

PART TWO

Cloudy Mirror
of Misunderstanding

SWINE COBBITT, of course, took advantage of his position to make us work late every single night between the old man's taking ill and the funeral. Even on the day of the funeral, after we had stood out in the sleet and the wind to watch the old man being shovelled under, Cobbitt made us go back, all damp as we were, and work on into the evening. Why, and what for, nobody knew, any more than anybody knew what was going to happen to the business. The old man had married twice, and once had a son, but he'd died; and now that there was no Kingaby left except girls and old women it was a kind of betting matter whether Groatan would buy us up or Bagworthy. In either case, said Cobbitt, we must have everything in order, and his idea of order was to have us clerks working from eight in the morning till nine at night, for, in Glasswell's case nineteen, in Middleditch's seventeen, and in mine ten, miserly shillings a week.

As a mighty concession, since there was coffee and sugar on the premises, and always a can of milk sent down from the house, we were allowed to make coffee if we worked after seven. Cobbitt was so beggarly mean that I always swore he liked working late so that he was using Kingaby fuel to warm himself and Kingaby coffee to drink. Glasswell was quite daft, though his penmanship was like an angel's; where he was didn't matter a scrap to him. And Middleditch had a wretched little house, a cross wife and four squalling brats; he didn't mind working on. They'd say to me sometimes, "What are you in such a hurry for?" And,

damme, could a fellow say that he wanted to get home
to his mother? So I used to invent all kinds of assigna-
tions for myself, and got myself a pretty reputation,
when actually, as soon as the blasted office did close,
I doubled off like a hare back to Fendyke Street to
make tea, cook Mother the kind of meal she liked,
play cards with her, or the piano for her, and try to
make up for the dullness of her days. And there was
no martyrdom about that either: Mother was the best
company I was ever in.

I was particularly mad at having to work on the
night of that funeral, for Mother had been very
mopish in the morning; in fact, ever since the old
man's death she'd been low-spirited. Once when I
asked her she said it was the weather; and then again
she said:

"When you're older, Jamie, you'll find that the death
of any of your contemporaries undermines you a little.
Besides, you've told me so much about Josiah Kingaby that I feel I know him quite well."

"If you knew him better," I retorted, "you wouldn't
grieve over his death, bullying old devil!"

"Oh, I'm not *grieving*," said Mother.

Still, at half-past eight that night I began to be res-
tive, and when I finished the page I was entering I
said, most politely:

"Mr Cobbitt, sir, I've finished. Can I go?"

"Finished, you young rip!" he said, "let me tell you
that when your work here is finished your services will
not be required any more. Take this drawer. Go
through the papers and make two piles, one prior to
June 30th this year, one since. Don't set the drawer
on a sloping desk top, zany, put it here."

And so it happened that I was behind him, and therefore out of his sight, and yet near enough to overhear a great deal of what was said a few minutes later.

There was a door at the back of the warehouse which only the old man ever used; it opened on to a kind of hot-house where he kept plants brought from abroad and led to the house. There was a kind of passage between the bays of the warehouse from that door to the back door of the office, and the top of that door and the upper part of the office wall were glazed.

Glasswell and Middleditch sat at the high desk away on my right, Cobbitt sat with his back to me at the table near the fire. He was so stoop-shouldered with peering for mistakes in ledgers that even if he had looked up his eye-level would have been below the glazed part. But I was standing up, and now and again straightened myself to ease the crick in my back, when suddenly, through the glass, I saw the door at the back of the warehouse open and a wavering light come through it.

The hair on the back of my head began to crawl. Nobody used that door except the old man, and we'd seen him tucked away that very afternoon—and they say spirits linger for a while around the places they were fond of—and he certainly loved his orchids. I watched, with my mouth gone dry, and the crawling feeling extending down my spine, while that little wavering light and a kind of a shape behind it, came down the cleared space between the crates and the bales and then paused by the half-glazed door. Then, of course, the light from our whale-oil lamps shone on the figure's face, and I could hardly stop myself from laughing. My ghost was a bit of a girl in a hooded cloak..

As soon as she laid hand on the door Cobbitt heard her and jumped up. She came into the office, shut the door behind her, and stood for a moment with a kind of remembering look—really rather like a ghost after all. Then she said, "Good evening, Cobbitt, you're working very late, aren't you? I just came down to have a look round. I didn't expect to find anyone here."

Cobbitt went through the motions of washing his hands, a habit of his that always makes me want to hit him. "I'm very glad to be here, Miss Sorrel. And, if I may say so, apart from the sad circumstances, very glad to see you again."

"And *I'm* glad of that," said the girl, "because I think you're going to see a lot of me in the future."

I took a good look at her, as I did at almost everyone I saw, for Mother, seeing no one but me and Mrs Petch, liked to hear about the people I met and what they wore. This girl was short, and when she laid her cloak over the back of the big chair the old man used to use I saw that her hair was reddish and curly, rather pretty, that her face was pale; and that she had no figure to speak of, though she held herself well. There was something oddly familiar to me in her face, too, and presently I put it down to a likeness, not very strong, but noticeable, to the old man's; though a girl could not have resembled him much without being downright ugly, which this girl was not.

She did not take the chair which Cobbitt pushed forward, but perched on the edge of the table, still looking round.

"It hasn't altered at all, Cobbitt. And neither have you."

I could believe that. There was nothing about Cobbitt to change. Every bit of human flesh had been dried off his bones long ago. His skin was parchment and there was ink in his veins. From being so bent his eyes had a queer upward tilt; you could see the white at the lower edge of the iris, which was mud-coloured, and that gave him the look of a hound, melancholy and faithful. Very deceptive, in that it made him look meek and harmless, whereas he was crafty and deep.

He proceeded now with a subtlety I could only admire (hate it as I did when it was directed against me, which was often) to discover whether this girl, who had recently come from the centre of things, knew anything at all about the fate of the business. He did it very cleverly, heaving a sigh when he mentioned that we were all working in order to have everything ready "in case of changes," and being ready for "any eventuality." It sounded like meandering, but it wasn't, and before he had been at it for five minutes the girl said, quite quietly, almost gently, but with oh, such satisfaction:

"Of course you don't know, Cobbitt, you couldn't, but everything has been left to me, absolutely and unconditionally."

Cobbitt said, "I'm sure I congratulate you, Miss Sorrel. Though for your sake I could wish it were ten years ago, when you would have had no difficulty in disposing of the business for a handsome sum. Things have changed since then, alas!"

"We shall have to go into that later," she said, "but in any case it is not a question of disposing of the business. I hope that I shall be able to carry it on just as before; and that means that I shall depend very much upon you, Cobbitt."

Perhaps I was more observant than the general run by nature, or possibly, with the desire to entertain Mother, I had grown to notice things closely and to work a good deal of guessing in with what I noticed; in any case, I knew a great deal more about Cobbitt and the Kingaby business, and even about such poor fry as Glasswell and Middleditch than they ever guessed. To them I was just the third clerk, Jamie Brooke, aged twenty, inclined to be swollen-headed on account of having had more education than the ordinary clerk, who lived with an invalid mother in Fendyke Street. They knew nothing about me as a person or they would not have believed the stories I sometimes told them to cover myself. *They* couldn't have deceived *me* so easily; and Cobbitt I understood as well as though he had been one of the much-explained characters in one of the books with which Mother whiled away so many tedious hours.

(It afforded me a certain sour amusement to look back and reflect that Mother was the one person who managed to deceive me.)

Cobbitt was never tired of telling how he had first entered the Kingaby office as a boy of eight, employed, I gather, to keep inkwells filled, the stove fed in winter and the flies under control in summer. He still firmly believed that there was no other really decent way to start in life and was horrified to learn that I had been at school when I was sixteen. He must certainly have been a bright little boy—and probably as crafty and sly then as later on—for he taught himself to read and

write and reckon, and had, by his own account, occupied the very stool upon which my unworthy behind
now wore out its breeches, when his feet only reached
the top rung. "I had, my boy, what you haven't got
and what I doubt whether you'll learn now, application." And by that I understood him to mean that he
gave himself up to the Kingaby business to the exclu-
sion of everything else. No drinking in taverns, no
cock-fighting, no wenching, no trips into Baildon to
watch the Players, for earnest George Cobbitt; he gave
every thought in his poking head, every ounce of en-
ergy in his ill-nourished body to the business—and
always cherished a grievance against us, me particularly, because we were ordinary human people, not
walking ledgers and ready reckoners like himself.

Of the first great disappointment in this model life
Cobbitt himself never spoke, naturally, since his remi-
niscences were all directed to the one end—to inspire
us. But our landlady's father, a very old man when I
talked to him, had been Cobbitt's senior in the office
and was fond of telling how old Jos Kingaby favoured
the young clerk and, whenever he quarrelled with his
son, Josiah, would threaten to take young George into
partnership. To the delight of the other clerks, I gathered, the threats were never fulfilled; old Jos died while
Josiah was in Jamaica and Cobbitt, now chief clerk
and general manager, was not mentioned in the will
nor left the smallest legacy; and when Josiah returned
he thanked Cobbitt for all he had done for the business
in the interval, but showed him very plainly that he did
not want a partner though he had a use for a humble
paragon.

After that—according to old Kennedy—Cobbitt

made several efforts to get a better post elsewhere, only to find that good clerks were ten a penny and that he was only unique in his specialized knowledge of one little business to which he had better stick. So Cobbitt stuck.

Of the next milestone in this plodding career we had first-hand evidence, for Middleditch was in the office on the morning when it happened. Creek Cottage, a really pretty little place, snugly built and well thatched and standing in an acre or two of paddock and garden, fell, by way of mortgage, into Josiah Kingaby's possession. Cobbitt, the old sycophant, congratulated his master, saying that it was a pleasing little property and likely to let well to some sea-faring man who wanted to settle down in sight of water, and who would, after the manner of his kind, make a good tenant. And at that Josiah took the deeds from a drawer and placed them in Cobbitt's hands.

"Here you are," he said, "it's yours. You've earned it if ever a man earned anything in this world."

It was worth, Middleditch reckoned, between five and six hundred pounds, and the old man handed it over as if it had been a cigar. So the good little office boy was rewarded after all. He let off half of it to some sea-faring man who worked the garden to perfection and kept fowls and pigs in the paddock. Cobbitt lived in the other half and one dreary drooping female looked after both establishments. Her reports on the different standards of living and comfort at the two ends of the cottage, which reached us through the grocer and butcher, were amusing and enlightening. Cobbitt was one of those rare people who are mean to themselves.

All this about our immediate overlord was, of course, common knowledge, but I knew more about the man himself. I had seen him when he and Josiah Kingaby had had an argument about policy, and on those occasions his expression was not—apart from those deceptive hound's eyes—that of a meek man overruled (he was, invariably, overruled, though often in the right) but rather that of an arrogant and ambitious man, thwarted. And when, sometimes it happened that events proved him right and the old man wrong, triumph would show under the deprecating sympathy of his manner; even those melancholy eyes would glint a bit. Ha, old Cobbitt, ordering me round, with: Now my boy . . . and You, young Brooke . . . and When I was your age . . . little did he guess that often, when I looked most blank and idle I was enjoying the only kind of drama which my life at that time afforded, and that much of it was provided by him.

On this particular evening I dealt very gently with the rustling papers he had set me to sort, and I kept my head down. But I missed nothing. And when Sorrel Kingaby said, "I shall depend very much on you, Cobbitt," I saw what happened to his face; and what is more, I understood it and thought—perhaps after all, you old swine, your mouldering precepts and stony adages are right; maybe if you do apply yourself and never swerve from one notion the reward *does* come. For with a girl as the new owner, drifting down perhaps once a month to make some twittering remark, knowing nothing, understanding nothing, what a position would be Cobbitt's. And my heart sank as I viewed the prospect. The old man had been a swine, too, in his own way, moody, cantankerous, bullying;

but quite often, and I believe with the idea of putting Cobbitt in his place, he would stand up for one of us. I've even known him stroll into the office on a fine summer's afternoon and say, "Great God, you are a pasty-faced lot. Get out all of you and let the sun shine on you." And he would remember Christmas; and when Middleditch's last baby, a boy, was born, after saying a lot of exceedingly nasty things about spawning like herring and filling the world with starvelings, he gave him five guineas in the afternoon "to buy the brat a rattle." There would be none of that under Cobbitt's rule.

And just as I was contemplating the new regime, with the stove damped down to save fuel, and an inquest held over a bit of wasted paper, a spilled drop of ink, a broken quill, and us working every evening until nine o'clock, Sorrel slipped down from the table and straightened herself.

"Well, Cobbitt," she said, "I'm very glad to see you again, and to have had a little talk. And now I think you'd better all go home. It's getting late."

I raised my head and sent her a look of blessing. Good wench, I thought. And she caught the look. Her eyes, very pretty, clear green and darkly fringed, met mine, and the expression of her face softened into a kind of half smile. After a minute she turned to Cobbitt and said, "Of course, I don't remember any of the clerks, except . . . yes . . . oh dear, the name begins with M—"

"Now fancy your remembering that, Miss Sorrel. Attention please . . . James Middleditch, Richard Glasswell, and Jamie Brooke."

Middleditch and Glasswell made bobbing movements with their heads as their names were mentioned, but I took care to bow properly, as I had been taught to do, long, long ago, at dear old Miss Bellamy's dancing class, when I was a happy schoolboy in Bury St Edmund's. Cobbitt glared at me; but the girl's eyes rested again for a moment. Then she said, "Good night," swung on her cloak, picked up the little lantern and walked to the door. Cobbitt ambled along with her; and I had the drawer back in place and my hat in my hand before he could turn back and decently cancel the permission to go.

I raced home and told Mother, "I'm late again, but for once it was worth it. I have real news."

"About the funeral?" asked Mother, with less than her usual interest. I had entirely forgotten the funeral.

"No. But I know what's going to happen to the business . . ." And I recounted the story of Sorrel Kingaby's arrival in the office and her inheritance. While I was telling the story I saw Mother's face going whiter; I always knew, because although she coloured her cheeks and lips very carefully, pallor showed around her mouth and eyes. I broke off my tale.

"Are you feeling badly?" I asked. "Is it the pain?"

"No. No. Go on. Did she say anything else? Is it all hers? No legacies or . . . anything?"

"She didn't say in so many words. But she said it was all hers, absolutely and unconditionally."

Mother's face began to twitch, as it always did before she cried. Then, very slowly, as though with great difficulty, the tears began to form in her eyes and spill over. She never made faces when she cried. There was just a twitching and then the overflow of tears.

"But, darling," I cried, "what has upset you? You

didn't expect the old man to leave each clerk five hundred pounds, did you?"

"Of course not, silly. But . . . hearing that. Oh Jamie, I have done badly by you. Why didn't I marry a rich man who could have left *you* a good business? Fancy all that being wasted on a *girl*!"

"Who's being silly?" I chided her. "I'm not saying that I didn't feel damned jealous when she brought it out in that satisfied way; but then I'm jealous of anybody who gets an easy living. And there are hundreds of them, girls, too. Why cry about one?"

"It brings it home so," said Mother. "The awful injustice of it. You, slaving away there for ten shillings a week. . . . And just think what she'll have." She took out her handkerchief and dried her eyes viciously as though they were her enemies.

"Now," I said, in a rallying voice, "do you want to hear what I believe about Cobbitt?"

All the time I was cooking and dishing up supper I talked about Cobbitt, how he would bully the girl, and pare down expenses and probably make me attend to the pack horse teams in the yard in order to save a stableboy's wages. I exaggerated wildly and was as amusing as I knew how to be; but Mother was not easily cheered that evening.

Before long, however, we had a real matter for sorrow. Ever since I could remember, to away back when I was a schoolboy. Mother had had a steady allowance. It wasn't enough to make for affluence, but it kept us both in comfort, and although we lived with Uncle Simon on his farm just outside Bury St Edmund's we were in no sense dependents of his, luckily for us, for what with his experiments and cross-breedings and

new crops, he was for ever on the verge of bankruptcy.
I had understood the money to be the remains of my
father's estate and that my father, dead since my in-
fancy, had been a cut above the farming class. It is
difficult to say by what means such ideas are borne in
upon the young mind, but I had always accepted
them just as I did my name, and the fact that my
mother had been crippled in an accident.

When I was sixteen, something happened which de-
creased Mother's income, and the matter of my leaving
school and getting a job arose. We moved, with a kind
of inevitability, to Bywater, and there, it seemed most
fortunately, I immediately fell into the job in the
Kingaby office. Mother apologized for it rather often,
but always insisted that it might lead to anything.
(Perhaps she had heard the story of Cobbitt's meteoric
career!) With my earnings, seven shillings at first, and
then ten, we were still quite comfortable. We had the
best rooms in Mrs Petch's house in Fendyke Street,
and for the money we paid she cleaned and cooked for
us, washed our clothes and did the bulk of the shopping. I only cooked in the evening because Mother
liked to lie on the sofa and direct things, and I quite
enjoyed muddling with the food. We certainly weren't
rich; I never, for instance, had the kind of clothes I
should have liked, but we were comfortable.

Now, all very mysteriously, after Mother had written notes and received visits from a lawyer, and spent
hours in furious meditation on the sofa, and wept, and
sent more notes and had further visits, I learned that
the income had apparently quite disappeared. We
were, apart from my earnings, penniless. And Mother
needed almost constant attention, could do no hand's

turn for herself, liked a good fire day and night, since immobile limbs feel the cold, liked the best Su-Chong tea at frequent intervals throughout the day, liked a supply of books, liked lace on her gowns. . . .

Financial trouble can become all-absorbent, like a severe pain. I found myself waking in the morning and beginning to go through possibilities, fears, schemes, as steadily and monotonously as though a voice outside my head were putting them into words and shouting them in my ears. I worried as I ran to the office; I worried in the office and so made mistakes upon which swine Cobbitt pounced with sadistic pleasure; I worried again on the way home and all through the evening. When I was in bed my mind, like a performing dog, went through the same old performance; and if, having got to sleep, I had the misfortune to waken in the night, then it was hell. Things that looked badly enough during the day seemed a thousand times worse at night. I began to emulate the Cobbitt of long ago and look out for a better-paid post; I tried Groatan and Bagworthy, who were both in the same line of trade as ours. Groatan wanted nobody; Bagworthy offered eight shillings. I went as far afield as Baildon with no better luck. I would plan in the night such wild measures as turning highwayman or smuggler; but the sane light of day brought sense with it and convinced me that such thoughts were folly. I wouldn't even know how to begin. If there had been smugglers in Bywater I would have joined them gladly; but for some reason this corner of Essex had escaped the Owlers' attention; and how could one young man, without a boat, without money, without connection, associates or experience suddenly embark upon it?

We economized, God, how we economized! Our comfortable rooms on the ground floor were given up, and we moved into two attics with uneven floors and sloping walls and windows so high that they afforded no view. The inner one I made into a bedroom for Mother, and I slept at night on the couch upon which she had spent the day. We dispensed with Mrs Petch's cooking and cleaning services. She, who had always been servile, changed with our circumstances and became truculent and familiar. She raked up an old account for washing some lace for Mother, and for some game which she said she had obtained for us cheaply, and since, by that time we were without ready money to pay it, offered to take instead the spinet and the little French escritoire which Mother had brought from home. They were worth about two hundred times the paltry sum of debt which she had invented, but we were in no position to bargain. Moreover, it would have been difficult to get them into the attic, so they stayed in the parlour and Mother mourned them almost every day.

With all this private worry I took little share in the almost fantastic interest which the whole of Bywater was taking in Miss Sorrel Kingaby and her resolution to carry on the business. Echoes of it reached me, as they were bound to do when, for about a fortnight one could hardly enter a shop without someone asking facetiously what petticoat government was like. Doubtless the poor wench had had some stiff opposition to face; Raikes the lawyer said in the bar parlour of the "Ship" that he had told her frankly that he would rather see his daughter dead than in a position where she must meet men on an equal footing. Dr Burnett,

Josiah's oldest friend, reported that he had paid her a special visit in order to dissuade her from adopting a course which would not only ruin her reputation but impair her health as well. The old woman, Mrs Fennigard, a kind of aunt, who had a malicious tongue and did quite a lot of gossiping, told one of her cronies that the other old lady, Miss Louisa Kingaby, had been in a state of hysteria for a week when Sorrel made her intention known. But that, said Mrs Fennigard, was because Louisa had hoped that Sorrel would sell out and set up house in a town where there was some polite society, with Louisa as chaperon and mentor.

"Pour Lou, like all old maids, is an inveterate matchmaker," Mrs Fennigard is reported to have said. I sometimes wondered how often these old ladies, gossiping over their teacups, stopped to consider how much of their chatter was overheard and passed on until at last it was retailed for the amusement of the groundlings. Mrs Fennigard, who thought highly of herself, would probably have been shocked had she heard her words repeated by Mrs Petch, for instance.

Bywater gossips, of course, both high and low, seized upon the subject with delight. In a town of that kind, with no theatre, no real society, illiterate and narrow-minded, the people were bound to find their drama in other people's lives. So they embroidered every story and very soon people were asking us if it were true that Miss Kingaby wore man's clothes, swore like a trooper and could add up pounds, shillings and pence columns simultaneously. They went so far as to suggest that Josiah had kept her at school without intermission for seven years because she was so peculiar and hideous that he was ashamed to have her about.

They were frankly incredulous when we reported that she was small, quite ordinary looking, almost pretty, baffled by any but the most simple reckoning, and, unless given cause for anger, more than usually pleasantly spoken.

I suppose I gave, during those few weeks before Christmas, this account to an eager inquirer a couple of dozen times or more. And each time, with increasing certainty, I knew that my description was as full of errors as the wildest gossip's picture of an Amazon. I described a perfectly ordinary young girl whom circumstances had placed in an unusual position; but as the days followed one another and financial worries became so familiar to me that they no longer could absorb all my attention, I became aware that Sorrel Kingaby was not a perfectly ordinary young girl. She was like a box with which I used to play when I was small. It was square and the sides were painted; and inside it there was another square box with other pictures on the sides: and within that there was another, and another, until the last cube was too small to have a lid and was like a dice, solid, but with infinitesimal pictures on its tiny sides. And each box, although only part of the whole plaything, was complete and perfect in itself.

Of course, that was a thing which I could tell no one. But what I could report and did, as did the others, to the infinite amusement of some critics and the disappointment of others, was that even in her own office Miss Kingaby was thoroughly chaperoned.

It really was funny. Behind Sorrel, when she made her next appearance in the office, came what I can only call an apparition, the very essence of spinsterhood.

Tall, gaunt, flat-chested, with greying hair severely dressed and that discoloured look, neither brown nor pale nor quite purple which some women get in their fifties—that was Miss Louisa Kingaby. Her face was as long as a fiddle, and she had large hands and feet, the former encased in mittens, black ones, and the latter in flat felt shoes with fur linings that hugged her ankles under her voluminous, multitudinous skirts. She wore a small shawl over her head and a large one round her shoulders. At her waist there jangled a collection of small silver objects, and on her arm she carried a big-beaded bag. Her expression and attitude gave evidence of two conflicting emotions, determination and trepidation. Sorrel had the air of accepting a defeat good-humouredly. She held the door open for the old lady who marched in and stood, as if ignoring her surroundings, until Sorrel pulled the chair which had been the old man's into a corner by the stove.

"There you are, Lou," she said. "Make yourself comfortable."

The old lady sat down, put the bag, gaping, upon her lap, exchanged one pair of steel-rimmed spectacles for another and took out a piece of slate-coloured knitting.

I nudged Glasswell and murmured, "Mary had a little lamb."

Sorrel said, "Now Cobbitt, I want you to come round with me and tell me what everything is, where it comes from, what it's used for and where and how we sell it. Then perhaps the books will mean something. Just now they look like Greek to me."

I wondered whether the watchdog would trail after them about the warehouse, into the bays, and up the steps to the lofts. But no, she sat quite still, except for her rapidly flashing fingers. She knitted until eleven o'clock, when she rose, collected the kettle and the coffee pot, took two pretty rose-painted cups from the bag and brewed coffee for us all. From the same capacious bag she took a packet of little sweet cakes which she offered to us with a kind of shy good-fellowship before going to the office door and calling to Sorrel that the coffee was ready. There was something rather disarming about her smile and her little domestic activities, and I began to think that she was not such a dragon as she seemed; and my good opinion of her was established upon the third day when, as Cobbitt laid some papers aside saying, "Young Brooke can copy those when he's finished what he is about, if he ever does finish," she thrust in her knitting needles and said grimly, "I write a very clear hand, Mr Cobbitt. I will copy it. I might as well be useful, since I am here."

In the course of months she saved me many hours of extra labour, and although, for some reason which rather puzzled me, she liked me much less than she liked Glasswell and Middleditch, I grew fond of her, and thought, now and then, what a pity it was that men chose women for their faces only and not for their other qualities. Louisa Kingaby would, I am sure, have made some man an excellent wife, and some children, doomed to remain unborn, a splendid mother.

As it was, of course, all her affection and solicitude were lavished upon Sorrel who endured them with varying degrees of tolerance and impatience according to her mood. A little later, when I heard, through Marian, more about the life that went on inside the house at the other end of the orchid-filled passage, I knew that although Sorrel and Cousin Lou sometimes quarrelled fiercely, their differences were always quickly settled by the need for maintaining an unbroken front in their dealings with Mrs Fennigard and the old man's widow.

Christmas came and went, the dreariest Christmas I had ever spent, despite the gift of a guinea from the firm and a wonderfully lavish supper to which everyone even remotely connected with the business was invited. We owed money at various shops; my clothes, always the weakest item, were badly in need of replacement, and it was with difficulty that I kept Mrs Petch paid. Nor was it the easiest of lives, in the depths of winter, to get up early, prepare breakfast, help Mother to dress, get the fire going and plenty of fuel within reach, make some kind of arrangement for the mid-day meal and be at the office by eight o'clock. I felt like snarling when anyone wished me a Happy New Year. And yet, curiously enough, it was the new year which brought me a temporary, a perilous, but a welcome respite.

Swine Cobbitt had always had a grudge against me. Glasswell and Middleditch were his kind; in shape, in colouring, in speech and background they were his brother clerks. He bullied them, as he would have bullied anyone in his power, but without spite or special enjoyment; he enjoyed making me feel his authority. And if ever there was an extra job to be done, an extra hour spent in the service of his god, I was chosen to do that job and spend that hour. Mostly he waited to see me do it; but occasionally he would go home, having locked the door between office and warehouse, and leave me with the key to the main door on the wharf.

The locked office door was nothing to me, I had found another key to fit it, and ever since our pecuniary troubles I had taken tea and coffee and sugar on each occasion upon which I had been alone.

But early in the new year, having left me a whale of a task, he had gone off to a free dinner which Groatan was giving to all who had done business with the firm in the last year, and to which Cobbitt was asked as a kind of compliment, there being no Kingaby to invite. I gathered up my tax of staples, tea, coffee and sugar, stowed them in my coat pocket and settled down to the job, determined to make as short work of it as I could. Suddenly I heard the door tried and, going to it, was hailed by a customer of ours who lived at Halstead. He had come over for Groatan's dinner. He dealt with Groatan then because, for more than two years, he had owed us one hundred and seventy-five pounds. We had written him another letter about the debt when the old man died and we were straightening things out, but nothing had been heard from him. Now, taking a greasy leather purse from his pocket, he paid me the sum and waited while I wrote a receipt. He was, incidentally, very drunk.

When he had gone I looked at the money and thought of all I could do with it. I found up the original entry of the debt and saw that the 7 could, with the utmost ease, be converted into a 2. I altered it. I went through the books, and in every place where the debt was carried forward I altered the figure. I knew that it was devilishly possible that on the morrow when I said to Cobbitt, "There is the one hundred and twenty-five pounds which Simpson brought in last night," he would turn and say, "One hundred and

twenty-five. Don't be daft, it's one hundred and
seventy-five he owes." Cobbitt had that kind of mind.
On the other hand, it was New Year, money was coming in and going out with unusual rapidity, and the
debt was two years old. It might be months before
Cobbitt noticed the deficit. And in any case it was a
chance, the only chance I had. And I took it.

I was not, of course, trusted with the cash-box key,
so I put the money into a drawer and locked it. I entered the sum of one hundred and twenty-five pounds
in the receipt book and went home. I paid Mrs Petch
for some weeks in advance; I settled with the shopkeepers; and I slept the sleep of the debtless. In the
morning Middleditch unlocked the cash box; I put the
money in. All through the day other money came in,
and in the middle of the afternoon Glasswell carried
the lot along to Mr Thorley's bank. Cobbitt, who, like
many misers, enjoyed good food at another's expense,
looked rather drawn and yellow all that day, and perhaps was a little less spry than usual. I did not guess
then that Cobbitt, too, was nagged by an uneasy conscience.

About three weeks went by. It was unusually mild
for January. As a rule, we in Bywater were almost
completely cut off from the rest of the world from
early in the new year to the end of February. The
roads were so bad that horses foundered and coaches
sank in the axle-deep mire. But in this year it was
possible for Sorrel and Miss Lou to be driven into
Colchester to interview a governess. I do not think the
object of their journey had been mentioned in the
office, but the little drain of gossip that ran downhill
from the tea-cups of Mrs Fennigard and her friends

to the ale mugs of Mrs Petch and *her* cronies, had
yielded another trickle; and it was known in Bywater
that Miss Sorrel Kingaby had differed again from her
great-aunt, in that she had argued that education for
young ladies should enable them to do more than em-
broider firescreens and sing popular songs. She said
that she found herself, after seven years of schooling,
woefully ignorant, did not understand about tides,
and had no idea that one gained or lost a day by travelling round the world. Mrs Fennigard's reply to that
was that she herself had had three husbands and not
one of them had ever inquired into her knowledge of
tides; and that the statement about gaining a day by
travel was frankly impossible, otherwise every human
being would be rushing in that direction in order to
lengthen life's span. Mrs Fennigard was all for packing
the girls off to school, to be made into ladies and learn
how to get themselves husbands. Miss Lou sided with
Miss Sorrel; the widowed Mrs Kingaby, who did not
like the presence of her step-children, had supported
Mrs Fennigard; and, so ran the gossip, the house had
been torn by a fierce and long quarrel during which
many speeches, more pointed and pithy than polite,
were made by either side.

However, on this January day the pair had left early,
muffled to the eyes, to meet and inspect the governess
in Colchester. Cobbitt, who since Groatan's dinner
had been fairly peaceable, suddenly decided to raise
hell, behaved like a maniac all day, and kept us all
working until seven o'clock. I spent the day in agony.
Cobbitt did so much, routed out so many things that
had been left undone, referred to so many accounts,
dragged out so many old files that I was almost re-

signed to the fact that I should be discovered before the office closed. So my attention was not on my work and I made three genuine mistakes. He pounced upon them with delight, threw back at me the long sums for re-casting, and then, to emphasize the fact that I must stay on, dismissed Glasswell and Middleditch. Then he wound his scarf round his head and put his hat on top of it and wriggled into his coat.

"I have an errand," he told me, "but I'll be back. Don't leave until I return." He shambled off. As soon as he had gone I made my usual raid on the warehouse, and had hardly hidden away my booty when the passage opened and Sorrel came, walking quickly and yet wearily, into the office. She was still in her outdoor clothes, and under the wide brim of her black beaver hat her face looked very small and pale, like a wedge of cheese. She said, "Good evening, Jamie. Has Mr Cobbitt gone?" She spoke brusquely, although she used my name.

"Only on an errand. He said he would be back."

"Is he at Groatan's?"

"I don't know."

"I'll wait," she said. And seizing the poker she set about the stove, in which Cobbitt had carefully damped down the fire before leaving, with such vigour that she shook away what little heart was left in it.

I got down from my stool and took a handful of sticks from the basket.

"Let me try," I said. And so, coming close to where she stood I saw that she was distressed and at the same time angry. The lower part of her face looked stubborn and ugly, but there was something about the set of her lips and the expression in her eyes that

informed me tears were not far off. Experienced with
Mother, I knew that there was one cure for that state.
I said, "You've had a long day, Miss Kingaby. Let me
make you a cup of tea."

She looked at me as though it had been a most revo-
lutionary suggestion. Something that was almost wari-
ness came into her face—as though she suspected me
of trying to make up to her in order to . . . but that
was nonsense, surely. My guilty conscience again. And
with no more than that second's hesitation she said:

"Thank you. That would be very nice. I've only just
got back from Colchester."

While I plied the bellows under the kettle she said:
"You're working late again." And then, "You're
not very good at figures, are you?" Once more the
warning feeling jumped through my bones. Was that
leading up to something?

"I'm very bad at them," I muttered and bellowed
vigorously,

When I had made and poured the tea I imagined
that she avoided looking at me as I handed her the
cup, and neither of our hands was quite steady. I went
back to my desk and bent over my work, but I could
see only one thing: a seven altered into a two. Transportation, I thought. And then what about Mother?

A footstep, and a bout of the little dry fussy cough
which lasted all winter, heralded Cobbitt's approach.
Now I shall know, I thought.

He was surprised to see that I was not alone.

"Why, Miss Sorrel," he exclaimed, "I would have
waited upon you at the house had I known that you
wanted to see me. Such a long day you must have had,
too. I always think the journey to Colchester . . ."

"Yes, I've had a long day—and a great shock, Cobbitt. That is what I wanted to see you about." There was a great deal of suppressed anger in her voice. And my heart missed another beat.

"Just a minute, Miss Sorrel, *if* you please. . . . Brooke, you can be off."

"I don't suppose what I have to say is any secret from him," said Sorrel, in that same hard voice.

"Nevertheless. . . . Brooke, you heard me!" I was by that time all but certain. And when I had snatched hat and coat and closed the office door behind me my first impulse was to run—run anywhere, in any direction. Yet some fragment of my mind retained its reason. If it were the matter of that fifty pounds, why had she let me go? Might it not be something quite different? Something that maybe I could turn to advantage, use as a defence when the moment of exposure came.

With these mixed feelings I did not go through the big doors, although I banged them convincingly. I turned aside, skirted the half-glazed side of the office, and crouched down at a spot where I judged that there would only be the thin matchboard partition between them inside the office and me in the warehouse. I could hear perfectly well.

The opening shot had evidently been fired by Sorrel while I was manœuvring into position, and at the first speech for the defence from Cobbitt I experienced a sensation of relief.

"I intended to tell you myself as soon as I had fully considered the matter. Mr Groatan made me an offer and I was thinking it over."

"The story I heard in Colchester varied from that.

It credited the approach to you. But no matter. May one ask what he offered you?"

"Another fifty pounds a year and ten per cent on the year's turnover."

"A very flattering offer. Shall you take it?"

"The answer to that rather depends upon you, Miss Sorrel."

There was deep significance and a subtle threat in swine Cobbitt's voice. And I thought, you're making a mistake, my man; you're judging the whole thing by the outside of the biggest box. You know she depends on you and is abysmally ignorant, and that is all you do know. Strip off the outside box and you'll find other things—that she's one of those who would cut off their noses to spite their faces, pig-headed, and almost incapable of being frightened. The light girlish voice said:

"Upon *me*, Cobbitt? In what way? How can I advise you? I know so little. I couldn't even guess—could you?—what ten per cent of Groatan's takings would be worth."

"We had not yet carried the discussion to that stage. But his is a good business, and he is a shrewd, lucky man. To tell you the truth, Miss Sorrel. . . ."

"Yes, by all means let us have the truth."

"The thing that has held me back has been the deep attachment which I feel for this business, and if I may be allowed to say so, for yourself."

"Then why did you go to—encourage Groatan in the first place?" There was a pause. I could imagine him swallowing hard and fixing those faithful-hound eyes on her face. And I thought, my dear, can't you guess? Your good industrious clerk isn't satisfied. It isn't money he wants, the chuckle-headed old screw, it's a partnership. He's trying to frighten you into giving it to him. And sure enough, out it came.

"I don't want to go to Groatan, Miss Sorrel. But there comes a time when a man must think of himself. For fifty years now, man and boy, I have worked here. For your grandfather, your father, and now for you. There isn't a detail of the business which I don't know. . . ."

"No one would deny that, Cobbitt."

"No one *could* deny it, Miss Sorrel. For fifty years then this business has had my labour, my unswerving attention, and my—my love. And it has given me—a living!"

"What more does it owe you?"

"Owe is perhaps a strong word. But I think I am not speaking wildly when I say, a place, Miss Sorrel. A share, a recognition that all the world could see."

"You mean a partnership?"

"Something of that kind."

"Be frank, Cobbitt. A partnership is a partnership, not something of a kind. Tell me, have I heard about this a little too early? Will Groatan offer you a partnership if you keep him dangling long enough?"

"We hadn't . . . I didn't . . ."

"I think you know the answer all the same. He made you an offer just good enough to frighten me with. Well, I'm sorry. If it were money you wanted I shouldn't quibble. I could hardly pay you too highly. And distasteful as it is to have to buy you, Cobbitt, I am prepared to outbid Groatan. But it will remain the Kingaby business, until I am dead or bankrupt. And that is my last word."

There was a long silence; and then Cobbitt spoke in a shaky, lachrymose voice.

" 'Outbid' and 'buy,' Miss Sorrel, are ugly words. Have I deserved them? What have I asked, as the price of a lifetime's service? Didn't I serve your grandfather and not get so much as a guinea for a mourning ring? And your father, who tossed me my cottage as you'd toss a bone to a dog? And now you, just out of school. Where would you be if I left you? What would you do to-morrow morning if I wasn't here? I only ask that. Is my request extortionate, in the face of the circumstances?"

"No. Not extortionate. Merely impossible. You heard me say I was sorry, Cobbitt, and I *am* sorry. But you know, and I know, that if my brother had grown up and inherited the business this situation would never have arisen. And I made up my mind long ago that despite everything, I would do, and have, what my brother would have done and had if he had lived. So there you are. If you don't come to-morrow I shall manage somehow. Perhaps I could bribe somebody from Groatan or Bagworthy, somebody who knows the trade and understands the value of money. And I could make do. Oh, for God's sake, Cobbitt; don't cry; or you'll have me crying. If only I could make you understand. It isn't my fault. It's something outside me. I have to make a success of it, by myself, otherwise it shows how right *he* was. Right to make that difference between Little Joe and me, I mean. I know all about the gossip and how people have laughed at me. But I don't care. I wanted this business for my own, and for my own I shall keep it. You couldn't frighten my father, and you can't frighten me." And her voice began to tremble, too. "In fact, I think I'd rather you went to Groatan, or anybody else, than stayed here feeling discontented all the time. That wouldn't be a very happy state of affairs . . ." She stopped; and there was a long silence. And then, mow me down if Cobbitt didn't break out into proper blubbering; and mow me down again if I, who hated his guts and not without reason, didn't feel quite sorry for the poor silly old swine. Fifty years, I thought, tied to the Kingaby wagon wheel, fifty years of meekness and industry and loyalty to an idea; and now to be defeated at the end, to have the last hope scotched. I heard him blow his nose, and could see, in my mind's eye, the violent colours, purple and yellow and green of his big pocket handkerchief, pressed against his sallow wrinkled face. And then he said, in a choked, flat, defeated voice:

"I do beg of you to forget it, Miss Sorrel. I was mad. Please, let us never mention the matter again. And don't worry about the future. We're in low water at the moment, but I've seen things worse, both in your grandfather's time and your father's. We shall pull through. We shall manage."

Having heard all that I wanted to, and a bit more, I got cautiously to my feet. My head came level with the glass in the partition and I took a peep inside. They stood there like people in a play; one on either side the narrow table, each with a handkerchief in one hand, and their free hands, hers small and white, Cobbitt's big, nobbly and discoloured, clasped across the table. Highly entertaining. And I suddenly realised that I was becoming like everybody else in Bywater, a seeker after entertainment from other people's lives. Dear, dear!

I was round the corner of the office, making for the outer door when I heard my own name.

"Cobbitt, what does Jamie Brooke earn?" Ah yes, she had recovered first, as the victor generally does. Cobbitt had to blow again before he could answer.

"He *earns* about six shillings, Miss Sorrel, but your father engaged him and arranged to *pay* him ten. I'll reduce him to seven on Saturday, if that is your wish."

"And the others, what do they get?"

"Glasswell nineteen, but then he pens all the trade cards and saves printer's bills; Middleditch seventeen. Of course, he is married and has a family to keep."

"Does the boy keep anyone?"

"He lives with his mother; but I believe she has a competence of her own."

"I wonder. I noticed to-night that his breeches were patched, and his shoes so badly cobbled that they can't be good in this weather. Could we give him a rise? To fifteen shillings, say?"

"He's overpaid as it is. Besides it would cause the others to be dissatisfied, Miss Sorrel." Ah, the old stoat, digging in his heels. Whack him again, Sorrel, I thought!

"Perhaps we might give the others a similar increase."

"That means an outlay of . . . thirty-nine pounds in a year," said Cobbitt stubbornly.

"Well, I think we must make shift to afford that. I once had a pair of shoes rather like that, in the winter. It wasn't a pleasant experience."

"When I was his age I earned seven and sixpence;

and did as much as that lazy young cub and Middle-ditch put together."

"Poor Cobbitt, what a shame. So we'll give them all the extra on Saturday, shall we? It'll be a surprise."

Now I wonder, I thought, as I slipped out through the warehouse door, is that little scheme a tribute to my shoes, or my charms, or to that timely cup of tea? And what endless possibilities it does suggest. But hard on the heels of that thought anger came. Damn her, and damn my shoes and the circumstances that forced me to wear them. I was a pitiable object, I supposed, to fortunate Miss Kingaby who could hand out five beggarly shillings and feel beneficent.

And so, on that evening, somewhere about mid-way between hope and hatred I resolved upon a course of action.

February brought a spell of hard weather. The pack-horse teams stayed in their stables, growing sleek and glossy as seals. The boys loafed about mending harness, swopping yarns, quarrelling and gambling away their wages. The coach failed to arrive on three successive weeks; and the roads were deep with snow and then with slippery slush. It was a wretched time; the roof of our attic dripped and I was perpetually moving pieces of furniture from under a new leak, placing pots and pails to catch the water and wringing out the cloths with which I staunched the less aggressive holes. No amount of stoking seemed to raise the temperature of the rooms and the windows, being so high and exposed, caught the full blast of the north-east wind which rattled the loose old casements and billowed the curtains. Even under piles of clothes and coverlets, Mother looked pinched and blue. It was, however, the slack period at the office, and I was always home by six o'clock and once or twice by five. And so February passed, and still I was not exposed.

The snows melted, the creeks swelled, the fields lay like sheets of silver and then came the winds of early March, bitter and searing, licking up the floods and setting dust a-swirl at every corner. And then the wind swung round. Where the leaden sky had hung, great white clouds, like full-sailed ships, drifted across the blue, and spring had come to Bywater. Sorrel brought half a dozen primroses in a tiny glass and set them on the office table; and all day through the familiar blend of scents in the office I was conscious of the thin clean perfume of the flowers, and thought of the woods at Fornham where they had lain like blankets under the trees. All the nostalgia of spring was in those few flowers.

One afternoon, early in April, Cobbitt gave me an errand to the corn-chandlers', and added, with unusual consideration, that as it was on my way home I need not come back. The tide was high in the estuary, so that the ugly mud did not show; the top of the church tower and the upper branches of the red-budded elms in the churchyard were still awash in golden light. It was an exciting afternoon. I changed one of the last of Simpson's guineas without the usual accompanying thought of transportation and bought one of the small chickens which were hanging in the shop where I went for butter. Heaven knows what prompted me to plan a little feasting that evening, but I did. And Mother, whom the softer weather had greatly cheered, entered into the spirit of it and made me get out a pink wrapper, edged with lace which she had not worn for some time. True, the silk was cracking along the folds and the lace was torn in places and not very clean, but the colour suited her, made her cheeks pinker, her eyes bluer and her hair almost dazzlingly white. I served up the chicken with a necklace of well-browned sausages round the dish and we pretended that we were having supper in a fashionable place and made remarks about the other merry-makers. It was all very silly, but pleasant.

I had piled the dishes and set on the kettle to heat for washing up and was out on the landing at the top of the stairs fetching in the second bucket of logs which I had dragged up earlier in the evening when I heard Mrs Petch, our landlady, give a shrill cry. Then I heard a voice which I recognized as Sorrel's. I had never noticed her voice much, but hearing it now I knew I was not mistaken, it had a velvety undertone. Mrs Petch replied to whatever Sorrel had said with a volley of abusive questions. I ran down the two flights of stairs in a twinkling, and as I dropped off the last step Sorrel almost ran to me, crying in a relieved way, "Oh, Jamie."

"What is the matter?" I asked, conscious that I was in my shirt sleeves and that my shirt was a garment of which the less seen the better. Mrs Petch answered me:

"Bursting in here at this time of night as if the fiend was behind her, gave me the turn of my life."

"It was only that I was just stretching up for the knocker again when you opened the door," said Sorrel. "There was no need to strike me." She straightened her hat and tucked away a curl. "No, no, it doesn't matter," she added hastily, as I turned upon Mrs Petch

angrily. "It doesn't matter at all. Jamie, I must speak
to you. Is there anywhere we could go?"

"The parlour's engaged," said Mrs Petch hastily,
"and I've got friends in with me. That's why I didn't
get to the door so sharp."

"I'm afraid then we'll have to go upstairs," I said,
"Or did you want me to come back to the office?" I
knew what had brought her; or I thought I did; and
the thought of it all coming out in front of Mother
made me feel sick. And yet Mother was bound to
know, somehow, sometime. Oh, God, what a fool. . . .

And yet she had twice said "Jamie" in a voice
which, whatever else it might have in it, carried no
trace of accusation. I led the way upstairs. And I
thought, as we climbed, of what I should say suppose
the worst had happened—nothing more or less than
the bare truth; and in the face of that story of penury
and privation it was unfortunate that our eyrie should
smell so richly of roast chicken and sausage; and
would Sorrel ask herself why I hadn't sold the silver
candlesticks and the sofa and a few other things and
so staved off the need for dishonesty for a little longer.

I opened the door and stood aside for her to enter;
and as she did so I seemed to see the apartment with
her eyes, unblinded by familiarity. The torn, dirty
brocade of the sofa and the chairs, the overcrowded
furniture, damp-patched walls and ceiling, the dirty
dishes on one corner of the table.

I said, "Miss Kingaby, this is my mother," and
Mother after one look of surprise, stretched out her
hand and in her best manner told Sorrel how very
pleased she was to see her, and apologized for not
rising and ordered me to push a chair forward, as

though a visit from my employer was the most natural thing in the world. And all the time through my own confusion and terror I was conscious of hatred flowing out of Mother towards Sorrel as real and tangible as the steam which belched from the kettle.

"Miss Kingaby has come to see me about something important, Mother. I'm sorry to disturb you, but there was nowhere else to go." I hoped, I almost prayed that at that she would say, "Help me into the bedroom." But she only smiled and said:

"Where else should you go, dear? I've heard so much about Miss Kingaby, and I am delighted to see her. But she has taken quite a walk to honour us. She would find a cup of tea refreshing, I am sure."

"Oh, no! No, indeed," said Sorrel. "I'm not at all tired or in need of anything, thank you."

"Well," said Mother, "even if you won't share it you won't mind if I have mine. I usually drink tea at this hour, and in my life it is difficult to break these little habits." I tried to shake my head at her, but her eyes met mine with a kind of glitter, and I knew that in some obscure way that cup of tea mattered, that it asserted her position in this room, and her authority over me, her son.

I knew too that Sorrel Kingaby was inclined to impatience; I had noticed that at the office. And to-night, though her manner was subdued, even a little shy, I quite expected her patience to crack suddenly and for her to blurt out something in front of Mother. I had slipped on my coat again, and my shirt was sticking to my back with the sweat which agony and embarrassment were wringing out of me. But I made the tea. Sorrel accepted a cup after all, and Mother sipped and

chatted as though she were at a tea-party, and all the
time, pretending to a right to frankness through her
greater age, she kept letting fall the most double-edged,
barbed remarks. Every one of them fell on me like a
hot coal. Sorrel sat almost silent, never reacting to the
malice in the remarks, but apparently taking them at
their face value. If she had been Mother's very worst
enemy, forced into her company under a veil of politeness, Mother could not have been worse. She said for
instance:

"I assure you, Miss Kingaby, all the stay-at-home
women in Bywater are watching your career with the
greatest interest. Such a brave decision to make. Such
an undertaking. And you know, when I heard that a
Miss Kingaby was taking over the business and learning the ways of it and doing all the things that have
always been regarded as the special province of the
menfolk, I gained quite the wrong idea of you. Jamie,
the naughty boy, never explained how small and pretty
and altogether feminine you are. My dear, you're
blushing, I declare. You mustn't waste your blushes
on an old woman's compliments."

I reached the point where I could no longer bear it.
I said quite firmly, "Now, Mother, I'll help you
through."

"You see what it is to be old and not have the use
of your limbs, Miss Kingaby. And also what a blessing
a good son can be. If I could wish a wish for you it
would be to be married before you are a day older
and to have six sons and no daughters."

And with that unsurpassable *faux pas* she allowed
me to help her into the bedroom. I would have gone
to the gallows at any moment until then swearing that

Mother had absolutely no vice in her. My God!

When I came from the bedroom Sorrel had pulled her chair nearer the table and sat with her elbows on it and her head in her hands. She looked up as I entered, and I saw that her face was full of misery. I said, "I'm sorry about all that delay, but she never sees anybody except me and Mrs Petch."

"That's all right. Sit down, will you, Jamie. I don't like what I've got to say, but it must be said. Cobbitt found out this afternoon about that fifty pounds."

I suppose I might have fenced for a moment. There was no absolute proof that I had taken it. Middleditch had handled the money, and it was possible that he might have altered the books. But I didn't want to involve him, poor devil, just to gain a temporary respite which wouldn't do me any good. So I merely said:

"What are you going to do about it?"

She looked towards the bedroom door.

"I can guess now why you did it. I've often wondered. But Cobbitt said she had money of her own."

"She had. An allowance. But it stopped last autumn. I wouldn't steal from choice. I'd tried everything else, economizing—as you see, trying for a job with better wages. And a cripple isn't like a sound person. Take away her little comforts and she'd be better dead."

"I know." We were silent after that. Sorrel looked at me with a curious expression, and then looked away, and I sat there awaiting the verdict, shamed, helpless. After a space which seemed to stretch endlessly she sighed and gave herself a little shake.

"Cobbitt, you see, is furious; partly, I think, because he has been so long discovering the alteration. I think the best thing to do is for you to take him the money

in the morning, say that you borrowed it for a little
while and can now pay it back, and ask him to overlook it."

"But I've spent it. I owed so much, and the rest I
have been spending a little at a time ever since."

"Yes, of course, I knew that." She brought one
hand out from under the table, and I saw in it a netted
purse confined by a brass ring. She pushed it across
the table.

"It's my private money. Some I drew for the housekeeping," she said, as though, dear God, it was for her
to explain to *me*.

I gasped out some sort of stumbling protest. I was
almost speechless from surprise and confusion and
relief, and none of the words I muttered made sense,
but they drew from her an urgent, "Please, Jamie!"
which seemed to sum up the whole fantastic situation.
It might very well have been that she, the thief, was
pleading with me, the accuser, for leniency.

I was just jerking out some further incoherent words
about never being able to repay and so on when I
heard the rapping of the stick by which Mother bade
for attention. With an apologetic glance to Sorrel I
went to the bedroom door and said, "Yes?"

"Jamie, you'll see Miss Kingaby safely home, won't
you? It's too late for a young lady to be out alone."
She meant, clearly enough, that Sorrel's coming alone
had been unladylike.

"I'd rather you didn't," said Sorrel, as I called back
the necessary assurance to Mother. "Somebody might
see us. And I think the essence of this plan is that I
should be out of it, and then I shall have a free hand
with Cobbitt."

"I'll come along behind you then and keep my distance. And I am so very grateful . . . which is such a trivial thing to say. I can't think why you should . . ."

She gave a brittle little laugh, though her eyes, fixed on me, were almost mournful in their gravity.

"Put it down to fellow feeling. I've known the time when I would have stolen had there been anything to steal."

But as an explanation that didn't quite meet the case, and when I had seen her safely back into East House, I walked home slowly with more mixed thoughts milling together in my mind than had ever been there at one and the same time before. Relief had first place; and then a wonder as to how Cobbitt would behave on the morrow, and speculation as to the cause of Sorrel's amazing action, a speculation which now and again hovered upon the verge of thinking she must be in love with me. And I was grateful, too, though oddly mixed in with the gratitude was something that was very nearly hatred. Fifty pounds, so much when you had to steal it, to risk everything in order to get it; so much when you considered the difference it made in the tradespeople's attitude and to the amount Mother and I could eat; and, at the same time, so little when one could hand it over in a netted purse and know that you would hardly miss it—"my private money . . . housekeeping." A damned unfair world.

Sorrel was not in the office next morning. Cobbitt accepted the money and the explanation, locked away the cash and formally dismissed me. I did not know how seriously to take the dismissal. Sorrel had men-

tioned a "free hand with Cobbitt," but it seemed unlikely that she would quarrel with him on my account,
and I knew that he would oppose my reinstatement
with every effort within his power. He enjoyed sending me off more than he had enjoyed anything in his
life, I believe. It was the final act in a long hatred. At
the same time, in case something might be done, I decided not to risk Mother's questions by returning
home. So I went for a walk.

It was a perfect spring morning, all blue and white
and golden. I got on to the Baildon Road and walked
as far as Layer Wood, where I left the road and took
the path along the edge of the trees. I found a sheltered bank, warm in the sun, and lay down on my
back, staring up through the thick-budded twigs and
things. As near as I could judge to noonday, I ate the
piece of bread and cheese which always composed my
dinner, and after that I slept for a while. I woke when
the sun had left the bank and the wind turned chilly.
Then I remembered having heard someone mention
that daffodils grew in Layer Wood. I hunted round for
a bit and came suddenly on a great patch of them, not
quite fully open, but with the yellow bursting through
the green. I gathered a great armful. They had a poi-
gnant, earthy, unflowerlike scent, and the thick white
sap from the broken stems ran over my fingers. They
would look well, I thought, in a big blue and white
Chinese bowl which Mother cherished, and I could
always pretend that I had bought them for a few
pence. But just before I reached Fendyke Street I had
another idea. I turned sharply, crossed the Green, cut
through the churchyard and along Stag Lane, and so
reached Water Street without the risk of meeting Cob-

bitt or any of the others coming from the warehouse. The quiet street was empty as I went up the steps of East House and pulled the bell chain. An elderly servant, with a hard face and a suspicious eye, opened the door. Suddenly I felt God's own fool, standing there in my shabby working clothes with a great bunch of little, half-open, wild flowers in my arms. But I held them out and asked her to give them to Miss Sorrel Kingaby.

Surprise and scorn mingled with the suspicion in her eyes, but she let the door swing wide and held out her hands. The transfer took a few seconds because one or two of the flowers broke free and had to be recovered. And during this operation I raised my eyes once and looked into the dim, rich-looking hall. The stairs sprang straight ahead of me, and after nine steps or so, curved. At the moment when I looked in that direction a girl came round the curve of the wall, resting one hand on the rail. The door seemed to shut in my staring face and I was left with a memory of a graceful, rounded figure, some richly glossy dark hair, warm, glowing skin.

Is it so foolish to admit the possibility of love at first sight? Perhaps it is, if by love you mean the appreciation of a person's character, intelligence, integrity, the kind of things that outlast the charm of shape and colour. They, I grant you, cannot be judged in a moment or a day. But that other sort, the leap of the pulse, the thunder of the blood, the lust of the eye and of the body, that can strike in an instant. Who has not known the moment when, in some shop window, one object, only in detail differing from those around it, has leaped up crying, "I am the one. I am meant for

you. In me shall you know the joy of possession." And
to be obliged to deny that instinctive choice, to pass
by and leave the object for another man's possessing,
is the worst curse of penury. I had made many such
instant selections and been forced to renounce them
all. And in the same way, on that April afternoon,
when Marian rounded the curve of the stairs and stood
for a moment hesitant, the itch to possess began to
torment me, and went on tormenting me through all
my reasonable reflections about being twenty years
old, poor, obscure, worth fifteen shillings a week when
in work and now unemployed on account of dishonesty. A fine fellow indeed to go falling in love; a
suitor any girl might welcome!

Mrs Petch had a message for me when I arrived
home. A small boy had been sent to say that I was to
call at the forge on my way to the office in the morning, as the new padlock would be ready then.

A cunning, tactful message; Sorrel's signal of victory without mention of battle. And again I wondered
what feeling in her could possibly have evoked such
delicacy of touch. I also wondered how much of the
story was now known to Glasswell and Middleditch. I
did not look forward to the morning with any great
pleasure. However, in the morning everything was so
ordinary that I had moments when I could almost believe that I had dreamed the whole interlude of the
night and the day, Sorrel's visit, my idle hours in the
wood and the vision of the girl on the stairs.

Yet, although those few hours had a dreamlike
quality, they had been lived through, they were significant, and they bore results. I was to remember that

knotted within that short space of time were the threads which tied me to the three women.

Sorrel, through the rest of that April and the early weeks of May, seemed to pine and dwindle. There were plenty of things in the business to worry her, and gossip reported domestic upheavals as well. But when, because she seemed to grow thinner and paler, I was tempted to pity her, I used to think that the business could easily be left to Cobbitt, and she could have cleared the house of Mrs Fennigard and Widow King-aby, at least. Her worries were not like mine, riveted on her neck. The fifty pounds were spent long since, and despite the most cramping economy we were in debt again. I shrank from another attempt at larceny; it was too risky, and I was not clever enough. But I was, for once, lucky.

One bright May morning Miss Lou came into the office before Sorrel, and she was limping badly. Cobbitt, with fussy solicitude, inquired the cause of the limp, and the old lady, who often made a confidant of him, span a long tale. Miss Sorrel had had terrible headaches about which she had for a long time said nothing, but she had at last asked Dr Burnett's advice, and he, after repeating that she was leading an unnatural and unhealthy life for a young woman, had advised at least an hour's walking every day. She, Miss Lou, had naturally wished to accompany her, and had walked a blister upon one heel, and it had festered and now she was in agony.

I overheard this story, and I judged that if Sorrel walked that evening she would walk alone.

I swear that I set out with no more in mind than to

meet her, engage in private talk and hope to lead to
the point where she might realize that I needed, if I
did not deserve, a pound a week.

It was, outwardly, a strange evening. The sky was
a deep purple, heavily hung with clouds. And everything that had a bud to unfold or a petal to spread had
done it that day. The effect of the white-smothered
hedges and orchard trees against that dark sky was
breath-taking. I followed Sorrel at a distance until I
saw her take the path along the side of Layer Wood;
then I cut through the wood at a run and joined the
path almost at its end, where I sat down on a fallen
trunk.

I was hardly in position before she was in sight,
walking swiftly and lightly. She had, that evening, a
nymphlike air, with her almost curveless figure and
cool pallor. She wore a grey dress with bands and rib-
bons of the same bright green as the young leaves that
spattered the white hawthorn hedges, and she carried
a wide flat green hat in one hand.

I jumped up at what I judged the right moment,
greeted her politely and stood aside, as though to
allow her pass. Now, would she halt? She did. Her face
suddenly blazed scarlet and the hand which was not
holding the hat flew to her neck, where, above the
edge of her dress, a little pulse had begun to beat
furiously.

"I'm afraid I startled you," I said. "I'm so sorry."

"No. No. It's only . . . you know how it is when
you're thinking of somebody and then you suddenly
see them?" The colour was already dying down. It
was not the first, nor the last time that I had cause to
admire the rapidity with which she could regain con-

trol of herself. As though by way of explanation she added, "I saw all the dead daffodils, and wondered about those you brought me. Were they from here?" I nodded. "I never thanked you properly. But then I've never been in a position where I could do so without somebody wondering."

She looked at the tree trunk upon which I had been sitting.

"Is that dry? I should like to rest for a moment. I've not walked so far for years. Dr Burnett said walk for an hour, but it has always taken Lou an hour to walk as far as the old Fort and back. And even then she blistered her heel, poor dear." She sat down and smoothed the grey skirt over her knees. "Do sit down, there is plenty of room."

I sat down, and there was a short silence. I was not quite sure what to say first. I need not have bothered. Sorrel twisted round so that she faced me, and her green eyes seemed almost to probe me as she said, "I've wondered lately, Jamie. How are you getting on?"

"Badly," I said. And even if I had planned to say otherwise I think I should have had to respond to the honest inquiry of that gaze with an honest answer. "We're in debt again. I suppose we're bound to be."

"It seems inevitable to me, too. And yet I believe Glasswell and Middleditch manage. They never seem to be in distress. They're married, too."

"I know," I said. "But their wives aren't crippled. Glasswell's wife has a lodger, and I believe Mrs Middleditch takes in washing."

"I'm bothered about the whole question," she said frankly. "My household seems to cost so much. It is a constant problem, for instance, to keep Lydia and Dinah and Phœbe properly clothed. They grow so fast. It seems as though Miss Phillimore lives at the house. What do the Middleditch children do?"

"Go without," I said. "It's the way of the world."

"And it used to be worse. Cobbitt once told me that when he was twenty he earned seven and sixpence and worked . . . like two men. And it was on that base that my grandfather built up the business."

"Money was worth a little more than it is now."

"I suppose so." She sounded relieved. "All the same, he never had enough to keep a wife in comfort, or children. It does seem unfair. Do you ever read the paper, Jamie?"

"Sometimes. Petch works at the Vicarage and she occasionally brings one home and gives it to me."

"All this about France," she said musingly. "Liberty, Equality and Fraternity . . . I sometimes think that *behind* all the horror they meant well."

"Perhaps they did," I said, covering my ignorance of the subject.

"You see," she went on, "I was deceived myself. My father always seemed rich; but perhaps that was because I was a child and didn't understand. But I do remember his giving fifty guineas to the Assembly Rooms at Baildon because that was then . . . but that doesn't matter. All the same, whatever I suggest now Cobbitt says can't be afforded. It seems that you can *look* rich, and have plenty of business and own ships and things and yet not have much to spare. I'd like to give you all more money—but honestly Cobbitt would talk about ruin, if I did."

"It is a matter of comparison," I said. "Mother and

I, for example, are poorer than the Glasswells because we've always had more. If I had never seen her eating butter, I shouldn't want to buy butter now. It's the same with hundreds of things—candles we'll say. If every night of your life has been spent with a rush-dip, then you can see by it; if you've always had candles you need them still." That brought the conversation back to us.

"Look," she said. "Perhaps I had better wait a little while before I upset Cobbitt again by suggesting a general rise, but I would like to help you, Jamie . . . because of your mother. Add up what you owe, will you, and tell me. I must be going now. I'm sure Lou will have her eyes on the clock. Can I get back along this path, or must I turn?"

"The lane at the end here leads straight back to Bywater," I said, getting to my feet. "And . . . I will try to be worth it; I'll do more in the office."

"Perhaps," she said, ignoring those words, "I could see you sometimes like this. For one thing a proper walk does me more good, I feel much better this evening. And it is pleasant to talk to someone outside the house, and not . . . so old. My Aunt Carrie likes to have her friends the Kerrisons in some evenings, and then Lou makes the number even for cards. I'll see if I can make one evening certain for them."

She gave me another long steady glance. And I thought, by Heaven, she *is* in love with me. She may not realize it herself . . . but it is a fact and it should be turned to advantage.

The lane sloped steeply up to the cross-roads, and just before we reached them I halted. "I'll say good night here," I said.

"And I must put on my hat," she murmured, as though my withdrawal and the donning of her hat were twin tributes to the proprieties—which was true enough. She tied the ribbon under her chin and the brim of the hat took on a lovely curve, from under which her eyes, greener than ever against such a background, looked out with a clear level gaze as she extended one hand and said, "Good night, then, Jamie."

I bent my head until my lips just brushed the fingers of her hand. The fingers, small as a child's and a little chilly for such a sultry evening, closed on mine convulsively and were then hastily withdrawn. I raised my eyes to the base of her throat; the little pulse was hammering again.

I stood with my hat in my hand and watched her to the top of the lane. The patch of grass in the middle of the cross-roads was white all over with daisies, and the hedges on either side the lane were solid walls of blossom; she passed between them, under the strange light of that purple sky, a slim straight grey and green figure, was outlined for a moment against the background of daisies and was gone from sight.

I plunged back into the lane and retraced my steps, going home by the longer way. I had a good deal to think over.

A few days later, before Sorrel and I had met again except in the office, I was doing my shopping on my way home one evening and had just come out of the bakehouse when a voice behind me said:

"Please, could you direct me?" I turned quickly and was face to face with the girl I had seen on the stairs at East House. She carried in her arms a bundle swathed in calico and pinned at the corners; her lips were parted and she was breathing rapidly. I had an idea that she had run after me from the corner of the Square.

"I'm looking for Miss Phillimore, the dressmaker," she said. "They told me the fifth house, but that is a butcher's shop."

"I believe she lives over the butcher's shop," I said.

Her red lips pouted entrancingly. "Oh, what a bother. Now I have to go back. And this bundle weighs a ton." She shot me a lively glance.

"If you like to carry my loaf . . ." I said. We exchanged burdens and went back together to the butcher's shop where I pointed out the side stairs and the little card which bore the dressmaker's name.

"I shan't be a minute," said the girl, one foot poised on the lowest step and her yellow skirt lifted to show a froth of petticoat, a neat round ankle and small arched foot.

"I'll wait," I said, grinning.

"You weren't asked to," she said saucily.

"I'm going to buy some meat," I answered and turned into the butcher's.

I stayed out of sight, but with a good view of the stairs, and after a moment or two she came tripping down, and looked to right and left with a ludicrous expression of disappointment on her glowing face. Then I stepped out of the shop and joined her. She feigned surprise, but fell into step beside me and said, "Give me back the loaf. I'll be your porter for a little while. Tit for tat." There was a dimple that came and went in her left cheek when she smiled.

"Why do you have to do the shopping?" she asked.

"Because my mother is practically bedridden."

"Oh, yes, I remember hearing. I do know a little about you, Mr Brooke. That is why I thought I could ask you the way. Because we aren't strangers. Fellow slaves of the family as it were."

"For a slave you look very well."

"Thank you. And the same to you. Oh, yes," her voice lost its bantering note. "I'm well housed and fed, but so indescribably, intolerably bored. Soon I shall have been here three months, and do you know, until this moment not a word have I exchanged with anyone except old women and children."

"Miss Kingaby and Mrs Josiah Kingaby surely come in neither category," I teased her.

"Mrs J is a nonentity and only addresses me in order to complain that I have shown favouritism to the elder children. And Sorrel is a freak. Or do you admire her prodigiously? Some people do, I'm told." She flashed me a sidelong glance from eyes so dark and lustrous that they seemed to glitter.

"She's good to work for," I said non-committally.

"Oh, I admit that. I've never worked for anyone so good. She said exactly what she wanted the brats to learn and comes up about once a week to see that they are learning it, and apart from that never fusses or changes her mind. But that bears out what I said, it's freakish in someone who is only eighteen herself. Not to mention all this other business . . ."

"You mean the office?"

"Yes. Don't you agree?" That sidelong glance again. "Can you imagine any girl in her senses, and not bad looking, shutting herself in on one hand with a lot of tea and molasses, and on the other with three children and a pack of women who will quarrel about anything under the sun. Do you know, there isn't a joint served at that table but, if Mrs Fennigard says it's too red, Miss Lou says not red enough, or the other way around. It's a perpetual wrangle. And after a meal like that and a day in the office, her ladyship shuts herself into her study, which is more like a tomb than any room I ever saw, and practises *sums*. It takes her about an acre of paper to work out fifteen per cent of two hundred pounds. Truly."

"I suppose, being a governess, you find sums easy."

"Put it rather that finding sums easy I became a governess. And I have had good places and bad places, but never one so deadly, deadly dull. I might have known, of course, coming to a town where there wasn't even a theatre."

"Are you fond of the theatre?"

"Inordinately."

"So am I. Before we came to Bywater I saw a play every week."

We covered the distance to the mouth of Fendyke Street, telling of plays we had seen, plays we wanted to see. I think for both of us it was like meeting, in an alien country, a person who understood one's mother tongue.

At the end of the street I halted and held out my hand for my loaf.

"Do you ever go out except to shop?" she asked.

"Do you ever go out except on errands to Miss Phillimore?"

"Yes. I often take long solitary walks, surveying the scenery and thinking melancholy thoughts."

"Upon what day, at what hour and in what direction will you next take a walk?" I inquired. "Because

I might introduce you to some new scenery and help to ward off the melancholy thoughts."

"I'm sure you could."

"Then when, and where?"

And so, with little adjustments in deference to our various duties we fixed our next meeting.

And so began that fantastic summer. Even the weather was to become a legend, a measure of comparison for sun and drought. "The year when you could go dry-shod from the Fort to Foul Point," which meant that the marsh had dried out completely. And it was a year of blossom. All about Bywater the lilacs and laburnums massed their purple and dripped their gold; every little garden brimmed over with wallflowers, lilies, roses. And out beyond Layer Wood, before we turned along the lane, we could look out over the valley, where the Lower Road ran; and there were little snug farmhouses, set amongst hayfields white with ox-eye daisies, and young corn, green, with blue paths where the wind brushed it, and every ditch creaming with meadowsweet. Those evenings had the very scent of summer. Up from the valley would come the call of some milkmaid bringing in her herd, the bark of a dog, answered again from a distance, an untimely cockcrow. And always the cuckoo with its brief, most seasonable song.

And there would be Sorrel.

I could, I suppose, have done differently. I could have let Mother become a charge to the parish, or moved into even more squalid rooms and eaten less of worse fare; and so have managed on what I earned and preserved a certain integrity. And then, perhaps, looking back, I should not sometimes feel this prick of shame, nor wonder whether some of the ill-fortune that has since befallen me, was not well deserved. But I did not take that hard path. I saw in Sorrel a young woman of considerable possessions who was willing, even eager to share them with me, and I let her do it.

That I never made love to her is not to my credit. At that time I would have given my right hand to do the thing properly; to silence the question that was so often in her eyes; to respond to the plain invitation which she made again and again. But something always stopped me. She was pretty, she positively blossomed in that summer; she was so generous to me in such a fastidious, delicate way that there were times when from gratitude I would have let her walk on my face. But the hard fact remained that the mere thought of physical contact with her sent a pang of repulsion through me; and the more I tried to reason myself out of it the more stubborn did the feeling come. It grew with our acquaintanceship. Occasionally I was forced to offer my hand at a stile or an awkward place, and then there would be that tightening of her fingers on mine which I had noticed on the night of our first walk. It was terrible to be obliged to withdraw my hand with churlish haste, but I was so obliged.

Fortunately Sorrel never guessed the reason for my restraints and retreats. She laid the blame on our positions; and as though to make up to me for what she thought diffidence and shyness, would become even more generous, both with gifts and with friendship. Our restoration to the status of "parlour boarders," the reclamation of spinet and escritoire, a new suit and several shirts for me, books and little luxuries for Mother—all were Sorrel's gifts. I exploited her quite shamelessly and brought begging to a fine art. I had only to look worried, to sigh once or twice, or seem a trifle distraint, for her to say, "Jamie, something is troubling you. Tell me." And I can only say that if I could have given her what she wanted, clasped her in my arms when she leaned against me, kissed her when, as she sometimes did, she held up her face in innocent invitation, I would have done so, very gladly. But it was impossible.

Sometimes I wondered whether it was the innocence and the immaturity. If I had only seen her during our trysts in Layer I might perhaps have believed it and so come to credit myself with either scruples or discretion which I did not possess. But it was not so. I saw her for hours on end in the office and I knew that she could be, and often was, hard and cunning, eager for the last penny in a bargain and for the last word in an argument. And not by generosity or by innocence and immaturity had she, in six months, made such an impression, even upon the roughish fellows in the yard that you could tell in a moment whether she was in the vicinity or not, just by looking at the way they were doing their work. Sometimes even I forgot that we had a secret footing, and would inwardly wither when she pointed out to me, without violence or abuse, but with a cold, relentless precision, exactly where and how I had made a mistake.

And so, again, I sometimes wondered whether it was that inner hardness which repelled me, and made me, within physical reach of her, suffer a mild form of paralysis. But that was rubbish; because I knew perfectly well that Marian, under all the gay provocativeness of her manner was harder than the nether millstone. But her hardness, her greed, her ruthlessness were always a challenge that I was ready to take up. At that time nothing that she could have said or done, no mere word or action could have wiped away the attraction she had for me.

So there I was, with one woman whom I could not love in love with me, and in love with a woman who was not in love with me. For, pretend as she might, Marian could not quite deceive me. There were moments when I hoped, moments when I knew a little triumph, but they were few and far between. She liked me, enjoyed talking to me, was delighted when I gave her presents bought with Sorrel's money, but no woman loves a man whom she will entice and provoke and tempt up to the very point and then refuse. She knew that I was mad for her; she was flattered; she took a certain amount of pleasure in dangerous embraces; but the kiss that lasted a second too long, the caress that verged upon intimacy was always met, not by any answering passion, but by hasty withdrawal. Not that I blamed her. I did not. I admired the cool head and the icy heart that had brought a girl so lovely to look at and so reckless in behaviour as well as so exposed in situation, untouched through twenty-four years of life. But I did know that when she languished in my arms and murmured that she loved me, she lied.

My absences during at least two evenings of the week had not gone unremarked by Mother. She tried rallying me archly, proceeding by way of hints and innuendoes to direct questioning. (The one question which she might have asked, and for which I was prepared—regarding the source of our new prosperity, she never once touched on.) I replied that we were beginning to be busy at the office and often worked late, and then I confessed to occasionally taking a walk. Then one day she asked point blank:

"Jamie, are you seeing Sorrel Kingaby? Out of the office, I mean."

I lied at once. "No. Why should I? Why do you ask that?"

"Because I wondered. You never mention her now. And I thought on the evening when she came here that she was pretty and young; the sort of girl a young man might fancy if he saw much of her."

"Did you? Well, I can assure you that here is one young man who has not."

"I'm glad of that. It would be a terrible thing."

"Why?"

Mother put on the Irish brogue with which she often screened an unpalatable speech. "Sure now, and wouldn't it be the terrible thing for a poor young man to be after falling in love with a rich young woman? Wouldn't he be breaking his silly young heart?"

She let the matter drop then, but reverted to it later, and at last, when we were reinstated in the parlour, and Mrs Petch had been bribed to clean and polish everything, I invited Marian home. Mother rose splendidly to the occasion and behaved in her grandest and most gracious manner. Nothing was lost on Marian. I saw her eyes notice, and her mind began to assess every single scrap of evidence of our better days, the candelabra, the bits of fine china, the few articles of good furniture. And Mother, in a way too subtle and delicate to be called boastful, managed to make the Suffolk farm where Uncle Simon lived from hand

to mouth sound like a country estate. It was a successful evening, and when I returned from seeing Marian
home, Mother said, "So that's it. And as pretty a girl
as even your father could have chosen." And the tears
welled suddenly in her eyes and she was crying as bitterly as I had ever seen her do. I thought of the sad-
ness which must come over a woman who has been
pretty when she is pretty no longer, and is confronted
by someone as young and lovely as Marian; I thought
of the natural jealousy which a woman must feel for
the girl whom her son chooses. But, damn it, I was
not proposing to marry Marian. How could I? And
surely even Mother must understand about being
young. Besides, she was not crying miserably; she was
crying bitterly and rebelliously.

"And how can you hope to marry—that girl or any
girl?" she demanded through her tears. "Oh, Jamie,
my boy, I have done badly for you. No woman ever
did worse. Your life should have been so different. . . ."

"I'm not quite sure that I hanker after marriage," I
said, with a degree of truth. "You must remember that
for me the domestic interior has lost the charm of
novelty."

I meant it kindly, but it seemed a bad thing to say.
Mother broke into a tirade of self-recrimination, saying that she had made an old man of me before my
time; that she had reduced me to the status of a
kitchen hand . . . and so on. It was a bad ending to
an evening that had gone well.

The summer wore away; there came the evenings
when Sorrel and I, looking out over the valley, saw the
harvesters working late, dark figures against the golden

stubble, and the brighter colours of the bonnets and aprons of the gleaning women caught the eye. The evenings grew shorter and then chillier. And in the same week, about mid-way through September, both Sorrel and Marian spoke bodefully of the future.

Marian said, "Well, the summer is over, Jamie. And I don't think I can bear the idea of spending the winter in Bywater." My heart sank like a stone, and my mouth was so dry that I could not have said anything even if I could have thought of words to say. "And the next place I go to is going to have a theatre and a pleasure ground, and more than one presentable young man." She smiled as she said it, and the dimple flashed, but there was a kind of savage relish in the speech for all that. I was stung by it.

"And then you say you are in love with me," I sneered.

"But, Jamie, I am. I like you far better than anyone I've ever known. But what's the use? We get on well together and amuse one another. But there's no future for us, is there?" She waited a moment and then repeated, "Is there?"

Commonsense and reason compelled me to say, "None that I can see."

"Well then." She lifted her shoulders and spread her hands in one of her pretty gestures. "After all, Jamie, you say you are in love with me. But you don't let that affect your life or your plans, do you?"

"How can I?" I demanded, "You know what my life is—home, office, office, home. What plans could I make? Or alterations."

"In fact you are settling down to be another Cobbitt. One day when you're about forty and all dried up, you'll earn enough to get married on. And by that time it will be too late."

"Is that my fault? What else can I do? It's this damned unfair world that's to blame."

"What do other men do? You have had more education than most, and you have ability and—and—background. Isn't there anyone who could help you? What about that Uncle Simon your mother mentioned?"

"He has a farm," I said bluntly, "and he's slightly crazy. He spends all his time and all his money trying to grow some barley that will have two more kernels on an ear than any other sort; or breeding a bullock that will weigh more without wanting more food. I don't think his experiments are planned to include helping his penniless nephew. In fact," I sighed as I remembered the conversation, "once, about two years ago, Mother and I went back to Fornham for a week. I had been ill and had leave from the office. I told Uncle Simon then that I hated Bywater and the warehouse, and that I would rather be a cowherd at the farm. Do you know what he said? 'Boy, I have all the cowherds I need at six shillings a week. You stay at Bywater until you've money saved, then I'll talk to you.'"

"And you haven't saved any?"

"How could I have?"

"And no other relatives?"

"None that I know of."

To that she said, "Poor Jamie!" very sweetly and hugged my arm. And coming, as we did, shortly after that into the churchyard, I drew her into the shadow of a buttress and tried, by rousing desire in her, to make her content to stay in Bywater where I was. But it was no use, I only put myself in torment, and I knew that she was thinking that soon she would be twenty-five and if she would sell her charms advantageously she must get them to a good market quickly. I was merely a penniless clerk with whom it had been pleasant to while away an idle summer.

Sorrel's remarks about the season's changing were almost as blunt and straightforward. And yet how different.

"The weather has broken," she said, staring out across the valley. "And, Jamie, I've been thinking. I shall miss our evenings."

"So shall I."

I was conscious of a prick of anger. For all that I was not in love with her, and that it was, in a way, to my advantage that our association, particularly on the financial side, should be kept to ourselves, I resented the tacit assumption that because we could no longer meet in a corner of a wood, we could not meet at all. God knows any pride that I might have had at the beginning had been fairly tamed by that time, but I was still capable of feeling hurt!

Sorrel continued to stare ahead of her with her brows knotted and a sombre look in her eyes. Suddenly she jerked out a question:

"Jamie, have you ever mentioned our . . . walks to anyone?"

"No." It was the truth.

"Well, I have. Look, my dear, this isn't going to be a very easy thing to talk about, and I do beg you not to be hurt or angry. You know, or you should do by this time, that you are the only person in Bywater I really care to see or talk to. And the fact that you work in the office doesn't make a scrap of difference to me." She paused and I saw her fingers wrestling together. "About a week ago, when I saw the weather changing and the evenings growing so dark, I began to think about the winter, and I knew that I couldn't *bear* it if I didn't see you sometimes; and I didn't see the slightest reason why you shouldn't come to supper sometimes and spend the evening. But, of course, my household is very peculiar, old fashioned . . . so just to try out the matter I mentioned to Lou that we had met and walked. She wasn't . . . she wasn't very nice about it. So, Jamie, when you do come, as I hope you will, please don't mind if the old women make it— rather awkward."

I knew then what it was that had changed Miss Lou's always frigid manner towards me into definite dislike. The change had taken place about a week ago, and I had, at odd moments, wondered what I could have said or done to increase her antipathy for me. But that thought shot through my head and was gone, wiped out by the brilliant flash of inspiration which visited me almost before Sorrel's hesitating, halting speech had died on the air. It really could hardly be called a thought; it was as though I suddenly saw, laid out before me, a clear plan of action, just as you can see a map, with the road that you should take traced out upon it.

I began to play a part which came to me as I went along. I looked at Sorrel very gravely and said:

"My dear, you have been very frank. May I be equally so?"

"But, of course. Oh, Jamie, are you upset?"

"Never mind my feelings now. What you have said shows into what an impossible position we have fallen. Of course Miss Lou was shocked, and one by one as people get to hear about us they will, one by one, be shocked. Look at it fairly. There are you—young, pretty, an heiress; and here am I—a penniless clerk in your office with no prospects and a mother to support. Already I have let you give me so much that no decent person could fail to be contemptuous of me for accepting your charity. Suppose, as you suggest, I now begin to visit your home and meet, socially, your disapproving family. Just consider, Sorrel, how I shall be made to feel, and what will be said. I think my skin is as thick as most people's, but I haven't been blind all this long summer to the fact that I was snatching a little happiness at the risk of a great misery. And now that the misery is about to begin I am not going to make the cause public."

Her face had lost its natural creamy pallor and turned ashen.

"Is this damnable question of possessions going to end with your hating me?" she asked. "Because listen, Jamie. Once I swore that I would be like Lou and go to my grave a Kingaby, and that I would devote everything I had in me to running the business and pretending to myself that I was the successor whom my father so much desired. But that was a long time ago, when I was a young fool and didn't know anything. Now I see that if Little Joe had lived he wouldn't have had to crush down all his natural feelings and lead a miserable life in order to be a good business man. And I don't see why I should. *He* could have married whom he liked, and so will I. I'll marry you, Jamie, eagerly and gladly, if you will ask me."

I pushed aside my own plan and gave this one my serious attention. Complete security for ever; comfort for Mother to the end of her days; a pretty, loving wife whom I could, I knew, twist round my fingers. Not a man in a thousand ever had such a chance, and if I lived to be a hundred I should never have such a one again. And the damnable thing was that if it had been made to me by any other woman under the roof of the sky I believe I could have taken it. If the girl beside me had been cross-eyed, mean-spirited, fat, scrawny, vicious, anything, and had held out the Kingaby business with her right hand what time she offered her left for the wedding ring I should not have hesitated. The girl who *did* stand there, making that double offer of the hands, was loyal, generous, intelligent, pretty, almost everything that a man might wish his wife to be. But the idea of marrying Sorrel was utterly revolting to me. I could imagine then the horror of that marriage bed—the paralysis, the bewilderment, the terrible hurt. I closed my eyes against the dizzying wave of nausea that swept over me.

Yet I sounded convincing enough when having, in less than a moment, rejected her plan, I reverted to my own.

I said, "Sorrel, that is the dearest and sweetest thing that any woman has ever said to a man. But I can't agree to it. Just because you're noble and generous enough to ignore money and position you mustn't forget their existence. And a marriage like that wouldn't make either of us happy. I am sure of that."

She said, rather wearily, "It's the same wretched

business. If I were a man and had ten times what I
have, and you were the girl who brought milk to the
door and I chose to marry you everyone would gossip
for a bit, but they would find it *most* romantic and we
should probably be the happiest couple on earth."
Her full mouth with its pronounced curves took on a
bitter line and the green eyes, looking straight into
mine were stormy and angry.

I abandoned the plan for a moment to take up the
argument.

"I'm sorry to seem bigoted, Sorrel, when it is a
subject that you feel strongly upon—but there *is* a difference, though it isn't an easy one to explain. Nor
need that bother us at the moment. I can only say
that, flattered and touched as I am, I can't marry you
now. If I could once come to you with something—
however little—of my own . . . well, that would be
different."

"I did think of that. But, Jamie, what chance is
there of that? I am sorry to sound too downright, but
we might wait for years and still be in the same positions."

"I know. But if I could borrow enough . . ."

"Yes," she said eagerly.

". . . to start me off in a different line, and could
make a success of it. Then . . ."

"What line, Jamie?" The plan was working now.
She was giving the very answers I wanted, just as
though she too were playing a part.

"It's all rubbish," I said deprecatingly. "Where could
I raise seven or eight hundred pounds? What security
could I offer?"

"Tell me," she said. "Tell me all about it. What

could you do, Jamie, with that amount?"

So I told her just what I had told Marian, about
Uncle Simon and his need for capital and my love for
that way of life and how certain I was that I could
make a success of it. And although I never mentioned
marriage or committed myself in any way, I did basely
imply that given the modicum of success I might consider myself a suitor not unworthy. . . . Before we
parted she was deep in consideration as to how, without Cobbitt's knowledge, she could raise seven hundred pounds for me. May God forgive me, I went
home triumphant.

Marian continued her attempts to torture me; bringing me various advertisements of posts for governesses
and asking me to help her to compare their merits; or
requesting my aid in drawing up an advertisement of
her own. I was so unsure of her that I dared not face
the possibility of her securing even a temporary post
elsewhere; she would see somebody else, there would
be a son in the new family, or her employer would be
an attractive young widower, or a bachelor with a
ward; and then Jamie Brooke with a little share in the
Fornham farm would be as far beneath her notice as
Jamie Brooke, Kingaby's third clerk. So finally I was
driven to ask her to wait for a few days.

"Why should I?' she demanded. "Have you an eye
on a job for me?"

"In a way," I said. "But I can't tell you anything
about it yet. Just wait."

"I've given notice," she reminded me. "Unless something is settled by the twentieth of October I shall be
on your hands."

"We must risk that," I said.

I had written a discreetly worded inquiry to Uncle Simon; and although the delay before his answer came seemed endless, I heard from him before there was a sign from Sorrel. And the days slipped away relentlessly, breeding a kind of panic in me.

It was actually two days before the twentieth when Sorrel crossed the office and laid a paper on my desk.

"Check that for me," she said. Down the edge of a column of figures, in faint pencil, was written, "Come back to the office at nine. I'll let you in."

It was a pouring wet night with a wind that took handfuls of drenching leaves and flung them in my face. I was the only person abroad in Bywater that night. As I drew level with the "Ship" tavern I was drawn by the glow of candle and firelight through the windows, and went in and ordered and drank quickly, two large tots of brandy. I told myself that if Sorrel had failed to get the money I should need some support; and if she had managed it I should need the stimulus in order to act satisfactorily the part of a delighted, potential lover at last on the way to attaining his heart's desire.

The liquor, to which I was unaccustomed, since my budget seldom catered for anything but a little ale, sent a warm glow through me and made my head spin. I was less conscious of the wind and the rain as I completed my journey. I knocked gently on the outer door and Sorrel opened it immediately.

"You're so wet," she said. "And I tried to revive the stove, but it was too late."

She was wearing her hooded cloak, and the fur-lined hood, pushed back in soft folds made a becoming background for her face. I looked at her and thought—to-night, either way, I suppose I shall have to kiss you. Even with the brandy singing in my head the old, familiar repulsion laid hold of my vitals.

She watched me hang my wet outer clothes on their usual peg and then perched herself on the edge of the table.

"Jamie," she began, "I've been so angry to-day that I thought I should die with fury. I thought I had done with feeling like a pauper." Ah, I thought, she hasn't got it. Cobbitt was too fly for her, the old swine.

"I know I seem to have kept you waiting a long time," she continued. "But I've tried everything. And every way I thought of was baulked by Cobbitt. My own money and the housekeeping isn't anything to do with him, of course, but then that wasn't nearly enough. So at the end I thought I'd go and see Mr Thorley—or Edward Thorley—Quakers don't even like to be called Mr do they? He saw me at once; and apart from keeping his hat on he was very civil until I told him what I wanted. Then he was horrid, Jamie, horrid in the most insulting way. I explained that I wanted to take seven hundred pounds out of his bank without Cobbitt knowing. Then he said, you know how he talks, 'What dost thee want that sum for?' And I said I wanted to lend it to someone. Then he said that he would, for this past year, have been worried about me if he hadn't known that I had 'good George Cobbitt' to look after me; and as much as suggested that it was criminal for me to want any of my own money without Cobbitt's knowledge. I began to get angry then, but I kept hold on myself and he asked what security I proposed to offer. I said the house. You see Cobbitt needn't know about that either. I was more hopeful then; but after a bit he said his conscience would not allow him to accommodate me. He feared already that someone was taking advantage of me and he would not aid them in that . . ." She stopped and looked gloweringly at the opposite wall. I thought, oh, come along, don't beat about the bush, tell me the worst and have done.

"At that I was so angry that I got up and pushed my chair back and it fell over; and I said that if he wouldn't help me I would go to a moneylender—not that I should know where to find one or how to set about the business. Still, I was nearly to the door when he called me back and said rather than that he would let me have the money, without security and without interest, and I should pay it back as I received it from the person to whom I loaned it."

I drew a deep breath. "So you got it?" She nodded. "Then why are you still angry?" She gave me a look which accused me of stupidity, lack of perception and deliberate intent to annoy. Then she lifted one shoulder in a gesture of resignation.

"Maybe I'm a fool to mind. But to sit there and be treated like a child, and to have Cobbitt thrown at me every minute; it was humiliating past bearing. If I could have seen the glimmer of a chance of getting the money some other way I wouldn't even have answered his patronizing speech. But I couldn't. So you see, Jamie, it's his money in a way, not mine; and it's a draft on the bank at Bury." She handed me the paper as she spoke. Before I could say more than the bare "Thank you," which might have acknowledged the passing of salt at table, she had lowered herself to the floor and begun to walk restlessly about the office.

"And that isn't going to happen again," she said, almost as though talking to herself. "I'm going to have some money that I can use without good George Cobbitt's knowing. It's ridiculous. I won't be treated as though I were a child or a lunatic."

"I'm sorry," I said stiffly, "that helping me should have put you in such a painful position." She turned towards me swiftly.

"Oh, Jamie, I *am* so sorry. I didn't mean that at all. It was *because* it's really his money and because he dared suggest that somebody was exploiting me by borrowing from me, that I am so annoyed. Please, Jamie, you must know that I wouldn't hurt your feelings for the world." She came close to me, so that even in the light of the one little hand lantern I could see the smooth texture of her skin, like a pale petal, and the quivering shadows which her eyelashes made on her full upper lids in the upward-flung beam. I could even smell the dry clean scent of her hair. And I knew that in accepting old Thorley's offer she had done violence to her pride and to her own conception of herself as an independent person. She had done that for me. And now she was close beside me, asking forgiveness, begging. . . .

And just for once I was moved by genuine feeling towards her. Whether it was from gratitude, or from the brandy I did not know, but I felt, not passionate, but warm and kind. So I put my arm round her shoulders and drew her even closer, and bent my head and kissed, first her forehead and then each of the eyelids which had closed as soon as I touched her. I would have released her then; but she gave a little cry and clung to me. And her body was like a closely coiled spring in my arms, and her mouth, hot and avid, sought mine.

Such abandon in Marian would have meant Paradise; in Sorrel it merely disgusted me. I extricated myself as well as I could, with little mutters and little pats, and she released me with great suddenness, putting up one hand and running it down the back of my head as I jerked it free. "Dear Jamie," she said, "one day!" And I knew, with a sense of shame that ran all over me like a scorching fire that she was attributing my restraint to chivalry, and that "one day" was a promise of a time when there need be no restraint between us. Dear God!

Next morning, just after Miss Lou had made the coffee and handed me mine as though she hoped it might poison me, as was her way these days, Cobbitt sent me into the tea bay to open a chest of Su-chong. It was a job that I had performed a hundred times, and I set about it mechanically. My thoughts were far away. To-night I should tell Marian—I was looking forward to that. My letter to Uncle Simon had left Bywater that morning, and he would be prepared for my arrival at the end of the month. When, and exactly what, to tell Mother was the problem that was exercising my mind as I set to work with the chisel. She couldn't, I thought, she positively could not accept my announcement of a partnership with Uncle Simon in the same blind, unquestioning way in which she had accepted our move back to the parlour, the reclamation of the furniture and my new suit of clothes. I should have to make up some story, pretend I had won a lottery, or been secretly backing horses for five years. . . .

Just then the chisel slipped and struck my left wrist. The blood began to pour. I ran into the office, where I had left my coat, with my handkerchief in its pocket. Sorrel was sitting at the table nearest the stove, side by side with Miss Lou. Cobbitt was standing by the cabinet just behind them. Sorrel jumped to her feet, shocked, I suppose, out of all discretion and cried:

"Oh, Jamie, my dear! What have you done?"

I said hastily, "Nothing. It's nothing. Let me be," hoping that by brusqueness I could remind her that a cut on my wrist was no more in that office, at that hour, than a cut on Glasswell's. But she fussed round as though I had been her only child. She insisted upon bandaging it herself, using her own handkerchief and Miss Lou's as well as mine. Over her shoulder I could see the old lady's face, and there is only one word to describe it—stricken. If she had loved me instead of hating and I had cut my throat instead of my wrist she could have looked no worse.

Sorrel said, "You must come up to the house, Jamie, and lie down." Miss Lou looked beseechingly at Cobbitt, who said:

"That's quite unnecessary, Miss Sorrel. If a cut wrist makes Brooke feel the necessity for a bed he can go to his own."

"Some brandy then before he starts to walk. Here, Glasswell, take this key and go up through the orchid house and ask Mrs Fennigard to send down some of the best brandy. If she isn't there ask Agatha."

I sat on my stool in embarrassed discomfort, with Sorrel hovering about me, until the brandy came. I

gulped some hastily and assured Sorrel for the fifth
time that I was quite all right.

"Fit to go home alone?"

"Quite."

Cobbitt himself helped me back into my coat as
though he were anxious to get me out of the place; but
even as he helped me he called to Middleditch to go
and finish the job on the tea chest. "And try not to be
so clumsy," he added spitefully.

"It wasn't clumsiness," said Sorrel in a loud hard
voice.

I was glad to escape. There was, apart from Sorrel's
indiscreet behaviour, something very wrong in the atmosphere of the office that morning.

I am not a Stoic about pain, and I had lost a lot of
blood in a short time. When I reached home I was not
feeling very well, and wanted to eat neither my bread
and cheese, which had come back in my pocket, nor
the meal that Mrs Petch sent up for Mother. But I did
want to meet Marian, as I had arranged, that evening,
and I did not want to go to the tryst pallid and shaky,
so about halfway through the afternoon I went through
into Mother's room and lay down on the bed. She was
taking her customary doze on the sofa in the living-
room.

I fell asleep and dreamed a long, involved, unhappy
dream which culminated with Sorrel having cut herself and me trying to staunch the wound with the only
thing I could find—handfuls of Su-chong tea. At the
dream's end she seemed to turn to me and say:

"I have to ask you a very personal and, I am afraid,
offensive question."

"Well?" That was Mother's voice, light, mocking, unkind. I raised my heavy head from the pillow and saw that dusk was already in the room. But in the sitting-room the candles were lighted and a thin line of yellow by the door's edge showed me that I had not closed it firmly before I lay down. But I was still muddle-headed from my dream and bemused by the idea that I had gone to sleep in the tea-bay. Through the haze I heard Sorrel again, saying very earnestly:

"Do please believe me that I wouldn't ask if the answer didn't mean so much to me. And beyond everything I must know the truth."

"Dear me! How mysterious, and how very earnest! Well? I'm afraid I can't answer anything until you can bring yourself to ask the question." There was a silence. I was off the bed by this time. I must get into that room and take hold of the situation, I thought. Before lying down, however, I had struggled out of my dirty shirt. Even with a cut wrist I could not meet Marian in that. I had laid a clean one ready, and now began to don it hastily.

"Mrs Brooke," I heard Sorrel say, "this afternoon somebody told me that Jamie . . . that his father . . . was my father, too. Is that true or not?"

My legs suddenly went soft under me and I groped for the edge of the bed. There was a moment's silence and then Mother's laugh rang out, a little tinkling sound which had always sounded merry and infectious to me. It was not merry now.

"A very difficult question, my dear Miss Kingaby. And, one might say, more than a trifle insulting. May I ask whether you question the parentage of everyone

who has the honour to occupy a stool in your count-
ing-house?"

"Oh, please!" Sorrel begged. "Won't you believe
that I have real reason to ask? I must know!"

"Suppose you tell me why."

"Why? Well, I asked for the truth, I can't do less
than give it to you, though it was a matter between
Jamie and me. We have become . . . we are . . . very
fond of one another."

Mother laughed again.

"That is a pity. Unless you mean as brother and
sister. Because it is quite true. Josiah Kingaby fathered
you both."

I heard Sorrel cry out; I cried out myself. And in
less than a moment of time I saw it all. Mother's allowance which had stopped when the old man died.
Her peculiar behaviour over his death. Her avid interest in Sorrel and her obvious hatred, on that first visit,
hatred for the legitimate child. Her constant self-
reproaches about having done badly by me. All made
so plain now. And other things beside. That curious
repulsion which came upon me whenever the relationship between Sorrel and me threatened to become intimate. Some instinct in the male, the chooser, which
was not active in Sorrel. And Cobbitt had guessed and
hated me for it. Cousin Lou—*my* relative, too—had
known and feared for Sorrel. God in heaven! How
great enlightenment could lie in one sentence.

Possibly Sorrel's mind had travelled, as mine had
done, to those evenings in Layer Wood, with the doves
mourning and the scented evening closing round to
twilight; perhaps she was remembering how in that
hour of lovers no words of love had been spoken,

though their need cried aloud on the air. The caress withheld and the casual touch avoided—perhaps she was reckoning them.

She said, "There is just one more thing that I would like to know. Was Jamie . . . did he know about this?"

There was a perceptible pause and then Mother said quite lightly as though it meant nothing:

"Oh yes, Jamie knew."

More than twenty years of bitterness went into those words. I knew that in aiming that lie, like a sword, straight at Sorrel's heart, she was avenging herself for all the wrong that she had suffered at Josiah Kingaby's hands. And as though that were not enough she added, "So I think you may take it from me that the fondness of which you spoke was really all upon your side."

I heard the door of the sitting-room close, and a second after the heavier bang of the front door. After a time I stood up and, handicapped by my bandaged wrist and my shaking fingers, dressed myself carefully in my best clothes. A change of linen and a pair of shoes I put into the little valise which had accompanied me to school. I carried it in my good hand and went into the room where Mother was sitting more upright than usual upon her sofa. Her blue eyes were very bright and her cheeks pinker than they were painted.

"Why, Jamie," she said, "I'd no idea you were awake. I've been waiting for my tea, but I wouldn't call. Do you feel better?"

I said, "I've been awake for a long time, and the door was open."

Mother shrank a little, but she was defiant.

"It's time you knew," she said. "But these things

are not easy to put into words."

"Why did you tell her that I knew?"

The very quintessence of spite and hatred looked out from those blue eyes.

"I wanted to hurt her. It was her mother who robbed me of him. All her life she has had everything that you should have had, that my son should have had. She sat there and I wondered what would hurt her most. And I thought to believe that you had known and were playing with her. I was right, too."

"You were right," I said. "And I suppose I have played, as you call it. I've taken money from her . . . large sums of money. I've taken affection. I've deceived her. But I was going away and she would have forgotten me. She's young, and she's busy, and the hurt I did her would have been a clean hurt. You've made me into something filthy and obscene. To hurt her, to punish her for something she wasn't responsible for, you have deliberately blackened me so that now I can't even face her to tell her that it wasn't true." I gulped, on the verge of the first tears I had shed for ten years. "You're my mother, and I suppose a bastard owes more to his mother than most men do; but ever since I can remember I've tried to look after you. I even stole to give you what you needed. And then you must do this to me."

"But what have I done?" cried Mother defensively. "You say yourself you had deceived and exploited her. Why is this so much worse?"

I stopped and asked myself the question. Hadn't I shuddered away from Sorrel and gone hot-foot to Marian? Wasn't I, up to an hour ago, deep in a plan for buying a chance of happiness with Marian by using money wrung from Sorrel by false pretences? To these and a dozen other accusatory questions I must answer "Yes." And yet, dimly realized, so dimly that I found difficulty to put it into words, I could see a difference. It was somehow concerned with the betrayal of the blood.

And also, now that I knew the root of that strange repulsion, I could know and admit that I was fond of the girl who was my half-sister. It was as though a dirty window had wiped clean and I could see clearly through it. Now that the necessity to pretend a physical attraction had been removed, I could feel the pull of the other qualities in her, courage and frankness and honesty and generosity.

I said, "I must think about what to do."

"It will be all right," said Mother. "She'll probably start the allowance again."

"Good God!" I cried, and rushed from the house.

I met Marian in the empty boathouse which had been our trysting place since the bad weather began. She greeted me mockingly:

"Well, miracle-monger. To-morrow is the twentieth. Can I look to you for a roof?"

I said gloomily, "Everything was settled and I got the money I told you about. Now something has happened that has made it impossible for me to use it." I told her the whole story, only omitting any reference to Sorrel's feelings for me; though the omission was, of course, a fatuous defence.

"So our icy maiden with quills in her hair is in love with my Jamie!" said Marian. And, "So you are a Kingaby. What a lot that accounts for." And "You silly boy, can't you see that that gives you a clear *right*

to the money?" Presently I began to feel a bit ashamed
of having taken it all so seriously and to wonder
whether the idea of sending back the money hadn't
been that of a sentimental fool. And Marian said,
"What then do you think of doing? Staying here and
turning up at the office in the morning?" And, "After
all, Jamie, you might think of me. I've lost several
chances waiting for you and your secret plans." To
that I had an answer.

"I intended to leave Bywater to-night."

"And your mother?"

"I can send her some money. Mrs Petch will attend
her well, if she is paid."

"And what money will you use, if you don't keep
the loan?"

"I don't know," I said weakly, "I don't know."

"Come along now, Jamie. Be sensible. Is it better
to borrow from your employer, or to take aid from
your *family*? You were going to do the one, why baulk
at the other?"

And I knew then that I should never make anyone
understand. I hardly understood myself.

She pressed against me in the darkness, soft and
warm, sweet, infinitely desirable. Her hair swept my
face as she said, almost whispering, "We could go
away to-night. We could get as far as the 'Evening
Star,' lodge there, and go on to Suffolk in the morning."

"You mean that you'd marry me?"

"Do you think I would make you a dishonourable
proposal, my dear sir?"

Seven hundred pounds, the freedom of the farm,
and Marian, weighed in a balance against some scruple

which I did not understand and had no name for.

"Will you wait in Stag Lane while I gather a few things together?" she asked.

So we went back towards Water Street. It was dark and beginning to blow hard. As we crossed the churchyard I remembered the graves in the alcove of the buttresses, and the wide opening lined with green branches into which I had seen Josiah Kingaby lowered.

"To think that the old man was my father," I said.

"Now," said Marian, "no gloomy talk, please. Let's forget the Kingabys. We're starting our own lives." She slipped her hand down my arm until her hand clasped mine and, tugging at it, began to hurry forward. So, with mounting excitement, tripping over the rough places and laughing together at every stumble, we ran forward.

PART THREE

Bright Glass of Love

I RODE into Bywater for the first time on one of those days of false spring that so often follow close upon the melting of the snow. At the top of Fourways Hill I halted to rest my horse, for with six inches of mire on the roads the going had been heavy.

From the top of the hill I could look away in one direction over miles of marshes where the creeks, flooded by the melting snows, shone silver. Above them, on a level with the hill-top and following the higher and drier spits of land were the massed woodlands, no longer black and sombre, but holding within their shadows the suggestions of purple and tawny colour which spoke of rising sap and swelling buds. Within an hour, I knew, the sun would set, the creeks would run leaden, colour would drain from the sky and the woods and the marshes would cower under the renewed onslaught of the wind, which, it was said, could sweep, without interruption, all the way from the Russian steppes to this part of Essex.

Turning my head, I could view upon the opposite side, the line of the river, widening to the estuary and curving away to the sea. On this afternoon of sunshine and blue sky and white cloud it girdled the darkness of the land like a bright sash; and tucked into it, like a posy of red and amber and orange, lay the little town which was the end of my journey. From that height and distance it looked warm and old-fashioned and homely, with its crooked roofs of narrow tiles, mellow brick chimneys with lazy pennons of blue smoke, and its round Saxon church tower rising from the centre.

I was not prepared to find it charming; nor, on the other hand, was I surprised to do so. Dan's description of it had been given purely in professional terms. He prided himself upon having an eye for female beauty, but his æsthetic powers certainly carried him no further, and he would have been positively amazed to hear a town described as beautiful. He had, after weeks of searching the coast from Blakeney to Shoeburyness, selected Bywater as the most likely place for our new headquarters, and he would have mocked me had he known that my first long stare at it was innocent of any consideration as to its suitability or otherwise for the running of contraband. Dan had, in many ways, the simplest mind I ever met; he always gave his undivided attention to whatever he happened to be doing; he sat down to table to eat, he went to bed to sleep, he walked or rode in order to get somewhere: and I am quite certain that if, on his tour of inspection, he had passed through the Garden of Eden (unless he had seen Eve, when his whole mind would have been bent upon seduction) he would have looked at it without even knowing that it was beautiful, being engrossed in the question as to whether or not it would make a good smuggling base. A mind like that, because it so seldom suffers from distractions, was often a great asset; but, by the same token, it had its strict limitations. When Dan talked he gave his whole mind to expressing himself. He was not, as I was, capable, at the same time, of proffering an argument, watching the effect of it upon the other person, comparing the visible reaction with the spoken reply and planning the next move. And that was why, though Dan had chosen Bywater because of the physical advantages, the estuary, the marshes, the Eastern aspect, and so on; it was I who had been sent down to discover, in my own way, whether in other respects the place was as suitable as it seemed.

I soon found out that where smuggling was concerned, Bywater could offer a perfectly clean bill of health. The reason was not far to seek. This was no fishing village, where, between seasons or in bad ones, economic necessity or sheer boredom drive men to try their hands at moonlighting. It was a thriving little place, and as near being a completely self-contained unit as I had ever seen. It boasted no fewer than three flourishing trading houses; businesses that gathered up the natural products of all parts of the earth, graded, priced and packed them and sent them out again, mostly by packhorse, since the roads were bad, to the towns which studded the prosperous hinterland of Essex and Suffolk. A number of people worked for, or were in some way connected with the firms of Bagworthy, Groatan and Kingaby; and the others, the shopkeepers, the craftsmen and artisans depended for their livelihood upon the prosperity of the businesses. So whatever threatened the legitimate trade threatened the welfare of the whole community; and a week of careful, subtle, imperceptible investigation upon my part brought me only the certainty that contraband had no friends in Bywater. Even the landlord of the "Ship," the crooked little inn where I lodged, bought his tobacco and his liquor from the proper source, which in his case was the house of Bagworthy where his two sons and his son-in-law were employed.

At first it was discouraging. There were methods in smuggling as in other things, and I had always favoured the one which gave shelter and foothold and ramifications; the hit-or-miss, dig-it-in-the-sand and root-it-out and run-with-it system seemed to me both clumsy and needlessly dangerous. Unless we could find a friend in Bywater I was in favour of abandoning the place. Yet, as I sat in the snug bar of the "Ship," sampled the wares and the gossip of each shopkeeper in turn, lolled for an hour in the cobbler's while he stitched my top-boot, and listened and watched and probed, I became more and more certain that a place like Bywater offered—upon one condition—unique advantages. The Preventive men, however active and zealous they might be, could, like other men, be in only one place at once; by this time they would know as well as I knew, Bywater's reputation where smuggling was concerned. They would give it only the most perfunctory attention, if any at all. Moreover, not far away, were the notorious centres of Brightlingsea and St Osyth, which would keep them busy and at the same time appear to explain the presence of contraband in the district. (A clue which often leads to investigation, unless its source is already under suspicion.) These were considerations which made me unwilling to return to Dan and admit that Bywater had defeated me.

So I stayed on and altered the direction of my watchfulness; and almost at once I discovered that, although Groatan and Bagworthy would be useless to me, the third firm, that of Kingaby, had recently gone through some vicissitudes. The head of the house had died rather more than a year before and had left his

business in low water. He had, moreover, left it in the
hands of, of all things, a mere girl who had been
brought out of school in order to assume control of a
highly complicated organization.

She was an object of great interest, this Miss Kingaby. A year ago, I reckoned, people talked of little else
for a season. Even now gossip and speculation were
quite easy to evoke. The general opinion was that she
had her head screwed on the right way, would survive
the temporary reverses which were not, after all, the
monopoly of the house of Kingaby, and would probably make as good a business man as her grandfather
had been. There was, of course, another school of
thought which held that she was crazy, that all the
business was done by her manager, Cobbitt, and that,
unless she brought the firm to ruin in the meantime,
some rogue would marry her for her money. Somewhere, about midway between the two descriptions lay
the truth, I imagined; and I pictured to myself a young
woman who might be amenable to reason and suscep-
tible to the promise of profit. Anyway, I thought, it
was my only chance of getting established in the district, and it was worth the risk of a visit.

Afterwards it was strange to look back and remember how blindly, how blithely I ascertained the position
of East House and presented myself before it at about
half-past eight on that February evening. There was a
moon, almost full, that night, and a multitude of stars.
I mounted the worn, whitened steps and pulled the
chain of the bell which rang, with a deep muffled note
far away within the house. While I waited I studied
the place. An old-fashioned house, I saw, with gables,
an overhanging top storey and twisted chimneys.

Above the wall to one side of the house a great tree reared its leafless crown; to the other was a clutter of roofs, stables and outhouses I guessed. They must run back, garden and stables, to the very edge of the river where the landing places were; and I had noticed that the lane by which I had come, Stag Lane, it was called, did not end with the street where the house stood, but after crossing it at right-angles ran on alongside the yard of the house, towards the river. A more perfect position for my purpose could hardly have been devised.

The door opened at last in a reluctant and half-hearted manner and a voice inquired, warily, my name and business. When I was admitted to a lofty hall with candles burning on a chest near the door, I found myself under the scrutiny of an elderly, hard-faced maid who regarded me with deep and obvious suspicion. It had not, until that moment, occurred to me that in Bywater an unexpected caller after darkness had fallen was an unusual thing.

While the maid plodded away to seek her mistress I studied my surroundings. It was obvious that the house had escaped the prevailing craze for classicism; the panelling was dark and heavy, the staircase twisted so that its upper reaches were out of sight; no attempt had been made to conceal the old black beams. But it smelt warm and comfortable, though there was something mysterious about it. Yes, in that first moment, before I knew anything about the house or its inmates, other than the one I had come to see, I could feel secrecy in the air. It was a house through which many undercurrents flowed.

I had just decided that when a slight sibilant sound

caught my ear. I did not jump round and thus betray
that I had heard it; I stole a glance and saw that the
door on the right of the hall had opened a little, and
showed, besides the red velvet curtain whose whisper
I had noticed, two faces, one above the other, whose
eyes were staring at me with no little interest. They
were both old faces, one long and sallow, the other
hook-nosed and heavily painted. When my eyes ached
from my sidelong peeping I carelessly changed my position, and instantly the door was closed. The maid
returned and said that Miss Kingaby would see me.
She led me past the foot of the stairs, past a table on
which more candles were burning, and through a low
doorway into a small room, sombrely furnished but
brightly lighted and cheered by an enormous fire.

I advanced into the room and said, "Good evening,
Miss Kingaby. I appreciate your receiving me so late
without appointment." The maid servant, very slowly
and reluctantly withdrew at last.

There are moments, as was then the case, when
much is at stake, when I am afflicted by a nervousness
which might be considered a disadvantage in one of
my trade. Actually it is not so. It means that I glance
away and seem diffident, and that sets the other person at his ease and often off his guard as well. But it
also means that I am not one of those people who, in
the first moment of meeting a stranger, can know at
once the shape of nose, colour of eyes, expression of
mouth. So all I knew about Sorrel in the first five minutes of our acquaintance was that she was young,
small and slight, and wore a grey gown with some
green ruching about the hem. And that her voice,

quite cool and self-possessed, was unusual, with a
deepish undertone.

During those five minutes I said that I had come
upon business, and she replied that she usually did
business in the office.

"Ah," I said, "but mine is not quite the kind of business that one conducts in an office."

"Indeed?" she said a trifle dryly, and waited. My
eyes, on their way from her hem to her face, saw her
hands, small and thin, folded in the grey lap. By that
time my twitch of nervousness had passed and I was
able to look at her fully and in the light of what I saw
shape my next speech. Dan, by his own swearing, only
looked at a woman from one angle, so it was as well
that he never did business with them. He knew nothing of faces beyond whether they were prettily
coloured and shaped or not, so he often came to grief,
despite the times that I had warned him of treacherous
eyes, flaccid mouths and other bad signs. I studied
faces for their meaning, and was not often deceived.

But this was a peculiar face. While one part of my
mind was directing my tongue through intricacies of
an introductory and non-committal speech, another
part was busy with what it saw and guessed. In moments of animation the face before me might have
great charm, but at this particular moment it was not
animated. It was waiting, wary. It had a stubborn chin,
too heavy for so small a face, and compensated by a
fine intelligent brow, above which clustered some
shining curls in the kind of careless disarray which
fashionable ladies spent hours in cultivating at that
period. Somehow I felt that those curls gave their
owner the very minimum of concern. Her eyes were

greenish-grey, a sea-water colour and not one usually associated with beauty, but they were bright and lively and had a certain frankness, even now when their stare was wary. The nose I had seen before, and never yet on the face of one lacking in physical or moral courage, and very seldom on a woman, a jutting, pugnacious nose, with a square tip and firm nostrils. And I knew, when I had finished my scrutiny, that in a moment, when I had come into the open with my proposal, I should know the answer immediately. There would be no shilly-shallying. Either I should find myself cast forth with contumely, or she would promise to consider the matter, and I should know that the day was won. And I thought that that was the kind of face I liked to do business with. But even as I thought it I realized that it was a queer thought to have about a woman's face, and a part of my mind broke off to wonder what exactly was wrong with me—could the detached, academic attitude be carried too far?

Meanwhile I was explaining, as briefly as possible, that I had come to make her a business proposition which she was at liberty to consider or to reject and that I should be grateful if she would consider it as though I were offering a price for a quantity of tea in her legitimate line of trade. That prepared her for the revelation that mine was not a legitimate offer; and so, building word on word, as the dry-wall builders in my native shire rear stone on stone, I proceeded until I had laid the whole project before her. It was really very simple and perfectly summed up in her own words when she said:

"Yes, I understand. What you want is to use my business as a cover for yours."

My heart warmed to her.

"Exactly," I said. "How does the project appeal to you?"

She shook her head slightly. "Oh, I should want to know a great deal more about it. It looks to me as though there would be great difficulty when we came down to details."

"Details are my special care," I said. "I can arrange things that would, naturally, seem very difficult to a novice."

She regarded me curiously, for the first time interested in *me*.

"Smuggling," she said. "Smuggler. One reads and hears things, of course. I should not have expected anyone so engaged to look, or sound, like you."

"We vary like other men," I said modestly. "And, of course, we are much maligned. Sometimes I remember with comfort that there are thoughtful men, men in high places, too, who hold that our import duties are out-dated; and I sometimes wonder whether the term 'Free-trader' may not one day apply to a member of a reputable political body instead of to a hunted law-breaker. But that is just talk. . . . Tell me this, amongst the difficulties you mentioned a moment ago do you rank your own scruples?"

Her mouth—the most contradictory feature in all that contradictory face, being full-curved and red, a passionate, voluptuous mouth—stretched in a grimace that could hardly be called a smile.

"I am wondering whether scruples are not a luxury beyond my means. The amazing number of facts which you appear to have unearthed about my business difficulties" (I had mentioned that aspect in introducing

my case) "are all, alas! perfectly true. And besides
. . . I am peculiarly placed. Some time ago when I
wanted some money for a special purpose I learned
that ready money is not easy to come by. And I will
not deny that the prospect of turning an extra penny,
apart from the business, attracts me. I suppose this
contraband running *is* profitable?"

"It has, like other activities, its good and bad times.
But I can assure you that on the whole it is profitable
—otherwise I should not be concerned in it."

"I suppose not. Could you give me any idea of what
I might make—in a year, say?"

I started to explain that an accurate forecast was
rather difficult to make, but that, realizing as we did
the value of a base, she would not find us ungenerous
when it came to splitting the profits. She interrupted
me. "No, I see. The thing is that I happen to need
seven hundred pounds. It's for a . . . for a debt of
honour, and I can't pay it out of my business without .. ." She broke off and a strange unhappy look
came into her face, an old, sad, almost battered look.
She said more briskly, "But speaking of that has reminded me of so many things which would stand in the
way of what you want. I'm afraid it's a waste of time
to discuss the matter further."

"What things?" I asked. Have them out, I thought.
Set it all up like a chess problem and we'll soon see.

"Well, Cobbitt to begin with. . . ." She talked for
about ten minutes, clearly and concisely putting before me the character and position of Cobbitt, and of
an elderly female relative who, from apparently the
best of motives, must have a hand and a say in everything. But God save us! What were they to the puzzles

which I had had to solve in my years with Dan? I took up the thread of speculation and talked enthusiastically for about a quarter of an hour.

"You see," I concluded, "there is merely the matter of the hiding places to work out. And if you will allow me to look over your property once I can soon arrange that. The boat slips in with yours because you have a kind heart and wish to indulge an old sailor's whim, and I'll wager you a flask of French perfume that Cobbitt will introduce the extra packhorses of his own accord if you'll follow my plan. As for this cousin, since you yourself, your comings and goings, will not be affected in the slightest, we need not even think of her."

She smiled again, and this time her eyes shared it. "You have very boldly disposed of everything except the risk. I think you should have been a lawyer."

"In that you show rare perspicacity. A lawyer I should have been had things turned out differently. As for this risk—naturally, I cannot promise you complete immunity. But Bywater being what it is, together with the arrangements that I shall make, I think the risk will be minimised. In any case, I think I could make it look as though you had been quite innocent and most grossly deceived."

"How I should hate that," she said honestly. "And how all my critics, especially the Bywater worthies, who consider all women to be fools, would enjoy it!" The smile vanished as she stood up. "Well, Mr— Borthwick, was it? You have interested me very much. I shall think over what you have suggested and send you my answer to-morrow. Then, if I decide to try it you shall tell how to make Cobbitt suggest having more horses when already he is plaguing me to have fewer. I must confess that I am most curious to see how *that* can be affected." This time the smile brought with it a look of sheer mischief, and as her mouth arched over her small square teeth I saw suddenly that as a little girl she must have been very lonely. And at that same moment, by a coincidence of related evidence, my eyes fell upon the throat and part of her bust which the low-cut gown left bare above the ruching. The neck was so small and white and smooth, and the collar bones so prominent, that they gave her an almost plaintive look of immaturity. Some feeling to which I was a stranger stabbed at me. I ignored it, told her where and how to get into touch with me, and added, "If you decide to agree, well; if not, well, too; but to mention what has been said in this room to-night would not only *not* harm me, but would do yourself a grave disservice." Weeks afterwards, when we were upon a footing of friendliness, she reminded me of that speech, and said that the wolf pushed aside the fleece for a moment and snarled at her. At the time she gave no sign of discomposure, but said simply, "To whom do you imagine I could mention such a subject?" And that something within me stabbed again. The words sounded somehow the depths of her loneliness and defencelessness, and when I thought of Cobbitt and his controlling hand I felt as though I had been enticing a child out of its own sheltered garden into a wilderness full of dangers. But I banished such thoughts at the time. Had I been in the habit of indulging in sentiment I should not have embarked on that trade!

Within twenty-four hours I knew her decision:

though it was months before I knew the story that lay behind it—the heavy sum borrowed and lent to a young rogue, Cobbitt's parsimony over the private allowance, a mob of women, old and young, to be kept in comfort and contentment. And at once I set about laying the lines of communication, weaving my webs around the fabric of the house of Kingaby.

Perhaps I might have guessed that I was not the man I once was, had I fully realized the extent of the gusto with which I laid my Bywater plans. For over seven years I had bent my talent for trickery to Dan's service and the thing had become a matter of routine. I could present myself with a problem: How can this man be outwitted? How can this situation be handled? And after a few moments during which some part of my mind would go, as it were, to a place apart and brood, the answer would be presented to me, just as a serving man will present a reckoning. I enjoyed the process, as I enjoy any evidence of efficiency; but I never relished it as warmly as I did during those days when we were getting Bywater ready for Dan's arrival. For she enjoyed it, too. During those few busy weeks she lost that air of having been broken somewhere and not quite healed properly. She admired, out of all proportion, what were really very simple bits of trickery. Old Abel Fakes, for instance, with his cold, ruthless nature hidden behind the blue eyes and pink cheeks of a child, appearing "to end his days" in Bywater, with only one possession in the world, his boat, and finding no place of harbour for it until Miss Kingaby, coming into conversation with him one day on the wharf, offered it a home; so that the sight of Abel and the *Sea-Gull*, with its cunningly contrived hiding-places, wove itself gently and indistinguishably into the water-front pattern.

Getting the horses safely installed in the Kingaby stables was a little more of a test, but very simple. I bore in mind two things. Cobbitt had the good of the business at heart; and Cobbitt was thrifty to the point of parsimony. So I said to Sorrel:

"Is there any likelihood of all your horses being pretty far afield at any one time—or could it be contrived that they should be?" And at a time when one string was ploughing towards Chelmsford and the other well on its way to Sudbury on the Suffolk border, I sent in, from Halstead, a very pretty, bumper order for a new customer who should, rightly, have been served promptly and this impressed. Giving Cobbitt time to moan over the failure to execute the order, we arranged some business which demanded either his presence, or Miss Kingaby's, in Baildon. It was very cold weather, and when Cobbitt made a chivalrous, if perfunctory offer to carry out the errand, Sorrel accepted it promptly; only stipulating one thing—that Cobbitt should go to the "Green Man" at Baildon and treat himself to their two shilling ordinary, and a glass of hot punch. She gave him three shillings to meet the expense, well knowing that even the inclement weather would hardly move him from his usual custom, a two-penny pie bought at the cook-shop and eaten on the way home.

I should have known him, I think, without Sorrel's instructions to look for a red and black comforter worn over the head under the hat. He bore so clearly the marks of his vocation, the sense of fussy responsibility, allied to limited authority; he smelt of ink and ledgers.

The coldness of the morning and the excellence of the punch that we were both drinking, gave us a starting-point and soon I was telling him, with decent reserves, which he respected, of the trouble I was having on account of the trader with whom I had proposed to share six pack-horses having altered his arrangements.

"I may need them two days a week, or one day in a fort-night, mine is uncertain trade," I said. "For the rest they stand in the stable eating their heads off. And the charges here . . ." I raised my eyes to heaven and left the charges to his imagination. I drew from him the fact that he was a local man, and then invited his help. Did he know any reputable person in business who would give the beasts stabling and half their food, in return for the use of them at such times as I did not need them?

"When I said 'local,'" said Cobbitt, turning eyes that reminded me of an old hound upon me, "I meant in the widest sense. I am from Bywater myself—a matter of fifteen miles away. Now if the horses were there, I could suggest the very place for them." He gave a little sigh at the thought of a good bargain so nearly missed. I said, "Bywater. Yes, that is rather far. It would mean that I might have to fetch them away sometimes in the middle of the night if I wanted to use them in the morning. Awkward for everyone . . ." I mused. Then I invited him out to see the animals. "A lovely string," he said, covetously, "all picked and young. You know . . . I don't see why, if there were good will on both sides . . . the times couldn't be arranged."

"That would be for the other person to say," I said,

not very hopefully. "It's difficult to guarantee other people's goodwill."

"In this case I could. You see, the place I had in mind, is my own . . . not my business exactly, but certainly controlled by me. If you didn't mind the distance out, I can assure you that we should not mind the irregular hours." He smiled ruefully. "Only last week we were in a muddle for lack of horses; and yet, like you, we haven't full work for another six."

He went home and reported to Sorrel that I was "quite a gentleman." But, she demurred, I had not stated my business. Quite right, too, said Cobbitt, only fools shouted their business abroad. If I fetched out my team in the middle of the night I should disturb everyone, she said. Not at all, Cobbitt countered; I should be given the stable at the end, nearest the gateway. So, having made all the objections which Cobbitt would have made had the positions been reversed, and gained the plan an adherent that nothing could shake, Sorrel capitulated and at last congratulated the old man on having made an excellent bargain. A bargain which looked even better when it was discovered that with the horses came their keeper, Timothy, with his wages paid by me; and with Timothy came his old deaf father, known as the Gaffer. Neither of them was above lending a hand to the Kingaby horse-boys, though the Gaffer preferred loafing on the foreshore where he soon fell into company with Abel Fakes. The two old fellows became inseparable, although one could hardly have termed them friends. The pair of them in the *Sea-Gull* was soon a familiar sight.

And so, with the exception of our leader, we were all together again; and at last I could send word to

Dan that we were ready to begin.

I realized that I had missed him. It was almost six months since we had given up our place on the Sussex coast. Courage, which in Dan is unlimited, and wiliness, of which I have my share, are all very well; they serve for a time. But there comes another time when mere numbers are bound to tell, and at Tislehurst our gang and Benjy Head's fellows had worked so long and so successfully that the Preventive men had just to concentrate on it or admit themselves a useless body. They had got down from the north a fellow called Quantrill who had been a soldier and seen service in Spain. And he had made the place too hot for us. After all, smuggling, like any other business, is conducted for profit; and when, for a long time you go, not only in imminent risk to life and liberty, but in the certainty of losing on three runs out of four on account of stuff abandoned or captured, well, it just is not a game for sane men. And that is why we five had been looking for a small place, quiet, in a corner that was not too much exploited already, and had happened upon Bywater.

Dan had been in London most of the time, and had made two visits to France. I had hardly seen him at all; and now I found myself longing for his company, his resolute optimism, crude sense of humour, infectious courage, all the things that made him so different from and therefore so attractive to me.

I thought he would be pleased with my arrangements—in all but one respect. We had once, while we were working on the Lincolnshire coast, had an unfortunate experience with a woman innkeeper whose place we had made our headquarters. She had no bet-

ter taste than to take a customs man for a lover, and
no better sense than to blow the gaff. True enough,
the folly had been heavily paid for, for Abe Stockwell,
who was with us then, lost his son in the resulting running fight, and afterwards slunk back and strangled
the woman. But that did us little good, because another
fellow who had been partial to the female and refused
to believe her perfidy, was always out for Abe's blood
after that; and internal strife is fatal to a band. So, for
ever afterwards Dan had decreed that no woman was
to touch, even remotely, upon our affairs. And amongst
the five of us who had moved over to Essex there was
not one who had any female connection. Abel and the
Gaffer were old enough to do without women; Timothy, who had once been married, had a queer grudge
against the whole sex; Dan himself, though a notable
womanizer, kept a sharp barrier, and often a distance
of miles, between his work and his pleasure; and I was
self-doomed to continence, since I derived no pleasure from casual encounters and was not fool enough
to imagine that the kind of woman to whom I had
been accustomed or whom I should ever want would
be found in the circles where I now moved.

So I had decided not to tell Dan that the head of
the house of Kingaby was a girl barely out of her teens.
I thought I would let him realize the advantages of the
arrangement first; then, before the information could
reach his ears from other sources I would take him to
see Sorrel and trust his commonsense to realize that
she was a different kind of cattle from the drab of the
Lincolnshire inn.

By this time Sorrel and I were upon familiar terms.
For it is a fact that though two people can conduct

legitimate transactions for years and still be only acquaintances on surname terms, the same two people planning any evasion of the law, any deceit or chicanery, are instantly upon a footing of familiarity. The same difference may be seen between the orderly connection of a man and his wife and the unbuttoned freedom of the same man and his mistress. The mere out-witting of Cobbitt, the little ruses we must adopt to deceive the elderly female relatives, had set Sorrel Kingaby and me at ease with one another in a way that twenty years of steady trading would not have done. Cobbitt and the female watchdog were given to understand that I had a cousin of whom I was very fond at the Baildon Academy for young ladies in Miss Sorrel's time. The girl had died young, and it was not so unnatural that I should be drawn towards one who remembered her. This and my fondness for orchids constituted a link between us; and since I was already *persona grata* with the good Cobbitt and took pains to ingratiate myself with the old lady, I was soon able to appear in the office without question; had been invited, by the relative, to sup at the house; and had twice paid Sorrel evening visits which had, she reported, roused curiosity but no opposition.

(Dan said that I carry respectability about with me as a pipe smoker carries the aroma of his favourite brand. It may be true. My father was a gentleman, though a rogue, and I myself, had my grandfather not died, leaving me penniless, halfway through my training, might now have been a barrister. It was from the only thing I could fall back upon—lawyer's clerking at forty pounds a year—that Dan had rescued me.)

Dan arrived on an evening of genuine spring in
early March. There were catkins all along the edge of
the Layer Wood and lambs in a field when I rode out
to meet him. I had taken a lodging for both of us in a
little tavern called the "Evening Star," away out on
the marshes. I had, in those earliest, disappointing
days, marked it down as a possible headquarters at a
pinch, though its isolation and its greater distance
from the river were disadvantages. It was a poor place,
the kind where a certain guinea can purchase loyalty
of a kind (a kind which personally I do not despise.
People's hearts change and their allegiances with them.
But a guinea is always a guinea.) I wondered often,
how a tavern could grow up in such a place, upon
what custom could it count. Yet on most evenings
there were men in the place, heavy, slow-spoken fellows who at least asked no questions, perhaps because
they would themselves have welcomed none. The
place suited my purpose admirably, and I had engaged two rooms for an indefinite time.

Dan, like a horse that has been running free, had
put on flesh and was in marvellous spirits. He had a
new suit, of a bright raisin colour. It was elegantly
cut, but it emphasized, as all his fine clothes did, the
heaviness of his shoulders and the thick muscles of his
thighs and calves. He looked infinitely better in the
fisherman's jersey, the trousers rolled to the knee, the
heavy shoes and woollen cap which he wore during
the run; but once, long since, when I had voiced this
opinion, his vanity, which was childlike, had been
horribly hurt, and he had not spoken to me civilly for
a week.

We had a great deal to tell one another. I described the lay of the land and the arrangements I had completed. And then one day I went into the Kingaby office and said, loud and clear:

"Miss Kingaby, I have a friend visiting with me who is as fond or even fonder of orchids than I am. Would you do me the favour to receive him and let him see your collection at an hour convenient to yourself?"

"It is still light enough to see in the orchid house at half-past six, and that is as early as I can be free," said Sorrel, with just that right air of casual goodwill.

"This evening?"

"If that suits you, Mr Borthwick."

I thanked her and moved away to make my usual obeisance to Cobbitt. I could hear the female relative's sibilant whisper complain that six-thirty was a very inconvenient hour. It would make supper late; and wouldn't it have been more pleasant if the gentlemen could have drunk tea after supper.

"It would then be rather dark for seeing the orchids," said Sorrel, with a God-grant-me-patience note in her voice. And I wondered whether every trivial arrangement in that house was similarly subjected to criticism, either by this lady, or the one who looked like an old parrot, or the young one with the pale widowed look. Once again I felt myself seeing life as Sorrel saw it, and I sent her a glance as I went through the door; a glance which conveyed, I hoped, sympathy, understanding and fellow feeling.

At some hour during that afternoon I fell prey to a curious malaise of spirit. Such a heaviness descended upon me that I became physically slow and clumsy. I knew, of course, that I was dreading the moment when

Dan should meet Sorrel and learn that I had fixed a place with a woman as its very cornerstone—but although his temper was terrifying to me, there was more than the fear of that in this reluctance of mine to get ready and go with him into Bywater.

I remember that I dressed myself carefully in my best clothes. Not that it mattered what I wore, I always looked the same, neat and unnoticeable. Dan, whose delight in fine clothes was tempered by an innate carelessness in their preservation, rubbed toilet spirit into his hair, but did not change his shirt. The elegant brown suit was already marked with splashes of food and wine, a dab of candle-grease and a smear of oil.

He shouted to me that time was passing. We had arranged to walk into Bywater because there were footpaths that we wanted to explore, so we were starting early. Still I lingered. Presently he came into my room, stuffing his watch back into his pocket. Under one arm he bore a bottle of good French brandy.

"Sample of wares," he said, tapping it. "What's he like, this Kingaby?"

"You'll see," I said, and clapped on my hat hastily and hurried from the room. Bloody fool, I told myself; four simple words would clear this situation, which ought never to have arisen. But I did not say them.

As we went along we examined the terrain with professional eyes. Dan muddied his boots, and once almost bogged himself in his inability to stick to the path. We arrived on the steps of East House just as the church clock chimed the half hour.

Sorrel had obviously prepared for the visit with some seriousness. She wore a gown of bright green

with a bold black stripe that left her throat and arms
from the elbow bare. Her skin looked very white, but
again I was aware of the thinness of her arms and the
prominence of her collar-bones, which gave her a look
of touching immaturity. The side door of the little
study which led to the orchid house stood open; humid
air, faintly perfumed, drifted in and mingled with the
scent of the logs that burned in the old-fashioned
grate. Candles were already burning on the side table,
and the light of their little flames danced in the crystal
depths of the decanter and stemmed drinking glasses
which stood nearby on a massive silver salver.

I saw so much of the room because my affliction
came strongly upon me and I was momentarily unable
to look at either Sorrel or Dan. The maid who had let
us in shut the door in that same lingering fashion,
and I made an effort to meet what could no longer be
avoided. I said:

"Good evening, Sorrel. This is Dan Culver, whom
you know already by repute. Dan, this is Miss Kingaby, who has offered us, shall we say, hospitality?"

There, now, I could look at him. I did so and saw
first of all an expression of almost foolish bewilderment sweep over his face, followed by such a look of
fury as even I had seen there only a few times before.
The crimson colour mounted until his very eyes looked
red, while his lips, which did not share the suffusion,
made a hard pale gash.

"I'll kill you for this, Wick," he said in a choking
voice. His head came down and his hands came up. I
moved round so that the table was between us. As I
did so I saw Sorrel dart to the side door, drag it shut,
and twitch the curtain over it. Then she stood with her

back to it. And she looked alert, interested, not at all frightened. I said:

"Just a minute, Dan. Remember you're in the house. Let me explain."

"You'll explain," he said furiously. "You crafty little—! I'll learn you to play tricks on me." He made a bull-like rush round the table. I moved on as nimbly as I could, keeping my eye on him.

"Remember there is a lady present," I said. And suddenly the full ridiculousness of the situation struck me. There I was, skipping round the table like a cat and trilling out little reminders of good manners to a great angry fellow who would, at that moment, have liked to shake the life out of me. I suppose some sign of amusement showed on my face, for Dan gave a kind of bellow and made for me again. Sorrel left the door and came to the middle of the room.

"This must stop," she said clearly. "In another minute we shall have half a dozen women armed with brooms and shovels rushing in to save me from being murdered." I saw Dan look at her properly for the first time. She looked back at him with a cold level stare. "Will you please come out and look at the orchids before it is too dark for such an excuse to be valid—or else go away before you rouse the house."

"Orchids?" said Dan. "Are you both mad?"

"We are supposed to be orchid fanciers," I explained. "Young ladies of Miss Kingaby's station do not receive gentlemen alone without some excuse." I underlined the word 'gentlemen' with all the irony at my command. Dan snorted, but he strode to the door, tugged back the curtain, and held the door open for her to pass. I followed her, and as I came level with

Dan he hissed a few words of abusive obscenity in my ear. But I knew that the worst was over for the moment anyway. We all laughed at the idea of our inspecting orchids with anything but idle admiration; not one of us knew one bloom for another.

"I wish I did," said Sorrel, fingering a delicate pale purple blossom with vivid orange splashes at the tip of each petal, "but when I might have been learning I was hardly allowed to look at them."

"Well, we've looked at them now," said Dan bluntly, and began to walk back to the study door. Once we were within and the door closed he turned to Sorrel and said seriously:

"I'm sorry, Miss Kingaby, but you've got to understand that the arrangements made by my smart, funny friend here can't be carried out."

"But, Dan, listen . . ." I began.

"Hold your tongue, Wick, and let me speak."

"No, let me," said Sorrel. "Perhaps you'll be good enough to offer me some kind of explanation. I am prepared to receive you as a kind of partner; I have agreed, after a good deal of consideration and no little inconvenience, to everything Mr Borthwick has suggested. Then you walk in here, ostensibly to discuss business, fall into an incoherent fit of fury at the sight of me, and now declare that the agreement is not to be carried out. What does it all mean?"

Dan shot me a look of vivid hatred. "Wick knows what it means. He knew all along that we don't ever do business with women. I've got a reason for that, and he knows what it is. It was the thought of being duped, not the sight of you, Miss Kingaby, that put me in fury." He swallowed, and the red colour began to mount again. "How would you have felt," he demanded, "if I'd walked in here to-night and turned out to be an old woman in a chip bonnet?"

"But I," said Sorrel reasonably, "am not an old woman in a chip bonnet."

He included her in his look of fury. "Don't split hairs. Would *you* go into partnership in this kind of job with a woman?"

"No," said Sorrel after a moment's thought, "I wouldn't. And I'll tell you why. It's your part to go out and do things in the dark and the danger, and I don't think women would do those things as well as a man. But why my part can't be done by a woman I fail to see."

"Then I'll tell you. Because anything to do with this game demands a level head and a still tongue. I'm willing to pay for your inconvenience, and if you can put a price on your consideration I'll pay that, too, and have everything cleared out of your way to-morrow."

"But, Dan," I began again.

"Will you keep your mouth shut?" he shouted. "Can't you see I'm trying to keep calm?" Sorrel spoke into the silence, saying much what I had intended.

"Then, Mr Culver, do you intend to abandon Bywater as a base? Or do you trust me to keep a still tongue for nothing when according to you a considerable sum couldn't prevent it from wagging?"

Ah, I thought, the situation is now in hand. I sat down on the nearest chair and, in the very act of wiping the damp of agitation from my palms, could not forbear a glance of amusement at Dan. In any kind of argument he was so easily outwitted. He now looked dull and wooden. And when I looked from his face to Sorrel's I was surprised to see the resemblance between them, not that she at the moment looked dull or wooden, far from it. The resemblance lay deeper than mere expression. I realized that I had brought together two stubborn, wilful people, and that where one was handicapped by her youth and her sex, she had the advantage of a quicker mind. She spoke now in a different voice.

"Do sit down, Mr Culver. Now, couldn't we begin this interview over again? *You* are very disappointed to find that I am not my father; *I*—well, never mind. May I offer you a glass of Madeira? Or would you prefer some of your own brandy, which was, I suspect, intended for Mr Kingaby?"

"I'll take the Madeira," said Dan in a voice that meant that nothing would avail now except patience. I can bear anything for an hour, said his voice, and then I shall break Wick's neck and clear out of Bywater.

Over at the side table Sorrel slopped out three glasses of wine and brought them, with a dish of little cakes, to the table by the fire.

"Now," she said, "Wick came into Bywater looking for a suitable place from which to work. He chose mine, for excellent reasons. I, for equally good reasons, agreed to take the risk of accommodating you. In this house there are eleven women who are dependent upon me: six are completely dependent and five I employ. Will you ask yourself whether a woman with such responsibilities wouldn't contrive to keep a level head and a still tongue if paid to do so? I entered into an agreement with Wick in a sober and earnest

frame of mind, but I am prepared to overlook your
flippant prejudice if you can bring yourself to accept
me. If not—then you must take away your men and
your goods. But you need not fear that I shall say anything about your activities. Very possibly, now that I
understand the game, I shall be able to find a free
trader who has not your—weakness."

"As fairly spoken as anything I ever heard," I said.
But I doubt if either of them heard me. Across the
darkly polished top of the table, with the wet rings
made by the carelessly filled glasses and the plate of
silly little cakes, they were staring at one another.
And as, when flint meets steel there is first the sound,
then the spark, and then the sudden flare of the tinder,
so their eyes, meeting, ignited something. Defiance,
distaste, the sound and the spark, and then the
flame. I had no need to look at Dan; I had seen him
look like that at too many women. I looked at Sorrel
and saw the instinctive gesture of the woman who
would assure herself that she is dressed—the smooth-
ing of the skirt over the knees, the hands folded as
though protectively in the lap. Her eyes did not waver,
but I saw the hot colour begin at the edge of her
corsage and mount, slowly, slowly, to the curls on her
forehead. And I thought of the good comradeship that
we had shared in getting things ready for Dan's coming; of the frank easy laughter over trivial jokes; of
my odd vision of her as a little girl. Why did I think
of these things then?

I said, "Look, Sorrel we aren't making much head-
way, like this. We'll leave you now and talk things
over. I'm sorry about everything. I meant it for the
best."

"*You* have no apology to make, Wick," she said very graciously, "and I am sorry that you have done so much good work in vain."

We mumbled some leave-taking and got ourselves into the street. As we came down the hall I was conscious, for the second time, of the parlour door, slightly ajar and of someone watching from behind it. I thought how, in age, curiosity intensifies itself, as though the old, as their own lives narrow, begin to live vicariously. And then we were out in Water Street with a thin new moon curved like a sickle over the little town.

I was prepared for a burst of invective; so I stayed silent, waiting for it. But Dan strode along in silence, too, and we went past the Church and the Green, over the road and into the labyrinthine paths of the marshes. Presently he stopped short and said, "Damn! I meant to see Timothy and look at the horses."

"They are all perfectly well," I told him. "And you'll see them to-morrow when they're moved."

"I ought to break your neck," he said ruminatively. And then, with growing heat, "Why in God's name couldn't you have been honest with me and said there was no place here?"

"There was. If you could just have behaved yourself to-night we could have shown you. I'd like to see its equal. A landing-place with a straight run through, on private premises, into a hiding-place if you want to store, or into the stable if you want to load up right away. There never was such a place."

"Well, don't speak as though we'd been kicked out of it. It's still ours if we want it."

And suddenly, for no reason that I could see, I

began to argue against it. I even went so far as to say
that I agreed with him about women being better kept
out of nefarious business. I can remember with perfect
clarity the spot in the path where he stopped all at
once—it was just where, on a clear night such as this
was, one could see the light in the tavern window and
salute the rustic poet who had named the place the
"Evening Star." Dan stopped on the path and turned
round, so that he faced me where I trod behind him.

"Have you lost your senses?" he asked me seriously.
"First of all you fix up to use a woman's premises and
say it's the best spot you ever saw; then when I'm beginning to agree with you, you veer round and say all
the other things. What the hell is the matter with you?
I thought your *brain* was all right." He implied that
most other things were at fault. And stung by that, my
nerves, already rasped by the day's suspense and the
evening's scene, betrayed me into indiscretion. I
thought, all right, why the devil shouldn't *I* say what I
think for once.

"Since you ask me," I said, "I had forgotten one
thing. The girl is all right, she's got sense and her wits
about her and she knows the value of money. But she's
not unattractive, and I don't want you to be in danger
of muddling pleasure and business. . . ."

He spluttered. "Well, I'm . . . of all the . . . well.
And what in the name of Moses gave you the idea I
might find the little virgin attractive?"

"I know the look that comes over you when you're
wondering what a woman would be like in bed," I
said bluntly. "I've seen it before. And I saw it to-night
and realized that I had chosen unwisely."

He gave a great bellow of laughter that roused a

flock of birds and sent them screaming and wheeling towards the moon.

"Well," he said, "I'll admit you don't miss anything, Wick, my lad. But if it's any comfort to you to know it, your precious Sorrel—is that what you called her? sounds like a mare—is not my dish at all. So I think we will try this wonderful spot." He added, over his shoulder, as he began to walk again, "Virginity never had any charms for me, anyway."

And as I fell into step behind him on the narrow path, I thought that the stress upon virgin state betrayed him; until a man had thought upon a woman in one aspect, highly specialized, he would not use that word in connection with her—unless perhaps he was a poet, which Dan was not. And I thought, also, for the first time that, viewed from the back, his neck was too thick. I kept my eyes on it because I found that it annoyed me, and was prompting me to say that he had put me in a very undignified position this evening, chasing me round a table, with a woman looking on. I had just brought myself to the point of saying the words, when I realized that *I*, Tom Borthwick, was on the verge of picking a quarrel with Dan. I almost halted under the onrush of flooding memories; that time my leg was broken and he came back, under the very noses of the flashing barkers of the Preventive men, picked me up, threw me on his back, with my arms round that same thick neck and carried me up the cliffside that was little less steep than the side of a house; that other time when I lay insensible and raving with fever in a stinking little room at Porthsea and some sailor told the landlady that I had Yellow Jack, and not a soul would venture near me until Dan came

back and nursed me; those numerous other times, less
memorable, but no less important, when his cheerful-
ness and courage had given me heart, banished the
dark demon who sometimes could have his way with
me, pulled a mad quaking world back into shape and
substance and sanity again. That was Dan. And was I
to quarrel with him now? Not, I vowed in penitence,
for anything in the world.

Very soon life fell into pattern again; a pattern composed of idle stretches, periods of great activity, moments of danger and days of routine whose orderliness
and monotony might surprise those who have not
sampled a smuggler's life. Governed by the tides, the
moon and the weather, we worked through the spring
and summer of that year and in eight months never
lost a pennyworth of stuff. The Preventive men, con-
centrating upon the notorious districts of Brightlingsea
and St Osyth, gave us no trouble. The hot dry summer, the second in succession, sucked up the water
from the marshes, and Dan, riding out for long hours
in the daylight, planned us routes that sometimes led
for miles without touching a road.

Once, in late August, we ran into an ambush out
beyond Steeple Rising; an ambush set, we learned
later, not for us but for the "Toosey" men as they
called the St Osyth traders. Timothy and I got through
with the horses, Dan, the Gaffer and Abel fought to
cover our passing and to prevent our being followed.
Dan took a ball through the calf, but Abel had a flap
of flesh almost as big as the palm of one's hand, torn
and hanging from the side of his bald head.

Dan's was a trivial matter and roused no anxiety,

for at the "Evening Star" a little lameness would rouse no interest; or if it did, could be easily explained. But Abel's head was less easily hidden. It was possible, remotely possible that there might be an ear in Bywater which had heard of the skirmish at Steeple Rising, allied to an eye which would notice Abel's bandage and a brain which might draw a hazardous conclusion. Ordinarily, at Tislehurst or Porthsea, for instance, it would not have mattered in the least; there the people were our friends. But we were the rats in the Bywater house. So long as we operated unseen and unrecognized, we could fill our bellies, but once discovered, we should find every man's hand against us. So, after a little thought, I bandaged Abel on his wounded side, and the Gaffer on his opposite side, and sent them back to Bywater with instructions to speak and act as though they had quarrelled and come to blows. Abel was to behave as the more injured party, and the Gaffer was to be very penitent and attentive. By that means I ascertained that Abel received the attention which his state demanded, without becoming dependent upon any outsider. When, just over a week later, I saw them sunning themselves on the river wall, I wondered if anyone else had noticed, and noticing, had wondered, that Abel's bandage had been changed in the interval and was tolerably clean, while the Gaffer's was grey all over and quite black along the edges of its unaltered folds.

In that summer I saw Sorrel ten times for Dan's once. More than that, for I doubt whether, in the beginning of the time, he saw her at all. I remember thinking that he had forgotten all about her, and being startled when, a consignment of very fine French gloves coming into our hands, he selected a pair, almost flung them at me and said:

"Give those to Miss Kingaby next time you see her. Bit more suitable than my last offering."

It irked me to think that I had not thought of the gesture; and when, some weeks later, I did present her with some lengths of lace of a kind just coming into fashion and therefore in demand, it was with the uncomfortable feeling that I was aping Dan.

By that time, thanks to the partiality of the old lady, Cousin Lou, I was on easy and familiar terms with the strange household in Water Street. And I think it was this more than our nefarious dealings which bore in upon me that Sorrel Kingaby was a woman in a thousand. Any girl, given a modicum of sense and Cobbitt to help her, could make a show of running a business; any girl, with a desire to do so, suitable premises, and me for a mentor, could take a hand in the contraband trade. But that household! All those women with their differences, their prejudices, their preferences. The quarrels, the constant appeals to Sorrel as arbitrator, the never-ending flow of petty complaints carried to Sorrel for redress. And over it all there hung, as I knew more of it, more of its history, the shadow of the man who had been the head of it, who had gathered them together, or begotten them; and who could, and did, I have no doubt, keep them in order, silence their complaints with a frown, end a quarrel with a fierce word. They still, it seemed to me, as an impartial observer, missed him and traded on his absence; just as a class of boys, accustomed to a strict master, will take advantage of his successor who is more kindly intentioned and, perhaps, more just.

Of the collection of women, I liked best—perhaps it was inevitable that I should—the one who looked upon me favourably, the spinster called Cousin Lou. Everything about her, from her scanty faded hair to her long flattish feet, was ugly, and she wore dreary clothes—drab, black, grey and mud-coloured, occasionally disastrously brightened by a spencer or a bow of crude violet or cerise colour. At first sight I had set her down as a dragon, and she did, in fact, make many things difficult. But she finally accepted me as a respectable business man, and as I came to know her better I realized that she had that rare thing—a good heart—and that she was unshakably attached to Sorrel.

There appeared to be an old, deep-rooted enmity between Cousin Lou and the still older lady known as Aunt Carrie. What one liked the other automatically loathed. So since Miss Kingaby lent me her favour, Mrs Fennigard found it necessary to disapprove of me, to refer to me as "the wool chandler fellow," and treat me contemptuously. During my London days I had known her type very well. Usually they are widowed, in which case Mrs Fennigard, with three husbands dead, conformed to pattern, and usually they own a little property, in which respect Sorrel's relative differed from the general run. And they make wills every month or so, bequeathing their property to one relative after another, as one or another gives offence in some way. Then they die and it is discovered that the last will leaves everything to the Church or the Foundling's Hospital, or the curate with a stammer. It was this old lady, with her lined, raddled face and fantastic tower of dead powdered hair who always peeped round the edge of a door, or from behind the shelter of the window curtains.

Then there was Mrs Kingaby, Sorrel's stepmother, one of the most disagreeable females I have ever known or even heard about. She had retained some traces of a buxom, bucolic beauty, but they were deeply overlaid by a spiteful melancholy. She was always being affronted, packing a bag, taking her child by the hand and going away. But she always came back, and Sorrel always took her in. And every time that child was returned to the schoolroom Miss Jacobs, the governess, a wispy, mothlike creature, wept and gave notice and had to be given a present or promised a rise in salary.

"Why?" I would demand sometimes, when some particularly troublesome occurrence escaped from Sorrel's tactful concealment and obtruded itself, "why do you clutter up your life in this fashion? Why not send all the girls to school? Then you could get rid of the governess, and, if you must keep the old ladies, confine them to a part of the house where they could quarrel all day and not involve you."

"And what about Lucia?" asked Sorrel with a twinkle.

"A brick round her neck and the river some dark night!"

She smiled, but the stubborn look followed the smile.

"No, Wick. I inherited them. They go with the house, like the furniture."

And once, when Miss Lou had unintentionally annoyed me by a piece of prying curiosity in which I caught her, I said, more seriously, to Sorrel, "You know, your Cousin Lou is a dear old lady, but dear old ladies can be dangerous. Would nothing induce her to mind her own business?"

Sorrel sighed and pushed back her hair. "I am her business. I have been her business ever since I was born. And I remember how she started coming down to the office in order to save me from something that happened after all. Now it has become a habit, and she'll come down till the day of her death, I think. I know she is exasperating; there are times when I could strike her . . . but we've been through a lot of experiences together. You know how that makes you feel about a person."

I knew. I thought of Dan. But if Sorrel's behaviour towards Cousin Lou was regulated by the memory of shared experiences, it seemed to me that no such thing applied to the rest of the women in the house. And as the year went on and I saw and understood more of the household on Water Street, I could only admire the impatient good humour, the determined fairmindedness with which Sorrel dealt with its problems. And in her treatment of Lou and the three girls she showed an unexpected sentimentality oddly endearing in so resolute a character. Once or twice I caught myself thinking what a mate some man would find in her; how generous and all-embracing, with no taint of sickliness or evasion, would be her love. And yet, looking at the subject in what I assured myself was an impersonal and academic light, I could not imagine her married; nor could I picture the kind of a man who would, at the same time, be attractive to her and attracted by her. A weak man, I thought, who would give her her own way she would end by despising; a man strong enough to mould her she would probably come to hate. That I myself, a man neither conspicuously strong not unusually weak, had fallen in love with her meant nothing, since we were so far separated from one another that even my love must have an academic flavour, and I must, and did, comfort myself with the thought that it was my mind which was engaged with her, rather as it might be with a character in a book or a play. And that, I suppose, is the most foolish idea that can afflict a sane man; the most dangerous conceit that can be entertained by any sound, whole, male creature.

September came; to my thinking the loveliest of months, with the elms just bronzed at the edges, the mornings full of blue mist, the evenings a long drawn mystery of grape-bloom and hyacinth. All along the sides of Layer Wood the pink spindleberries trembled and every cottage garden was ablaze with homely flowers. (Dan said gloatingly, "The nights are getting longer. God send a dry autumn to keep the marsh open for us.")

Early in that month the *Mirabella*, one of the Kingaby ships, came in at the end of the East India voyage, and, according to custom, Sorrel said, she must invite Captain Swann and his mate to dinner. She meant to make it a big party and ask her lawyer, the local doctor, and a few other Bywater burghers. She mentioned the dinner party several times, and then, at perhaps the fourth mention, said rather shyly:

"Will you come, Wick? And bring Dan if you think he would like it."

I hesitated, thinking it over. She added anxiously:

"There isn't any reason against it, is there? You are

often here, accepted as a wool chandler; and Dan is never seen. I mean it wouldn't be dangerous to dine here, since nobody knows what you do."

"I don't suppose it would be *dangerous*," I said. "At Porthsea I believe Dan once went to a mayoral banquet, but that was because the mayor's daughter was in love with him at the time. But it might be unwise; if anything happened and it were remembered that we had been received formally by you."

"You once said you would make it look as if I had been deceived, Wick. This would only show how greatly I had been duped. Please say yes; it's going to be such a *nice* dinner." The child was uppermost, cajoling, irresistible; but I did not resist. I thanked her and I said I was sure it would be a most excellent dinner, and that I would speak to Dan about it. I had actually no slightest intention of conveying the invitation to him, but the devil was in the thing from the beginning. On the very next day, while I was in Colchester, he took it into his head to go and see Timothy and the horses, and when he was in the yard Sorrel saw him from the side window of the office and went out and asked him herself.

He did not, when he told me about it that evening, refer to my silence on the subject, but I thought he looked at me a little queerly, and I judged it best to say, "Oh yes, she asked me yesterday, but it slipped my mind, and I didn't think of it again until I was half-way to Colchester this morning."

It is strange how a house can alter. When we arrived on that evening the female element had been banished. It was a house of men again, and my fancy toyed with the idea of the old place stirring itself to

welcome the scents and sounds that it had missed and
mourned. Stealing through the odours of good tobacco
and rich cooking that hung about the hall was the
fragrance of damp soil and growing vegetation. I
glanced about in search of the source of it, and saw
three wide shallow boxes on the floor beyond the chest.
Captain Swann had brought home his usual offering
of orchid plants.

Sorrel, in the green and black gown, with a green
ribbon in her hair and a rare pink flush of excitement
on her cheeks, welcomed us. Despite the flush her
manner was cool and dignified, a little restrained.
Under cover of the move from the parlour to the dining-room she caught my sleeve and said quietly, "When
the others go, slip into the study and wait. I have
something rather important to tell you."

The words, the confidential tone of her voice, and
the touch of her fingers on my arm set me a little apart
from these burly sea-men and stolid burghers whose
little gallantries she accepted with that air of good-
humoured dignity; they consoled me for a place at the
table from which I could not see her without an un-
seemly craning of the neck. My neighbour on one side
was Cobbitt, who ate his way through the long, excellent dinner with a tempered enjoyment as though in
duty bound to estimate the cost of it all. On my other
hand was a dapperly-dressed, impeccably-groomed
old fellow, the now retired head of the Bagworthy business. He told me that he was ninety years old, drew my
attention to the fact that he still had his teeth and
could eat anything—a self-evident fact—and that he
could see to read without spectacles. He also informed
me that he never missed one of Josiah's dinners, they

were the best in Bywater, and that although Josiah
was not what he called a thrifty man of business he had
genius for muddling through on the right side of a
squall. That Josiah had been under the earth for
almost two years, and that a girl in a striped dress sat
at the head of the table, seemed to have escaped his
notice for all his phenomenal sight, and since I discovered that he was utterly and completely deaf, I did
not attempt to enlighten him.

When Cobbitt's few stilted remarks and the old
man's monologue palled I amused myself by listening
to the altercations which arose at the side table, directly behind me, where a waiter, hired from Baildon
to direct the maids, was finding himself opposed, con-
tradicted and bullied at every turn by the elder of the
two.

And all the time I knew that I was listening to Cobbitt, and to the Bagworthy elder, and to the quarrels
behind me in order to distract my attention. For although I could not see to the head of the table with
any great ease, I could see Dan, who sat nearer to the
end and upon the opposite side from me. And I could
see that he was laying himself out to be charming, with
an eye to the table's end, even when he was apparently
talking to the men on either side of him.

I knew him so well, was so familiar with every
change of expression on his face, that it was useless for
me to avert my eyes. He was not the most handsome,
but the most vital and engaging-looking man I have
ever seen. The months of work and activity had
stripped off the surplus flesh he had gathered, but the
massiveness was still there, a matter of bone and build.
His skin never lost its tan, even in winter, and the con-

trast between it, with its underlying redness of cheek,
and the light Saxon blue of his eyes was arresting
enough in itself to render noticeable a far plainer face.
His hair, thick and never quite tidy, showed two dis-
tinct shades, its natural medium brown and streaks of
straw colour set in it by the sun and the sea winds. His
nose was short, high at the bridge and widely flared at
the nostril; in profile it gave the whole head a resemblance to some of the Roman emperors whose pictures
I could remember in a history book. Like so many of
them, he would fatten and coarsen in his later years;
but just then, at the age of thirty-five, he was remarkably good looking in a vigorous and high-coloured
fashion.

I sat there, as the meal drew to its close and the
covers were drawn and the fruit, the sweetmeats and
the decanters were ranged in colourful display upon
the age-darkened oak, and I reckoned Dan in the
terms of the danger that he might constitute to a
woman. He had, certainly, no elegance, no refinement
of manner, was incapable of making a pretty speech
or turning a pleasing phrase. He was almost completely
unlettered, frequently ungrammatical and a stranger
to manners of the finer sort. But in the eyes of the
women with whom he had consorted during my acquaintance with him—and their name was legion—
these things appeared to be no drawback. Why should
they be, when even I, a man, accustomed to the dead-
ening process of daily familiarity with him, could sit
here now, in a critical mood, and acknowledge the
magnetism of his physical presence and that other,
most powerful, unnamed and unnameable thing—the
force which, if he came to me with some fantastic

project for passing a church by going up one side of the steeple and down the other, would compel me to feel that if he thought it could be done, then it could be. For whom else, in the name of the Saints, should I have abandoned safe and sure drudgery and ranked myself amongst the runners of contraband, after living the whole of my twenty-four years in the very odour of respectability and law-abidingness? From whom else could I draw, in the times of my darkness, such comforting draughts of light and comfort? No, if he had been small and sallow, ill-made or utterly ugly, and yet possessed that quality he would still have been a threat to any woman. Threat, because, although once his desire had been aroused, he could pursue a woman relentlessly, and while it lasted make an ardent and impetuous lover, there was no kindness in him and no faithfulness. The desire passed and the interest with it and the woman might have been dead for all he cared.

I knew this, so well. I had been confided in so often, sometimes by Dan, seeking help to elude some over-persistent discarded charmer, sometimes by the women themselves. I had never held it against him; why should I? It was part of his character and certainly not for me to approve or disapprove. Often, indeed, I was glad when some *affaire* of his came to an end, it meant more of his company, a restoration of the good companionship between men which each woman threatened and lessened for a time but proved powerless to oust. Why should I grieve over their defeats?

But now, now—it was not some mere female creature known to me by sight or name, or a stranger whose ascendancy I could only recognize from Dan's behaviour; it was Sorrel. And I knew, that evening, before the dinner drew to its end, that, with the gradual, imperceptible stages by which the most insidious diseases make their advances, I had fallen a victim to raging jealousy.

With good food in their bellies and good liquor in their glasses the company had thawed. There were toasts from the end of the table. My nonagenarian neighbour mumbled that Josiah always made a witty speech, and wasn't the port the best I had tasted? At last, bibulous and in some cases not too steady farewells begans to be spoken and the guests to drift away. Dan caught me and said, "Sorrel has something to tell us," and I knew that all hope of excluding him from the interview was lost. We went into the study together and stood by the grate where the fire had sunk down to a heap of grey ashes with a pink core of warmth.

"Pleasant evening," said Dan, speaking around the butt of his cigar and jogging it so that a shower of ash shook down over his chest. He kept his eyes on the door even as he dusted himself down. There was a sudden silence after the final heavy thud of the door and then Sorrel came in. The ribbon in her hair had worked loose and a loop of it fell forward on her brow, making her look roystering, a nymph turned bacchante. She dabbed at a wine splash on the front of the striped skirt with a handkerchief. Taking a place between us on the hearth she looked from one to another and said, "I believe a peculiar thing has happened. What was the name of the Preventive officer who hounded you out of Tislehurst?"

"Quantrill," we said, both together.

"I thought so," said Sorrel, with a nod. "Well, he's

been put in charge of the East Sussex customs and he paid me a visit to-night!"

"God!" said Dan in a soft voice. Then, more loudly, "It ain't possible. Somebody of the same name, perhaps. These fellows all work like hell to get their relations into jobs." I could hear his need to reassure himself in that speech.

"Short, thick, red-faced, with very pleasant manners and a funny little voice. He called me 'my deay Miss Kingaby' in almost every sentence. Would that be right?"

"That's him, the ——" said Dan. "Well, does that beat the devil? That he . . ."

Just then there came a roaring voice from the hall, "Miss Kingaby . . . Miss Kingaby . . . I've just remembered these plants. They ought to go into the hot house to-night. Can anyone give me a hand?"

"The Captain come back," explained Sorrel unnecessarily. "Why yes," she called back on her way to the door, "we'll all help."

"No need for that, no need at all," said the Captain, looking over her head. "If one of these gentlemen will just . . . No, no, they're damp and dirty, Miss Kingaby, you leave them alone." He motioned me to take the opposite end of the box he was already handling and as we lifted it from the ground started backing down the passage towards the door of the orchid house. Sorrel asked whether we needed a light, and the Captain retorted that the moon was as bright as day. She stepped back into the study and we jogged, like coffin bearers, down the length of the hall and through the baize-lined door.

"Had Satan's own job keeping the damned things

warm and wet all these weeks," grunted Captain
Swann. "I'm going to see they don't perish of cold their
first night home. Now where's a space?"

It was very light under the glass of the long passage,
the cold unearthly light that comes with the full moon.
I always hated it; it made me think of space, endlessly
stretching in icy silences, and of mortality and the
loneliness of being dead. And once I began to think
of these things the flaw in my mind opened and
widened. . . .

I looked towards the homely, comforting reality of
the candle-light in the study which could be seen
through the little bottle-glass panes of the study's side
door. And as I looked I saw Dan, not Sorrel, outlined
for a second against the warm light, and then blotted
out as the curtain was drawn across it.

I was a man, mature of mind and body; I engaged
in a hazardous trade for my daily bread; there were
weeks when I risked life and liberty almost nightly
with no more thought or timorousness than many another man. But I swear that the symbolism of that
drawn curtain, the shutting away of the warm, the
known, the mortal light, struck me deeply. Struck at
some part of me that was neither body, nor the mind
as we know it. I had a feeling of faintness, so that I
almost released my hold on the box we were carrying;
and a mile away, on the surface of my consciousness,
I knew that Captain Swann was looking at me hard
and thinking that I was carrying my liquor badly. But
what I was carrying badly was that unnameable
thing which distinguishes men from brute beasts; the
thing which must be carried unconsciously to retain balance, since, the moment one is aware of

it the mind rocks and living becomes a burden. It was the thing that I called, in my mind, my darkness; it was, I think, akin to the evil spirit that troubled Saul, the king of Israel; but in my case sweet music, especially harp music would only have aggravated the condition. It could start anywhere, at any time, from any cause or from no cause at all. To-night it was the deadly light of the moon and the curtain drawn over a candle's glimmer. . . . And I was no longer Tom Borthwick, man born of woman, an ex-law student, ex-barrister's clerk turned smuggler, standing upon two solid fleshy feet in a glass passage surrounded by orchids in the company of a red-faced sailor who suspected me of being drunk. No. In the hour of the evil spirit I saw myself, and other men, not as trees, walking, but as motes, infinitesimally small, blowing through the cold outer spaces of the universe, lost between star and star, exiled from all comfort under the icy light of the moon . . . a lifetime less than a breath's span, a person less than an ant. And I wanted to take this red-faced sea captain, and Dan and Sorrel and draw them together into shelter, away from the threat of dissolution. . . . Above all, I wanted to leave the moonlight, seek warmth and brightness, have a glass in my hand, a pipe in my mouth, some cheerful voice in my ears, so that I might forget the vision of a doomed human race, rushed along, like cattle to the slaughter-house.

The Captain, his duty once more impeccably performed, went away. I paced the length of the long passage several times, fighting with the shapeless, formless thing that had attacked me. At last, noisily, I went along to the side door of the study and opened it. Sorrel and Dan were standing at some distance from one another, and they had both started upon a sentence, as though my entrance had been a signal to them to begin reciting. But the very air was a-quiver between them; a rapid pulse beat in Sorrel's throat, her cheeks were more flushed and her breath came short and hard. As for Dan, although he turned aside and thrust a taper into the fire and fussed with a cigar, I had seen enough of his face to recognize the look that I had so often seen before; the look of the animal roused, the lust set on its course, the passion which can neither pause nor rest until it has found slaking. And I thought, in the five or ten minutes of my absence we have all three gone through our separate experiences; Dan's familiar, mine only too well-known; only Sorrel has felt something new. And now we must for a moment or two pretend that those minutes have no existence. I said brightly, "Well, and what of Quantrill? How did he smell us out?"

"He didn't," said Sorrel. "He isn't interested in Bywater at all. St Osyth and Brightlingsea are on his mind at the moment."

"Beware of him," I said. "He probably has a deep hidden motive even for telling you that."

Sorrel said with teasing affection, "Wick, you have such a twisty mind yourself that you credit other people with similar ones. Isn't that so?" she asked, turning to Dan. He regarded her sombrely; and although his lips answered her question, his eyes said other things in another language.

"Wick's right there," he said. "Quantrill is the craftiest thing on two legs."

But his mind was far away from any thought of

Quantrill, or contraband, or shots in the night. And damn me, if, knowing what I did of Quantrill, and our experiences at Tislehurst, I wasn't swept by a perverse feeling of admiration for the make of man, who, hearing that his most dangerous enemy had crossed his path again, could, in the next moment, draw a curtain and make a woman's heart beat that way.

It was, however, some weeks before Quantrill's appointment affected us in any way except to make us more wary. And wary we were and had need to be; for he was no ordinary man. Before long stories began to spread about of his activities around the districts that he had mentioned to Sorrel; and they were very similar to, blood brothers of, the stories which we had heard in Sussex. Who started them, I wondered. Surely that dapper, plump, scarlet-faced old soldier did not himself set afoot the rumours that he could be seen in two places at once; that a Spanish lady of high degree had given him an amulet that charmed his life and rendered him immune from ordinary peril. And yet here, in Essex, within a few weeks of his arrival the stories had begun again, lacing the ordinary caution with which the Owlers regarded an active and crafty foe with a thrill of supernatural awe. I was not, myself, superstitious, at least where Captain Quantrill was concerned. I believed that his reputation for being in two places at once depended upon rapid motion, the unreliability of eye-witnesses, and a tendency amongst the ignorant to prefer highly-coloured fiction to plain fact. And I did credit him with a unique, highly organized spy system, combined with shrewd observation and deep guile. I hoped the Toosey and Brightlingsea gangs would keep him busy all winter, and that some other notorious area would require his attention in the spring.

The mellow golden season ended, and with it my liking for the Essex coast. Even if the later months of that year had brought more comfortable happenings, the sad flavour of decline would hang over the memory of them. As it is, to recall them is to see again the havoc made by the winds in the painted stretches of Layer Wood; to hear again the sound of the wild geese squadrons winging through the night, and to feel the steady arrow flight of the driven rain over the dreary marshes where the creeks swelled leadenly under the sullen sky.

Looking back at that time I see a kind of pattern in it, like a piece of cord woven from three coloured threads.

There was our job. After a few rainy days which brought down the leaves into mud-coloured masses underfoot, a dry east wind began to blow and blew intermittently for weeks on end; so the marsh paths remained open for an unusually long season. That same wind made it easy to make the run from the French coast, so we were very busy and made good profits.

There was the relationship between Dan and me which was, despite every effort I could make, changing, and proving that nothing, however tried and proved, can be regarded as sure and unalterable.

And there was the state of affairs between Sorrel and me, a state which could not be separated from the other threads.

I remember the day when, as was my habit after a run, I called to tell her that the latest venture had been successful and to deliver her share of the result. She took the money and locked it away, saying with a peculiar smile:

"May this go on! I have yet another pensioner, Wick."

"Where do you find them?"

"They seem to find me."

"I think you're a fool," I said bluntly. "But then, you know that."

"I'm a fool," she said wryly. "But not in the way you think. You know, I think a lot of unhappiness is caused by people trying to compensate themselves for something they think they have missed. You believe, don't you, that I fill up this house with people because I am kind and sentimental. It's quite wrong. I fill up the house just to show myself that it is my house and that I can do what I like with it. And that feeling is necessary to me because there was a long period in my life when it looked as though it would never *be* my house. Can you understand that?"

"Perfectly well. It isn't very unusual. Dan, for example, buys numbers of new clothes because once he was ragged and barefoot. The clothes don't mean anything to him. Within a week they look just like the old ones; but it satisfies him in some way."

What perverse demon made me mention Dan, and watch, almost hungrily for that alteration of her face? Some buried instinct for self-torture, the kind of thing that makes one keep pressing a bruise. No, not perhaps from an insane desire to hurt oneself, but from curiosity to see how the injury is proceeding. Will it hurt as much this time as it did last? Yes, it did; no, it didn't; oh, about the same.

And about the same, indeed, was my feeling, when I saw the instant response that moved in her; heard the alteration in her voice:

"Is he all right?"

"Perfectly. I told you, it was a straightforward run."

"I'm always worried."

"I know. And you may remember that until the *Mirabella* dinner when you and Dan became really acquainted, you didn't know much about the game. He tells you too much," I said gruffly.

"He trusts me."

"So do I. But I believe that innocence is the best guard. And I think you'd be in a better position, if anything happened, if you were kept uninformed."

"But I hate being kept in the dark."

I thought that there was not much danger of that. Dan, either through carelessness, or to please her, had taken her fully into his confidence.

I had to set that fact against the conflicting evidence of the way in which he spoke of her. Or did he do that to tease me? Was he unwilling to admit that Sorrel meant more to him than all those other women? I shall never know. People may, through mutual liking, and confidence, through shared experience, intimate daily living and observation, attain great knowledge of one another; but there is always a great deal that is hidden; and there are some feelings that are, in fact, hidden from the person who entertains them. And so, although I knew Dan so well that I could often foretell his words, I never wholly understood his feelings toward Sorrel; and though she and I were frequently frank to the point of rudeness to one another, although she interested me and attracted me more than any woman I have ever met, I should still not like to commit myself upon the question whether it was love, or not, which she felt for him.

He spoke of her coarsely; but that was his way. Six weeks after the *Mirabella* dinner, which I always considered to be a landmark in their story, he was complaining that he had had nothing from her but kisses. (He put it very differently!)

"What did you expect?" I asked surlily. "Are you so dull that you can't see a difference between Sorrel Kingaby and your drabs at Porthsea and Tislehurst?"

He sneered. "Difference my ——! There's only two kinds of women—those worth taking to bed and those not."

"And those, apparently, not so easy to distinguish," I retaliated. "Remember the first night you saw her?"

"I was mistook there; but only because I like a little meat on my bone. A second look told me that you can light a good fire in a small grate sometimes."

"Two very poetical metaphors." He looked at me blankly.

"Oh, stow the lawyer's gab, Wick. I'd like to see you tackle the problem of how to bed a wench with an aunt or a cousin or some other gargoyle always just round the corner."

"Quite a teaser for you. Most of your females couldn't identify their mothers, far less an aunt."

"What about the mayor's daughter?"

"Just the same," I said. "The higher an ape climbs the more you see of its tail."

"All right, Mister Clever Borthwick, what do you wager that I don't have her within a week?"

I suddenly felt sick, and wondered whether by my attitude I had goaded him.

"Look here, Dan," I said seriously, "have a care what you do. We're in a good place here; you might make a mucker and we'd lose it. Let her make the pace for a bit. And you look round and see if there isn't another petticoat that might be upped without risk."

He gave me an odd look. "S'pose we do lose the bloody place, we've lost 'em before. The world's full of places. But there's only one Sorrel."

My God! I thought.

Yet on the very next day, or at latest the one after it, it looked as though he had taken my advice about the alternative petticoat. In any case, he was making obvious play with the woman who kept the "Evening Star." She had been, perhaps fifteen years before, a comely enough piece, but her teeth had gone and her hair was going, and her whole air of hopeless lasciviousness was pitiable enough to show why women should turn respectable at twenty-five whatever they have been before. There was a husband, but I always suspected him of connection with the Toosey men, since he was seldom at home, and when he was slept most of the time.

She perked up suddenly, curled her lank hair, raked out from some cupboard a paillasson more than ten years old which now fitted her evilly, and made some attempt to paint a face which wore an expression like that of a cat which has been given some utterly unexpected cream.

About a fortnight later Dan said to me, with the voice and manner which he used when he had done something about the business without consulting me:

"Wick. Quantrill is busying his —— self with By-water. There's been a leak somewhere. I'm going to move the horses and make our headquarters here."

"You fool," I said, "this is the most obvious place, if he should just think of it."

"He may not think of it. He's thinking of Bywater, and he's got his eye on Sorrel. God knows why!"

"But," I protested, "what if he has. That was the whole beauty of the thing: bales amongst bales, barrels amongst barrels, and pack-horses amongst pack-horses. He could search the place from end to end and be none the wiser."

His face took on a stubborn look, rather like Sorrel's, only his was stupid-stubborn where hers was wary.

"Well, I've done it. I've fixed it all with that draggle-tail out there." His expression changed to one of extreme distaste. "Wick, she's got breath like a bumby!"

And then suddenly I saw through the whole thing. He was protecting Sorrel; he didn't trust my arrangements; hadn't trusted me to see that in the final count she would not be involved at all.

Truly, men are strange creatures. I would no more have dreamed of going to bed with her and risking an illegitimate baby than I would have dreamed of throwing myself off the church tower; but I should have watched, unmoved, Quantrill inspecting the premises and even, if invited, accompanied him. Dan must move the horses and abandon the most perfect headquarters ever discovered, and yet the other, the real, the glaring risk never, I am sure, entered his thoughts.

After that he ceased to speak of Sorrel at all, and little of other things. He became very secretive, and I never made an attempt to probe into his doings. I could guess well enough and I was sick at heart. I began to meditate leaving him. I had not, owing to responsibilities that have no place in this story, saved much of the money that I had made by moon-lighting, but I had enough to save me from returning to the drudgery of an office. I could set up in business of some sort. I could go away and forget Bywater and Dan and Sorrel. I could buy books, one at a time, and settle down to a peaceful, uneventful life, the kind for which I was born.

I brought myself at last to broach the subject to Dan, who at first treated it as he did the onslaughts of my spiritual malaise. He threw his heavy arm about my shoulders, opened a bottle of Canary, and started to tell me a story, obscene but funny.

"I'm serious," I said. "I'm sick of the game, and even you can't blink the fact that we no longer pull together."

"I've noticed that you've been touchy lately," he said with an air of childlike naïveté. "Are you still holding it against me that I moved headquarters?"

"No. Though that was a straw showing the way of the wind."

"Then it's about Sorrel Kingaby. Ha, Wick, don't deny it, your face gives you away!" He was thoughtful for a moment, and then he said gravely, "I didn't know you were really serious about her. You had ample chance, didn't you? All that time before I came, and then later on when to me she was just a skinny virgin. Damn it, Wick, I can see it now though, ever since that night when you went for me out there on the marsh. Of all the goddam things, a petticoat coming between you and me. And you drivelling about taking off and leaving me. What'd I do?" He stared at me and repeated, "What'd I do, Wick?" Then he brightened. "No. I tell you what, I'll chuck her. She always was a bit masterful for my taste. You'd suit her better. You go in and see what you can make of her. . . ."

"Thank you," I said savagely. "Is there anything of mine you'd care for in exchange? 'Any old Cloe?' for instance."

"Honest, Wick, I haven't hurt her. And the whole bloody time it wasn't me she wanted. That's straight talk. I can't explain. I ain't a lawyer. She was using me, and I knew it. I was there because somebody else wasn't. Maybe it was you she hankered after. And I bet you never give her a sign, you old oyster." He added, with a kind of animal bewilderment, "That's the first time that sort of thing has come my way. I ought to have a grudge against you."

"Not on that score," I said.

"Then what are we snarling about?" He gave his wide beaming smile. "Come on, Wick. Here's you and me, two sensible fellows, squabbling over a green girl. Where's the sense in it? Drink up and to hell with the drabs. They got their uses, but there never was one —— worth a couple of men falling out over."

And once again I felt, under my limp, exhausted body, the mighty heave and strain of the muscles of his back as he toiled up that cliff face under my weight; knew again the sense of being cared for at last which had come to me in that stinking little Porthsea room.

"You may be right," I said reluctantly.

"Then for the love of God let's have no more of this deserter's talk!"

And suddenly I thought a strange thing. I knew that I had really deserted him long ago, on that night on the path through the marshes, when I thought that his neck was too thick, and had to remind myself, as I had just done again, of all I owed him. And that made me, who am not a religious man, though I take an academic interest in the matter, think of Judas and the betrayal of Christ. It has never been clear to me why Judas acted as he did. Thirty pieces of silver wasn't so much, and anyway, next day he was ready to do without it. Is it possible that amongst the women who followed Christ there was one who had caught the disciple's eye, and on whose account he was jealous of his Master? She might not have chosen Christ in any worldly or fleshly manner, but she might have been absorbed in Him, and so Judas was baulked and his vanity injured. Is there, behind the story of the greatest betrayal of all time, another story, Judas's?

Nonsense, of course, and blasphemous at that. But who shall govern where his mind shall run?

And in this case there was no betrayal. What happened happened in the ordinary nature of things. Though afterwards I was glad that I had smiled back at Dan that night, and that we had emptied the bottle together as we had emptied so many others.

For all that Dan had laid himself to win over the innkeeper's woman I don't think that once, in the time that elapsed after our move, we ever had contraband there. The horses lived in the ramshackle stable. Timothy and the Gaffer slept in the loft above it, Dan and I occupied the two best rooms in the place. Abel retained his lodging at the "Ship," and so his place in the Bywater scene, but he was often over at the "Evening Star." Five men with no visible means of livelihood, whose comings and goings were highly erratic, needed some explanation, which doubtless Dan had provided between his reluctant embraces. But the actual stuff was brought in Abel's boat up a backwater from Foul Point and hidden until eventually loaded from a place there which we had discovered by meticulous scouting. It was cut off from the land by a strip of marsh threaded with creeks, inaccessible to anyone who did not have intimate knowledge of the place. Actually I had discovered, hidden below the mud and the sandy ridges and the marram grass the remains of a stone causeway which I attributed to Roman workmanship. It provided firm footing to within a few score yards of the point which the *Sea-Gull* could reach by the backwater. It was, in its way, as unique a ground for action as the river and wharf and warehouse at Bywater had been, and the discovery of the causeway had consoled me for the fact that we were back in the more traditional way of carrying on.

Where the causeway ended there was a mile or two of tolerable path, with care easily negotiable, which followed a spit of higher land running through the marsh. At its end there was a choice of three directions, all leading inland. One path, the shortest, led direct to the "Evening Star"; the second, branching left towards Bywater, joined the comparatively good road that led by Layer Wood and Steeple Rising into Baildon; the third, bearing right, was a worse road and never used by wheeled traffic, being low and muddy except for a week or two in summer. The Baildon Road crossed a river by an old stone bridge, and

was sometimes known as the Stone Bridge Road. The
Lower Road, as it was called, crossed the same water,
but higher up, at a narrower and shallower point, and
those who travelled it were obliged to plunge through
the ford. Except in very bad weather we used the
Lower Road, which was the less frequented.

Abel Fakes, since his mishap at Steeple Rising, had
aged rapidly as some hale old men do after a long
period of apparent imperviousness to Time's encroach-
ments. He seldom now set out with us on our longer
journeys. It comforted his pride if we, to let him make
up for this inability to move quickly, allowed him to
take charge of the less arduous part of a run—the load-
ing and getting ready. So it had become our custom
to remain at the "Evening Star" until almost time to
start, then to set out and meet the horses, Timothy,
Abel and the Gaffer at the point where the paths ran
together.

During those weeks—and they seemed infinitely
prolonged—of harsh east winds I had often envied
Abel when we parted and he shuffled off along the
path that led to Bywater and the "Ship," the fire in
the bar and his warm bed. And he, I suppose, envied
me as I took my place along the line and moved away,
free of limb, to carry on the job, which, for all its risks
and discomforts, had a fascination of its own.

It was towards the end of December, and the wind
was still blowing, when Timothy, starting off with the
horses towards the causeway and the load, stuck his
blunt nose into the air and sniffed:

"Wind's gorn ter change," he announced pontifi-
cally. "There'll be rain afore morning."

"That'll be too late to spoil the path," said Dan

comfortably. "And once this run is over I don't care so much." Weather as weather meant nothing to him. He was never exhilarated by a fine day nor depressed by a dull one. Except for their effects upon his business all seasons were alike to him.

I shuddered as I turned back for the last hour or two under cover. "Nothing but a snowstorm," I complained, "could be worse than this wind."

"I never knew anybody fuss about the weather as you do, Wick. Whyn't you go down and warm yourself helping them dig out the casks and load 'em."

"I've heard worse suggestions. But if I did Abel's feelings would be hurt again." Already in a fortnight Abel's feelings had been three times hurt by Dan's restlessness driving him to take a hand in what the arbitrary old fellow had come to regard as his special province.

Actually I hated the hanging about just before a run. I had, of course, taken part in hundreds, and once we were on the road I was calm and cool; but I always suffered from a preliminary nervousness which evidenced itself in various irritating ways. On this evening it found expression in a curious preoccupation with the weather. I kept going to the door and looking out. True enough, the wind was changing, but it was veering north, not south, as I had hoped. Its character was changing, too; from the steady cutting drive which I had so disliked in the last weeks it was becoming squally and boisterous. One such squall, occurring when I was looking out, drove a dash of cold rain that stung like hailstones into my face. Soon the onslaught of the hard-driven drops could be heard on the windows.

"It's going to be rough," I said.

"All the better," Dan answered me. "Keep the molly men in by the fire." It was one of his fixed and comfortable convictions that the customs officers were much less virile than the men they hunted, and could be kept indoors by any inclemency in the weather. He had on occasion teased me by telling me what a wonderful Preventive man I should make.

We were just ready to leave with our lanterns, our flasks, and our packets of food to eat on the road; should, indeed, have been outside in the wind through which no voice would have carried far, had I not at the last moment thought of old Cobbitt and his red and black comforter tied over his ears. I hurried up to our sleeping room and came down again tying a scarf, not under my hat, but over it. Dan, with his woollen cap jauntily pulled on one side, roared with laughter when he saw me. "Next time I'm in Colchester I'll buy you a cardinal cloak, sink me if I don't!" he said.

The door of our room opened upon a little stone-flagged passage with the entry door at one end and the door leading to the bar and the kitchen at the other. Both doors, and they were solid things made of oak and nail-studded, were shuddering in the draught that swept the passage. As we walked to the outer door, myself leading, I remember thinking how very violent the wind must be to shake it so. And just as I laid my hand on the latch and, as it were, braced myself for the blast that would greet its opening, the door seemed to open of its own accord and somebody tumbled in.

For a moment I did not recognize her. When Dan mentioned the cardinal cloak I had thought how far behind the times he was in his knowledge of women's attire—cardinal cloaks, I thought, were fifty years old, and I could remember my grandmother wearing one and being thought old-fashioned. And here, before my eyes, *was* a cardinal cloak, its scarlet almost black with moisture, its hood pulled so far forward that the wearer's face was almost hidden. But in the next instant, before the door had closed of its own accord, I knew that inside the cardinal cloak was Sorrel, and that something horrible had happened.

She was in a state of collapse, blown into the place almost like a leaf. I slipped my arm around her and pushed Dan, who stood staring, back towards the door of our room. But as I was half-lifting, half-dragging her along the passage, he turned again, lifted her as though she had been a child, and carried her within. I kicked the door closed. But I had seen his face in which alarm and concern had been shot through by tenderness.

The small cask of brandy, good French stuff, the sort we smuggled, not the sort in the "Evening Star," from which we had been filling our flasks, stood on the corner of the table; the pewter mugs from which we had been drinking stood close by. While Dan lowered Sorrel into a chair by the fire which had been allowed to burn low, and she raised her hands to push away the dripping folds of her hood. I drew a measure of brandy and carried it to her. Between the water-darkened, bloody coloured cloak and the drenched curls of her hair her face was chalk-white, with enormous eyes staring as though from a mask, and a faint purple shadow lay around mouth and nostrils. She took a gulp of the brandy, gasped, drew in a deep breath, and laid her hand on her breast.

"Thank God I got here!" she said, and her voice was surprisingly strong and clear. "Quantrill's picketed the ford and the Stone Bridge."

"Did he tell you so?" I asked, my natural distrust of any direct statement of his at once in action.

"No. I overheard him."

"Oh!" In that case the information was probably correct and not intended to mislead.

She lifted the mug to her lips again, but stood up as she swallowed. "I must get back. He's sitting in my parlour waiting for his dinner."

"Quantrill?"

"Yes."

"Then how did you get out? D'you think he followed you?" There was urgency in Dan's question, the first he had asked.

"That was Lou's doings. One of you must help me with Lou."

"Where is she?"

"Back along the path under a bush. She may be dead."

As she said that her face suddenly crumpled as though all the bones within it had collapsed. A terrible shuddering laid hold of her so that her very heels chattered on the uncovered bricks of the floor.

"She came," she said wildly. "She did it for me. And I think it killed her." She turned to me and laid her hand on my arm in a clutch which, though as small as though a bird's claw had seized me, was painful in its urgency.

"Please, Wick, help me to get her back and indoors again before that old devil suspects anything."

And there, of course, I made my fatal error. Dan

could have gone back with her and carried Miss Lou with one arm and dragged Sorrel along with the other; and Sorrel's own mother wit would have done the rest. And I was as capable as he of rushing down to the point where the paths met, meeting the horses and making some arrangements for the disposal of the load. But when Sorrel turned to me like that and I thought of the poor old woman under a bush and Quantrill, sitting like a great red spider in Sorrel's house, spinning the web for our undoing, I lost my judgment—the judgment which, I say it in all modesty, had saved us in far worse passes than this.

"Take another swig of that and we'll go," I said.

"And what'll I do?" Dan asked.

"Get along to the others, turn them back and dig the stuff under again," I said.

"How about trying Old Nick's Jump? This stuff was promised, you know," said Dan, who disliked failure to deliver the stuff.

"I shouldn't risk it. But you must do as you think best," I said. "Come on, Sorrel."

Old Nick's Jump was the third way out of the marshes. We had tried it once and sworn never again. It *was* a path of a kind, but its surface was villainous, about as much worse than the Lower Road as the Lower Road was inferior to the Stone Bridge one; and besides being too great a strain on the horses when they were loaded, it involved a nasty crossing of the same water as, in the case of the other two roads, was crossed by bridge or ford. Old Nick's Jump, as its name implied, had neither—you jumped it if you were riding a horse which could jump, otherwise you plunged down a slimy chalk bank, through the water

and up on the other side. And I was so unbalanced by
Sorrel's coming and the need for haste in order to fore-
stall Quantrill's suspicions of her absence, that it was
only of the natural danger of the path, especially after
dark, that I was thinking. I should have known that
Dan had really neither caution or judgment . . . that
to tell him to do as he thought best was to invite trouble . . . that Quantrill . . . But I also had neither sense
nor judgment on that evening. I took hold of Sorrel's
arm and began to hurry her towards the door.

Then suddenly Dan spoke in a voice so unlike any
I had ever heard him use that I turned and stared in
amazement. He spoke like a child who had trans-
gressed, been savagely punished. and then, quite unex-
pectedly, forgiven. He said "Sorrel!" And she turned
and looked back at him over her shoulder. "It was
good of you to come. Thank you for. coming. I'm sorry
about . . . everything. I'll be back Thursday, even if I
make the run. May I come?"

She gave a kind of jerk of the head, but she was
turning at the same time and hurrying towards the
door. I pulled it open and the howling wind seemed to
reach in and tear at us. Dan shouted "Goodbye," and
plunged off towards the marshes; Sorrel and I turned
towards Bywater.

At first speech was impossible. The wind buffeted
the breath from our bodies and tore away the few
words we did essay. But after ten minutes there came
a period of slackening, and just then Sorrel said, "I
left her somewhere here."

I sharpened the look-out I had been keeping, and
presently the beam of my lantern fell on a clump of
bushes with a dense shadow at their feet. We stooped

and grasped at it. It stirred of its own accord under our hands, and Sorrel cried, "She's not dead; oh, she's not dead!" And as though in recognition of the voice Miss Lou said very faintly, "Sorrel, Sorrel!"

"When I left her she wasn't conscious at all," said Sorrel. She knelt down and put her arms around the old woman. "Lou, Lou, dear, can you hear me? Will you try to walk if we help you? It isn't very far and the wind is less. We must get back because of him, you know."

"Quantrill," said the faint voice. The poor old thing had understood and began to heave and move with much the kind of action with which a fallen horse will try to right itself.

But the mere action of rising seemed to exhaust her, and the rest of the journey into Bywater was like the worst kind of nightmare. It was worse, I think, than it would have been had the old lady been quite insensible and quite helpless. As it was it somehow smacked of cruelty to heave and push and pull her along as we did. And when, as happened three times for short periods, I managed to get her on my back and stagger along, it was, silly as it seems, an affront to her dignity, especially as she moaned and kept saying "Sorrel!" in a kind of piteous appeal.

At intervals, broken and interrupted by the alterations of posture and grip which such a journey demanded, I gathered from Sorrel the bare outline of the happenings of the earlier evening. Quantrill had made his first visit to Sorrel on the night of her dinner for Captain Swann, and had obviously desired to be asked to join the party. Since then it had been a joke with him that one day he would attain sufficient favour to be asked to dine at East House. On this afternoon he had arrived, craving, he said, not only for dinner, but a night's hospitality, since the "Ship" was unable to accommodate him.

"He had come into the office," said Sorrel. "And his manner was as genial as usual. If I hadn't known from Dan that you were planning a run for tonight I don't think I should have suspected anything. As it was, when he said that he would go and see about his horse, I went up to that little room where we store pepper and that kind of light stuff, and pushed open the window a bit. He *was* in the yard, so was his horse, and so was that cross-eyed fellow who rides the piebald. You know that corner of the yard; the wall is quite blank except for that window, and though they looked round a bit furtively I don't suppose it occurred to them that they could be overheard. . . ." She paused while we shifted our grip on Miss Lou. "I heard him say about the pickets at both the Stone Bridge and the ford. And he added that he was staying here for the night. The man on the piebald saluted and rode off quickly, and Quantrill himself led his horse into the stable.

"I left the office and hurried up to the house and ordered the dinner. I thought of slipping away then, but he must have followed me up, almost. I tried to think of someone to send with a message, but it so happened that both Glasswell and Middleditch were out; both teams were out. There was only the women, and it had started to rain and blow. I knew they'd never find their way either. So I got up every kind of drink I could think of, brandy, port, Madeira and rum; and I said he was to help himself and that dinner

would be late because after all this time I wanted to
serve him properly. I thought he might drink himself
a bit stupid. But he didn't. He just sat and looked at
me and sat and looked at me, and all the time my
mind was twisting about and I thought I should go
mad.

"Then I thought of Lou." And here, poor Miss Lou,
hearing her name, said "Sorrel" again, and Sorrel
broke off to reassure her and urge her to further
effort. "Yes . . . I thought of her. I ran to her room and
told her not to ask any questions, but to do just as I
said. In five minutes she was to come in, in a hurried
way, and say that Old Betty—she's a servant we had
before Agatha—had been taken ill and was asking for
us. I told her that I had to get out of the house and be
away for over an hour without Quantrill's minding.
And she did it beautifully. Then, of course, what with
the pace I set and the wind and the rain, she just collapsed. Wick, what shall we do? How shall I get her
indoors?"

I said, "Where does Old Whatshername live? The
servant?"

"In Fenn Row."

"Where does the doctor live?"

"On the Green. Why?"

"Coming from Fenn Row would you pass the Green,
or go anywhere near it?"

"Yes. The Green lies between."

"Steer for the Green then."

The first houses of the little town rose up on either
side of us now, and in a few minutes—few, but how
long, how agonized—we were in the space, flanked on

one side by the Church and on the other three by substantial houses.

"Which is the doctor's?" I asked. And when Sorrel had pointed it out, I said, "I shall pretend to be just a passing fellow who saw you two ladies in distress and pulled his bell. I'd better leave then—at least I'll help you to the door and then disappear. I think the flurry of your arrival with the doctor will allay any suspicion. I hope it will, anyway. It's the best I can think of."

So I pulled the doctor's bell and told him that a lady seemed to be indisposed just near his gate; and he came out and recognized Sorrel and weighed in the balance the respective merits of bringing Miss Lou into his house, waiting to have his horse harnessed and his carriage brought round, and of "This gentleman here," and himself carrying her just along Stag Lane, and so home. Sorrel chose the latter course; and as we neared East House I said firmly, "I'm afraid I can come only as far as the door, this has made me late already." I would have risked meeting Quantrill alone; but I thought that his behaviour already showed a suspicion of Sorrel, and that that devilish old Mrs Fennigard would have referred to my wool-chandlering and there was just a chance that something about my happening to be present at the crisis might have set Quantrill's mind working. So I accompanied the party to the top of the steps, accepted thanks from Sorrel and the doctor and disappeared into the night. In dragging the doctor into it I thought I had made a sensible move. Doctors better than anyone else can shut up idle questioners; they have authority; they are not often involved in questionable adventures. Moreover the poor old lady was in need of a doctor. And it is always valuable at a time when lies are being told to have one witness who has a simple truthful story to tell.

When the door of East House closed on the oblong of light and the street was left in darkness I was at a loss what to do, or where to go. Dan and the rest of them were, by this time, I hoped, well on the way back to the hiding-place at the end of the causeway. If I followed them there was nothing useful that I could do because by the time I reached them the stuff would be hidden. If—and I hoped desperately that he had done no such thing, Dan had decided upon trying to push through at Old Nick's Jump, I should now never overtake them.

There was one thing that I must know; and fortunately it was easily found out. I turned in the direction of the "Ship." I was soon answered. There were three rooms vacant, I could have my pick of them. I said that I would see how the weather turned out; and, ordering brandy, I went and sat in a corner.

One thing was plain. Quantrill, for some reason, suspected Sorrel; that was why he had wanted to spend the night in East House. And Sorrel, thanks to Miss Lou and Dan, was clear enough. There would be no activity about that yard; there was no incriminating evidence upon the premises. But where had we failed? Where had the leakage been? Rack my mind as I might, I could remember nothing that had been said or done, or left undone. . . .

I drank steadily for some time; but the liquor, instead of clearing my brain, clouded it, and at the same time failed to raise my spirits. I began to have unhealthy thoughts about Quantrill. There was a suggestion of doom about the way in which he had twice crossed our path. I remembered that he had appeared on the night when Dan had first become aware of Sorrel; and through my mind went the thought that that had been a significant night. All the characters had been assembled then and the action of the play had begun. And yet there was no ill connection between Dan's *affaire* with Sorrel and Quantrill's suspicion of her that I could see. In fact, it was otherwise. Dan had moved the horses because he feared for Sorrel. And yet, as the brandy fumes mounted, I could not banish the thought that it was, somehow, all closely interwoven, like a good play. For whose entertainment? That of the gods? Perhaps from their view the connecting link was plain. I could not see it because I was only one of the poor players.

I thought—Tom Borthwick, you're getting drunk. I looked at the clock, swallowed what remained of my brandy, and stood up. I told the landlord that I thought I would risk the journey. If Dan had done the sane thing he would be back now at the "Evening Star," impatient to know how Sorrel and I had fared. And there was a great deal that I wanted to tell him. Apart from the discussion of future plans for lying low, perhaps for disappearing for a little while until Quantrill's suspicions had quieted down, I wanted to tell him how right he had been to move headquarters; to ask whether he had any idea of where the leak had been; and to show him that he need no longer pretend to me about his feelings for Sorrel, because it was all plain now. . . .

I had much to say to Dan, who had been my friend for eight years. But of course it was never said; because while I was striding back over the marsh path, and Sorrel was watching Miss Lou breathe her last, and Quantrill was enjoying his special, celebrating meal, Dan, with men and horses and contraband scattered about him, was lying dead on the far bank of Old Nick's Jump with a bullet through his head.

PART FOUR

Green Mirror of Envy

Miss Louisa Kingaby's sudden death ridded me of the person who more than all others had grudged me the sanctuary of East House; and although, in order to underline my claim to be one of the family, I found up and wore an old black gown and pelisse, I could not even pretend to mourn her passing.

I never understood her attitude to me. She had known about Jamie's relationship to Sorrel, so she could not have considered that I had eloped with her precious pet's beau; in fact, she should have been very grateful to me for my share in averting, if not a scandal, at least an awkward situation. Nor was it as if I were robbing her of anything; although she was a Kingaby by birth she had nothing of her own. In fact all of us, Mrs Fennigard, Widow Kingaby, Miss Lou and I depended entirely on Sorrel's charity. But looking back to my first stay in Bywater, when I was governess to Dinah and Lydia, I can remember that Miss Lou never missed an opportunity to administer a snub to me; and after my return it was a hundred times worse. Perhaps with some kind of instinct, she sensed that I hated Sorrel as much as she adored her.

I can't quite say that I hated Sorrel Kingaby from the first moment I saw her; for at our Colchester interview she struck me as being a rather insignificant little person with slightly eccentric ideas about girls' education and not much knowledge of the value of money. She offered me an excellent salary and mentioned that she did not expect a governess to do anything in the house, or even to make and mend for the children. It sounded the kind of post for which one hopes in vain. In the place I was leaving, Heatherly Park, I had never finished, I was always dusting, and mending, doing flowers, washing lace and dressing her ladyship's hair. And so, although the new post was socially less desirable, and my new employer very ordinary compared with my old one, I took a favourable view of her, thinking she was sensible and kindly and a little overwhelmed at finding herself responsible for the well-being and education of three young sisters.

My first few hours in Bywater enlightened me. Dinah and Lydia came to help me unpack. I tried to be charming to them, because if one's charges are devoted one's labour is halved. But there seemed to be room in their minds for no one except Sorrel.

The room she had allotted me was certainly superior to the one I had occupied at the Park. It was spacious and light, well and sensibly furnished; but I tired of having amenities pointed out to me as Sorrel's work. Did I not think the hangings delightful? Sorrel had chosen them. Had I noticed the vase of flowers on the windowsill? Sorrel had given the girls permission to pluck them and told them to keep the vase replenished. The fire-screen—a very mediocre piece of work—had been made by Sorrel while they were all at Miss Gould's. Sorrel had saved them from going back to Miss Gould's horrid school and they could never be sufficiently grateful. Sorrel had said that black dresses were gloomy for young people, that was why, within three months of their father's death, they were both wearing such pretty colours. On and on and on until I was tired of the sound of her silly name. Perhaps on that first day it was the re-iteration of the name, Sorrel, which annoyed me. Each time they said it—always in that doting way—I thought, first of a weed that grows in meadows and then a sorrel mare, and I could not remember what colour a sorrel mare would be.

We "Sorrel worshipped" until almost supper time, when they reminded me that they always went down for the meal because Sorrel thought growing girls wanted more to eat than could be conveniently carried up on a tray; and they must be washed and tidied by five minutes to the hour because Sorrel liked punctuality. When at last they left me to change my dress, I realized that they had not remarked either the water-colours or the embroidered things which I had un-packed first of all in order to impress them; nor had there been a sign of that rather calfish admiration which my appearance usually rouses in girls who have themselves reached the gawky stage. Sorrel, I could see at once, was going to be more difficult to replace in their affections, then any mother or elder sister I had yet encountered.

At the supper-table (furnished with silver more massive than that at the Park, and far more lavishly spread with food!) things were even worse. Besides Miss Louisa Kingaby, whom I had met at Colchester, there was a painted old woman, dressed in colours that made her likeness to a cockatoo simply ludicrous, and a gloomy, disapproving, youngish-looking female, in rich bombazine and crepe. Relationships between the three of them were full of undercurrents and anything but happy or friendly, yet the word most frequently on all their tongues was "Sorrel." "Sorrel, don't you agree . . ." "Sorrell, I wish you could arrange . . ." "Sorrel, when you can spare a moment . . ." "Sorrel, will you please see . . ." It was like standing behind the throne of God and listening to prayers and praises.

I felt a kind of low-spiritedness come over me as I sat there and looked round. I thought how much I should have liked to sit at the head of the table in the place occupied by this little pale-faced, red-haired, green-eyed creature, and mean so much to all these people. And how much more charming I would have been to each in turn. Sorrel was often brusque and off-hand; but it didn't seem to matter.

The days that followed justified my first feelings of depression. I have an affectionate nature, a gay manner and good looks, and never before had I been long in a house without attaching *someone* to me. Even the allegiance of servants I never despised, since so much of one's comfort could depend upon their goodwill. But in that house, although it was so rent by dissension, there was never a scrap of affection left over for me. It was always Sorrel, Sorrel, Sorrel. Even the Widow Kingaby's child would run to meet her, leaving her own mother; and simply because Sorrel would bring her up goodies from the warehouse, or give her pennies to buy lollipops. Except in the case of Miss Louisa, the affections of the others were no less purchased.

I grew desperately jealous. As I learned more about the family and realized what despotism that little creature wielded, not only in the house, but at the warehouse, and in the yard, and as far away as the high seas where her ships travelled, the injustice of the world came home to me very sharply. I felt that I simply must take something away from her, if only to comfort my pride.

I tried the girls first, deeming Phœbe too young to count, and working upon Dinah and Lydia. Sorrel was very strict with them, most insistent upon dull subjects like sums and the use of the globes. So I became less strict only to be sharply reminded by them of what Sorrel desired and expected. "But Sorrel is so strict," I protested.

"Not nearly so strict as Miss Gould," said Dinah, twirling the globe and shooting a cold glance at me. "Look, Lydia, there's Madagascar, Sorrel's ship the *Mirabella* calls there on her way to India."

Next I studied the possibilities of attaching Mrs Fennigard to me. She hated Miss Louisa; the two old ladies could not even agree as to what constituted a nice day; and since one was such an ardent partisan of Sorrel, I did have hopes of the other. Moreover, Mrs Fennigard was very old, and although she was poor and dependent upon her grand-niece, she owned a great deal of jewellery, some of it valuable. I took pains to please her, holding her wool, helping her gather together her stick, her spectacles, her smelling bottle as she went from one room to another. I deferred to her opinions, which were all arbitrary and out of date. But once, when she and Lou had had words about something that Sorrel had said or done, and we were left alone, I said, lightly, "It's no use, Mrs Fennigard, Miss Louisa eats out of Miss Sorrel's hand," the old witch raised her eyebrows and stared at me in a way that accused me of unnameable sins, and said:

"So she should. That's where she does eat from. As do I, and you do, and Lucia does. Praise God it's a good open hand."

For all the quarrels and intrigues and back-biting that went on within its walls, there was not one person in East House who could be pried from her allegiance to Sorrel.

It became to me like the longing to buy something that one sees in a shop. I could have borne it if I could have found, as I had found so easily in other places, a male admirer. All the women in the world could have adored her then and been welcome. But in deadly Bywater there was not a soul at once suitable and willing; or if he existed I never met him. I took the girls on long walks, of which Sorrel approved most heartily, and I kept my eyes open. All to no purpose. I plied my needle, did a good deal of shopping with my better salary and Sunday after Sunday set the maids and matrons of Bywater staring at my toilettes, but for all it availed me I might have looked like Miss Louisa, a jumble of black and grey and slate-colour; or Mrs Fennigard, a shrieking bundle of yellow, orange, purple and green. The few young men who were in Bywater were stodgy and middle-class, respectable sons of respectable trading men; and such, I have noticed, lack the ease of approach which distinguishes both their superiors and their inferiors.

Then, one day, when I had been some weeks in Bywater and was low from repeated failures, sick and tired of being just the governess, Mrs Fennigard and Miss Lou had one of their noisier passages of arms. At such times they were apt to forget both dignity and caution, and it did not require much eavesdropping to overhear their exchanges.

"A ridiculous story," said Mrs Fennigard. "A story that only a credulous old maid would believe."

"Marriage doesn't confer sense," retorted Miss Lou, "otherwise you'd have more. I'm sorry now that I asked your advice. It's obvious that you don't care *what* happens to Sorrel, or what danger she runs, short of bankruptcy."

"Danger," the old lady sneered. "Don't you credit Sorrel with any sense or taste? Jamie Brooke indeed. A snivelling clerk. Run along with your bogy tales."

"Well, if I see any more of it, I shall *speak*," said Miss Lou, who, apart from the stab about marriage not bringing sense, was conducting this quarrel with rather less than her usual ferocity, a fact which led me to believe that she really had some urgent worry on her mind.

"That's the way," said Mrs Fennigard. "The young people who have been driven together by well-meant warnings would fill the bottomless pit. For myself, since I disbelieve your story, I'm thankful to think that Sorrel is human enough to go to the office for some other reason than to balance accounts."

With this information in mind I began to look out for a clerk in the Kingaby office named Jamie Brooke.

He was quite ridiculously attractive and I sympathized with Sorrel's choice. He had chestnut hair and eyes of the same colour, and even at the end of a long winter his skin had a slight tan as though the stain of gold from his hair had run down over his face. And his figure was slender without being gangling. Nobody, looking at him, would have suspected his humble station. To take him away from Sorrel, who had everything, would be a triumph indeed.

It was so easy. Perhaps the ease with which it was

done should have warned me; for nothing really worth having is easily come by.

Moral people, with tepid blood in their veins, who have never been tempted and never known hatred, would, I suppose, judge that the events of the next year brought me exactly what I deserved. In less than a month after our marriage I knew that Jamie had wanted me for one thing only, and he was openly accusing me of mercenary motives. The farm at Fornham proved to be a very different place from that pictured either by Mrs Brooke's snobbishness or Jamie's homesickness; it was a poorish kind of place and Jamie's Uncle Simon was a Bedlam case if ever I saw one. Despite all my reasoning, Jamie insisted upon sending his mother a hundred pounds, with orders that she was not to take anything from Sorrel. Later I discovered that Mrs Brooke's allowance had been continued from the day of our elopement, and that it ended only with the old lady's death. In July my baby was born, and in August the bankruptcy which the crazy old fellow had been staving off for years, actually came about; and there we were married, penniless, and with a child to support, all within less than a year of our flight from Bywater.

The uncle, who was not without friends, retired to an almshouse in Bury St Edmund's, and began to experiment with pig-breeding in the yard. Jamie said he could find work in London; and to London he went. There followed three or four months of beggary, bitter quarrels and utter misery. And all the time, at the back of my mind hung the thought of the comfort and plenty at Bywater. I suggested returning there; but Jamie said he would rather die.

"There is so much there that you have a right to," I argued.

"That's rubbish," he said.

"Sorrel would be the last person to wish you to starve."

"Sorrel would probably be kinder than God. All the same we are not going back there."

"Speak for yourself. I shall take the baby and go. Isn't it her grandfather's house?"

"If you do that it will be the end of everything between us."

I laughed. "Is there anything left to end?"

After that I endured things for a little longer, with the idea of Bywater tugging at me all the time. The baby pined in the London air. I lost more of my looks, until the face that stared back from the cracked square of mirror in our filthy lodgings was that of a woman ten years older than I. What could I do by staying?

Sorrel turned so white when she saw me that I thought she was going to faint; but she recovered her composure, and though she scrupulously avoided looking at the baby, her manner to me was cordial and ordinary. She saw, or pretended to see, nothing unusual in my return. I had come prepared to argue, if necessary truculently, and to point out, as I had done to Jamie, that the baby had a right under its grandfather's roof. But Sorrel herself forestalled me. She asked me only one question, "You are properly married?"

"Oh, yes. I took care to see that."

"I should imagine you would. Not that I mind for myself, but I told the girls you had married. Dinah is almost fifteen; at an age to ask questions." Her eyes flicked over the baby and away again.

"Very well," she said. "You're welcome to make your home here, Marian. There's room and food for all. And in a way you have a right to it. I'm afraid the governess, Miss Jacobs, is installed in your old room, but I can have the one opposite mine made ready at once."

She moved across the room and tugged the bell-pull.

"You call yourself Mrs. Brooke?" I nodded. And when Agatha appeared, looking just as usual, grim and disapproving, Sorrel said with a casual air, "Mrs. Brooke has come to stay with us, Agatha. Will you see that the spare room is prepared?"

It was over; I was safe. Never was beggar received with less fuss. I should, I suppose, have been grateful and devoted the rest of my life to being a Sorrel-worshipper. The fact remains, however, that my hatred, far from being assuaged by this treatment, was augmented and inflamed. It was so lordly, that careless hospitality—Come, it seemed to say, I have plenty of room, plenty of food, I can house you all. And it was actuated by love of power, not by any charitable impulse.

For a few weeks, with the memory of our lodgings, of Jamie's search for work and the meagre wages he drew when it was found, sharp in my memory, East House, with its careless plenty, its heaped fires, its solid walls, did seem like a haven; but as soon as comfort had become a familiar thing again I began to see myself just one more of Sorrel Kingaby's satellites. And my hatred for her grew.

For one thing it irked me that a year which, with its

misery, had lined my face, dulled and thinned my hair, ruined my figure, had left her untouched. So far as I could see, even the Jamie episode, which should have hurt her irretrievably, was lived down, covered over and forgotten; and in so short a time! There was still that untouched, cool, hard look about her which had made me call her an ice maiden. I had robbed her, but in doing so I had injured myself without, at least visibly, touching one curl of her red head. Indeed, one might have thought that all the inhabitants of East House—except the girls—had been dipped in the waters that are supposed to confer immortality. Nothing had altered in the least. Even the quarrels were last year's quarrels. Sometimes, sitting at the supper table I would look round, and it took the sight of Miss Jacobs' dim face, or the slightly altered contours of Dinah's figure to assure me that the past year had not been a nightmare from which I had awoken.

But of course nothing does actually remain unchanged, however it may seem, and gradually I came to see that there were differences in East House and in Sorrel herself. Below the surface new currents were moving.

Th first alteration which thrust itself upon my notice was the change in the girl Dinah. She was at a stage of growth where a year makes a vast difference. She began to show a furtive but avid interest in Clarabel, my baby, and in me because I had been married. Whenever a chance offered she would slip along to my room and talk to me and fondle the baby. Sometimes during these talks she would let fall a half-conscious criticism of Sorrel. "Sorrel thinks of Lyddy and Phœbe and me all in a lump. I don't think she realizes that I am almost grown up." "I *am* sorry Sorrel ordered all our new winter dresses off the same roll of velvet; it's beautiful stuff, and the green will suit Lyddy and Phœbe, but I am too sallow for it."

"Yes, you are," I agreed. "You need a warm colour. You would be quite beautiful in the new strawberry-pink, or what they call apricot bloom. Why don't you suggest changing it? I don't think Miss Phillimore has cut it yet."

"Oh, I couldn't. You see, it is the very same as Sorrel chose for herself, and it is so generous of her to let us have such good quality. I'd hate her to think I criticized it."

"Unless you do," I reminded her, "you never will get what you want, will you?"

"I suppose not," she said discontentedly. "And it's the same with my hair. I'm too big to have my hair hanging like this."

"In London," I said, "I saw a new fashion which would suit you. The hair was cut quite short and curled and worn with a ribbon or a fillet of gauze to match the gown."

She turned, without speaking, and stared into my mirror.

"*Would* it suit me, do you think? Or should I look too old, suddenly? Why don't you try it, Marian? Any fashion would suit you."

"My hair has lost its gloss lately," I said, "but I think it is improving again. Look, Dinah, if you will cut mine and curl it I will do yours. And before that velvet you mention is actually cut into I will say, as if it just came into my head, that I think you ought not to wear green, being the one dark one in the family."

"Will you really, Marian? Oh, you are an angel!"

Our new coiffures gave rise, as did everything in that house, to a good deal of varying comment.

"Twenty years ago," cried Mrs Fennigard, "that style was known as *à la guillotine*, and only revolutionaries adopted it. One hopes that its recurrence is not symbolic."

Miss Louisa administered one of her stabs. "The fashion is far too old for you, my child. You can see how much more suitable it is for Marian; quite rejuvenating in her case."

Sorrel paused on her way to the head of the table and laid her fingers on the curls of Dinah's nape. She said with rueful affection:

"Dear, dear! I hadn't realized that you were growing up so fast, Dinah. What are we going to do about it?"

A year ago Dinah would have turned her cheek and nestled like a puppy against that hand; to-night she merely smiled, and signalled to me in triumph across the table that Sorrel had not made one of her fusses. It was a petty victory, but after so many defeats, very sweet.

The other change partook of the nature of a mystery. Something was going on in and around East House, something that had begun in the year of my absence. There was a man named Borthwick who appeared to have been made free of the house, and was violently partisaned by Miss Louisa, and as violently decried by Mrs Fennigard. He was engaged in the wool trade and seemed to be prosperous. He was a gentleman, too; he had that unmistakable ease of manner combined with an inward aloofness. His attitude towards Sorrel puzzled me. Sometimes I thought that he was in love with her; yet, if that were the case, there was something restraining him all the time. I wondered if he could possibly be married already. Certainly there was an air of romantic melancholy about him which suggested a mystery, an unhappy past perhaps. He and Sorrel called one another by their Christian names in a remarkably friendly fashion. And although I was beginning to recover my looks he had no eyes for me. Miss Louisa encouraged him. She would often suggest asking him to supper at such times as he was known to be in Bywater. I suppose she thought he was eligible and steady. He was, without being in the least handsome, quite good looking, and during our first few meetings I laid myself out to be pleasant to him; thus inviting sour glances and words from the spinster. Between her venom and his lack of response I often grew despondent, and would study myself in the mirror before going to bed. Perhaps, I thought fearfully, the improvement in my appearance was imaginary and visible to my hopeful eye alone. Sorrel was at the beginning, I at the end, of the best years in a woman's life.

But one evening something happened to cheer me. A small thing. I came out of the parlour, carrying Clarabel up to bed. The study door opened and Tom Borthwick came out, accompanied by another man. Maybe he was as old, or a little older, than Tom, but he struck an immediate note of youth and vitality. He was tall and broad and thick without being clumsy, and he was ruggedly, not romantically, handsome. The first sight of him waked something in me. He had been bending his head to say something to Sorrel, and he looked up suddenly and saw me as I lingered by the

parlour door, deliberately waiting to let them pass. A
look of interest and admiration came into his face. I
was mortified that I should be wearing an old gown,
that my hair should be disarranged and that I should
be carrying the child. Nevertheless, the expression in
his light, bright eyes restored my self-esteem suddenly.
I hoped that Sorrel would pause and make an introduction. Tom Borthwick wished me good evening with
his unvarying politeness, but apart from that no word
was said. Sorrel went with the two men to the door,
exchanged a few words, and closed it behind them.
Bitch in the manger, I thought, and went upstairs in a
fury. Next time I determined I should not wait to be
spoken to. But although for many evenings after that
I wore my best dress and took special pains with my
curls, and let Dinah mind Clarabel to her heart's content, my efforts were wasted. I got no further than the
knowledge that the man whose memory nagged at me
was a friend of Tom's, and named Dan Culver. I
never saw him in the house again.

    But there was a third visitor who, although he came
at infrequent intervals, always managed to make his
presence felt. He was an old Army officer named
Quantrill, rotund, red-faced, hearty and boisterous.
He—like everyone else in this bewitched place—was
Sorrel Kingaby's slave, but he did not devote his ex-
clusive attention to her. He was lavish with flattering
glances and compliments; eager to engage in conversation; always ready with an amusing story or scrap of
gossip, a breath, in fact, from another and livelier
world. Sorrel was flagrantly selfish about him. She
would hustle him away into the study before he had
done more than exchange a few words of greeting, if

she could. She was curiously less at ease with him than anyone else, and this, combined with her jealous guardianship of him, made me suspect that she might be taking his attentions seriously. True, he was no longer young, but he was sprightly, healthy, always impeccably groomed and laundered and dressed, and his manners were as irreproachable as Tom Borthwick's. He was obviously attracted by Sorrel. I could tell that from the way in which he looked at her. Besides, I could see no other reason either for his visits, or her slightly formal and yet rather confused manner when he was about. And I thought it not unlikely that despite the difference in their ages, he was the kind of man whom a frigid girl like Sorrel might fancy as a husband.

But I had hardly taken my bearings after my return to East House and become familiar with these new visitors before something happened which set me wondering and watching.

Sorrel had given me the room that opened opposite hers across the landing near the stair head. Clarabel, naturally, slept in my room, and was fretfully and with difficulty cutting her first teeth. As a result my nights were often disturbed. On one such night, late on in the autumn, I thought I heard the door of Sorrel's room open and close again very cautiously. I scurried across to my own door, opened it a crack, and peeped out. There was a dim light on the stairs moving, disappearing even as I stared at it. The stairs curved. I crept to the bulge of the wall and stared downwards, and could just catch sight of Sorrel, moving stealthily down the last few steps, her old-fashioned cardinal hood drawn over her head and a small hand-lantern in her hand.

She was not on a legitimate night errand. Almost the last thing that Josiah Kingaby, her father, had done, and certainly the only modern improvement that he had allowed at East House, was to install a water closet near the top of the back stairs. (I had often thought of that water closet when we were in London, in those filthy lodgings with one rickety privy to serve the whole yard!) Besides, the cloak and the furtiveness argued a longer, more secret errand.

I knew, by the sudden disappearance of the light, that she had not gone across the wide lower hall to the front door, or she would have been longer in my view; she must have turned sharply at the foot of the stair-case, and was making either for her study or the orchid house. Clarabel was hushed for the moment, so, without waiting to don either slippers or wrapper, I tiptoed along the passage to the spot where, in an angle of the wall, there was a window which looked down upon the roof of the glass passage where the orchids grew. A good many leaves from the sycamore tree on the lawn upon one side, and from the walnut tree in the yard on the other, lay on the faintly shining panes, but I could see the light moving now and then, and growing fainter until it disappeared.

I was so curious that I found my heart beating hard with excitement, the first excitement I had known for a veritable age. I went back to my own rom and care-fully arranged the door so that it was just ajar; I meant to lie down with my eyes on the chink so that I should see the light and be able to time Sorrel's return. But I fell asleep and did not wake until morning. At breakfast I looked at Sorrel carefully; she was always pale, with that clear white pallor which is so different from sallowness. This morning her eyes looked a trifle heavy-lidded, that was all.

After that I carefully opened my door and propped it every night for a week, but I heard and saw nothing. Towards the end of the week a draught from the window or chimney blew harder than usual, and my door banged twice, heavily. Next morning Miss Louisa said plaintively:

"What was happening in the night? There seemed some commotion."

I saw Sorrel stiffen, but the movement was so slight that unless I had been watching I should not have noticed it.

"I was moving about after the baby," I volunteered, "but you'd hardly hear that, would you, Miss Kingaby?"

"I'm a painfully light sleeper," she said, more peevish now that she thought I was the culprit. "It's not the first time I've heard movements and noises."

"Well, I'm growing deaf in my old age," said Mrs Fennigard, "and I thank God for it!" Two equally untrue statements. I had never known her to miss anything either with eyes or ears, and she was certainly not the person to thank God for an affliction.

Sorrel, who often treated such complaints with a noncommittal indifference, paid attention to this one.

"Would you like to change your room, Lou? Marian must move about to attend the baby. I believe we could make a proper re-shuffle to everyone's satisfaction. Dinah would like a room to herself, I know. Then the two others could have the smaller back room and

you could have theirs. It's the warmest in the house,
being over the kitchen. And then Marian could have
the one where you are now, and you wouldn't hear
her whatever she did."

Very clever, I thought. All on the spur of the moment, too! For under all the verbiage and unusual
pandering to an old lady's whim, one fact stood out
plainly. When the general move was completed Miss
Sorrel would have the landing at the stair head to herself, and the room I now occupied would be the spare
room again. And by that I knew that the excursion I
had witnessed was no chance thing.

I thought—if I don't sleep for a week I will know
where you go and what you do. I discovered that my
new room gave me a view along the passage and ended
with the blank wall by the stairs. I should not see
Sorrel, but I might see the light if it caught the panelling and made any kind of reflection. And if I did, I
should be ready.

I had only one abortive vigil. On the second night
after the move, I saw far along the passage the pale
diffusion of darkness as the light of the lantern struck
the wall. And to-night I was ready in my soft-soled
slippers and warm wrap.

I had always thought that there was something cat-
like about that girl, about the soft manner that she
adopted so often, and about the sudden clawing flashes
of temper; about the green eyes and the wiliness. On
that night some instinct seemed to warn her of something, and her behaviour made dogging her very difficult. She hesitated once or twice and turned back once,
retracing several steps. I thought of the green eyes and
wondered whether, truly cat-like, they could pierce

the shadows that concealed me. Superstition chilled
my spine, but I overcame it. Step by step I followed
to the warehouse door, sweating lest she should lock
it behind her; but she did not, despite whatever instinct was at work in her, take that precaution. I followed her in.

From a distance I saw it all. She, who had so much
must have that much more; she who had no need of
marriage for security or for position; she whom marriage could only have hampered and confined, must
have that strong and ardent lover. Must know love
with all the embellishment which secrecy and precari-
ousness can lend it. Must possess, and be possessed by
this Dan Culver, whom, ever since that first meeting
and that first long promising stare, I had wanted for
myself. Sorrel, whom I had thought of as frigid and
undeveloped, an ice-maiden. Sorrel, who had asked me
with that offhand insolence whether Jamie had married me or not. Sorrel, the woman of business who pretended to despise purely female matters. Sorrel, who
had all along had some peculiar hold upon Jamie, so
that borrowing a paltry sum from her had weighed
more heavily upon him than ruining my whole life.
Sorrel, the whore!

Oh, I was mad with jealousy, sickened by envy!
Fury moved the flesh upon my bones, as I remembered
the glance of those hot blue eyes, the bulge of those
muscles. She could have had Tom Borthwick, with his
gentle melancholy, or Captain Quantrill with his age-
ing sprightliness, and I should have laughed to find
her no better than the rest of us, and no different
from the common run. But to have such a lover, added
to money and power, to adulation and sycophantry, to

real love from old Lou, and friendship from Tom
Borthwick, as well as deferential court from old Quantrill. It was too much. It was unbearable, ludicrous,
absurd. No woman on earth ever had so much.

Tears of self-pity ran down my face as I turned away
and made my way back to the house. I had not realized
until then what a great deal of comfort I had been in
the habit of drawing from the thought that there was
just one experience in which I was richer than Sorrel
Kingaby. Now that was gone, and compared with her
I had nothing, absolutely nothing except a baby. And
although I loved Clarabel she was going to be a drag
on me until I was too old for freedom to matter very
much. In order to satisfy my love for her I must stay
with her, and so could never again have a post or expect any man to take up with me. Why should my life
be so different from that whey-faced little trollop's?
What had I done? Merely been born poor. Compared
with her I was *good*. I had never let Jamie near me, in
that way, until we were married.

Thinking of Jamie reminded me of the money. She
probably cursed it, I thought, as soon as she knew I
was to share it. That would explain why Jamie's uncle,
after staving off bankruptcy so long, had collapsed
almost directly he had hold of what should have been
a resuscitating sum of money.

And, I thought, as I crept back into my chilly bed,
she had ruined my life in other ways, too. It was her
damned hold on everything which had upset me and
made me jealous in the first place, so that I had
grabbed Jamie in spite, and in the excitement of
wresting him away from her had overlooked the fact
that he was not worth taking, stupid, unenterprising,

unlucky. In short, ever since I had first set eyes on her my life had gone awry, and it was all her fault.

I could hardly bear next morning to look at her along the breakfast table. Ah, that heavy-lidded look, what it implied! And that mouth, always arrestingly red and full and in a small white face, fuller now, more curved, almost swollen, with a bee-stung look. It made me think of that other mouth, hard and compelling. I should have liked to lean along the table and mutter an obscenity, and then, in the shocked silence which would follow, explain to them all. So bitter were the feelings boiling within me that I might have given vent to them had I been alone in the world. But I had Clarabel to consider. So I sat at the table, mim as a mouse, and ate her food and hated her, and dreamed that somehow I might one day know the sweet taste of vengeance.

It is strange to look back and see the links in the chain which are made blindly at the time of their forging.

I had kept my promise to Dinah and murmured the word about the green velvet; and Sorrel, as sweetly as though she knew that Dinah's allegiance was shifting, said instantly that of course the child must have the colour she wished, and that she was vastly sorry not to have noticed the unsuitability of the green herself. Wouldn't I, she asked, like to take Dinah to Colchester and choose some material that we did think becoming? Sam could drive us in the gig.

She came up to me on the morning of the jaunt and handed me some money. "Buy Dinah what she fancies, within reason, of course. And Marian, you yourself . . . it would be an unenviable job buying finery for

another with never a bit for you. Do get yourself anything you need or fancy. I think there will be enough
—if not my credit is good at Stapleton's and Meevey's
—don't hesitate to make use of it."

Out of the strong—as the Bible has it—came forth
sweetness; and out of the maw of plenty came the kind
permission to spend a guinea or so on myself. Largesse
. . . vails . . . money for pins. God, how I hated her
at that moment!

We shopped satisfactorily and I gave Dinah her
head, and exercised, as the case seemed to demand,
my most arrogant or my sweetest manner with the
shop assistants, and could feel the girl every minute
adoring me. When it was finished and the parcels were
on their way to the "Cups" yard, where the gig was
waiting, Dinah hung on my arm and coaxed:

"Could we have tea at the Blue Parlour? It is re-
puted to be all the fashion to be seen there. A girl at
school told me about it. She had been in the holidays,
and swore that beside the fashions to be seen, the
cream buns were the best she had tasted. Do let us
go?"

"I see no reason against it," I said.

We were crossing the narrow strip of cobbles outside the tea house, which apart from a blue door and
windowsill looked a modest, ordinary place enough,
when we were hailed by a hearty voice, and, turning,
saw Captain Quantrill, with his red face beaming
above the dazzling white folds of his voluminous neck-
cloths. His first question, after greeting us, was,
naturally, whether Sorrel was with us; and, his second,
whither were we bound. When we told him the Blue

Parlour, he begged permission to accompany us, saying, in just his way, that he had heard well of the honey toast served there, but had never dared penetrate the sacred portals without feminine escort. "The gods evidently intended me to wait until to-day and have all my sweets at once," he declared. Dinah giggled and blushed.

We were very gay at tea. The beverage, the honey toast, and the buns were all delicious; and the knowledge that I was out, free of East House, in the company of a lively and charming gentleman, sent the blood to my cheeks and set my wits working, and I knew, in the way a woman does, that he was admiring me and wondering why he had never noticed me before. And all the while, at the back of my mind, there wriggled like a maggot the thought that here, too, was a slave of Sorrel Kingaby's who, at our next meeting, would toss me ten cheerful words and then follow her gladly into her study.

Having disposed of four cream buns, very quietly and neatly, Dinah suddenly gave a cry, "Oh, I promised Cousin Lou to match her some wool at Meevey's." She fished in her glove and brought out an inch of the sullen purple in which Lou was knitting a new spencer. "Shall I run along and do it while you finish your tea?"

"If you like," I said. "Then you needn't come back here, Dinah. Go straight along to the gig and I will be waiting for you there."

The Captain kept up his amiable chatter while we emptied our cups, and then announced his intention of accompanying me back to the gig. When we were walking along the street he asked suddenly, "Mrs

Brooke, you are familiar with Bywater—who is this
Borthwick fellow?"

"A friend of Sorrel's," I said.

"So I gathered. In the wool trade, isn't he? Pretty
prosperous I take it."

I naturally attributed this interest in Tom Borthwick
to the concern one man does take in his rival's worldly
station and prospects. And it shot through my mind
that I might with advantage put in a word.

"He seems so. His team lodges in the Kingaby stables, you know. I think that is really the foundation of
the friendship. Poor Mr Borthwick! If he has feelings
other than friendship towards Sorrel he is doomed to
disappointment, I fear."

"Indeed. Why is that?"

"Ah, why indeed!" I countered. "And why should I
let you into a secret, Captain Quantrill? For secret it
is, I can assure you."

"Imagine East House holding a secret!"

"Yes, imagine it. And the worst of it is that the
more favoured gentleman is Mr Borthwick's best
friend, and was introduced by him to the house, I
believe."

"A sorry situation. Now I have often wondered
what kind of man our Miss Sorrel would favour. Is
this one handsome, young?"

Poor old thing, I thought, trying to be so clever!

"Extremely handsome," I said, and launched into a
description of Dan Culver's charms. I was so engrossed
in telling him, in this subtle manner, that his own case
was as hopeless as Tom Borthwick's, that I missed,
until much, much later, the significance of some of his
little interrupting questions.

I thought his manner was subdued as he handed us into the gig.

"Remember me to Miss Sorrel," he said. "I'm afraid it will be some time before I get to Bywater again." And I thought as we bowled away back to Bywater, perhaps after all I have succeeded in losing Miss Sorrel one of her admirers.

Yet within a fortnight he was back, bouncing, gay and gallant as ever, inviting himself to dinner and to stay overnight at East House.

Such confusion I never saw. I thought that Sorrel had missed him, even in that short time, or had divined, in that cat-like manner of hers that she must make some effort to retain his admiration. The dinner she ordered was enormous, and the hour of it was put back until it was later even than the hour gradually becoming fashionable in very smart circles. The room opposite Sorrel's, which had been mine, was lighted and warmed and prepared, and although Miss Louisa, who was competent, as such old sticks are, had taken charge of the preparations, Sorrel seemed unable to sit still in the parlour and leave things in her hands. I was most surprised to see her, usually so cool and off-hand, so much put about; and I thought that to offer port and brandy and rum and Madeira to a gentleman before dinner was vulgar ostentation. I think Captain Quantrill shared my view, for he refused to drink anything except one small glass of brandy.

Into the parlour, in the midst of one of the Captain's best stories, Miss Louisa burst suddenly, very agitated and pale.

"Sorrel, you must come with me to see Old Betty.

She has sent word that she really is dying at last, and must see us before she goes."

"But, Lou, I have a guest. It's most highly inconvenient," said Sorrel, but she rose all the same.

"I'm sorry, but you can't let the poor old thing *die* without a farewell. Remember all that she did for your poor dear mother, Sorrel."

"Well," said Sorrel. "I don't leave you without company, Captain Quantrill. And I shall be back before the dinner is cooked. But if I should be delayed I trust you, Aunt Carrie, to start as soon as it is ready, and to see that after all this time Captain Quantrill has no reason to complain of Bywater hospitality."

Of course I knew that Mrs Fennigard was the oldest lady present, but what with her great age and stiffness she was hardly the person to leave in charge of a dinner party when there were Lucia and myself at hand. But the two Kingabys were going out, so the honour must be left to the only blood relation remaining, even though she was only a penniless dependent like Lucia and me. That was just like Sorrel. She could administer that kind of stab almost automatically.

Time passed. Once or twice I saw the Captain's eyes stray to the clock; once or twice he drew out his watch and consulted it furtively. The rich dinner smells began to permeate the house. At last Mrs Fennigard sent me into the kitchen to see how things were progressing. The meal was ready to serve. Headed by the old lady, with her cane in one hand and the other hand bearing heavily upon Captain Quantrill's arm, we trooped into the dining-room and our guest made numerous speeches congratulating himself upon being one gentleman present amidst such a bower of beauty.

It was one of the merriest meals I have ever known at East House; with no Sorrel to appeal to it seemed not worth while even Mrs Fennigard and Widow Kingaby differing about anything, Miss Jacobs—"Jacob's Ladder" as Dinah and I called her between ourselves —who usually went in dread of Sorrel, perked up wonderfully and allowed Mrs Fennigard's suggestion that the girls should all drink port with their dessert.

In the midst of the laughter and chatter we heard the front door bang; and a kind of restraint fell upon the table, rather like that which comes over a schoolroom which has been unsupervised when the governess suddenly returns.

Then we heard Doctor Burnett's voice; and Lucia said, "That's the doctor." Whereupon Captain Quantrill leapt to his feet crying, "My God, there's been an accident." He seemed very agitated, but he begged us all to keep calm and remain at table. I did, however, push with him into the hall. I don't know what he expected to see, for even at the doorway he tried to dissuade me from looking.

But it was only Miss Lou who had collapsed on the Green quite near the doctor's house. She died within an hour. And next morning, just after Captain Quantrill had taken his departure, some incoming traveller brought the news that his men had ambushed some smugglers on a marsh path at a point known as Old Nick's Jump and that two had been killed and the other captured.

The news caused great excitement, for it had not been known that smuggling was going on so near Bywater; but that excitement was nothing to that which followed the further information, namely, that one of the killed men was Borthwick's driver, Timothy, and the other Dan Culver himself.

And still Sorrel Kingaby's luck held good. Borthwick's horses whose stabling might have drawn suspicion of complicity upon her, had been gone from her premises for about a month. People went about saying, "Ah, that Miss Kingaby, she's a fly one. Guessed what was afoot and give him the sack, I reckon." And at the same time she could mourn her dead lover openly because her pallor and her tears and her grief were all attributed to sorrow over Miss Lou's death. And now that the old woman had gone, both Mrs Fennigard and Widow Kingaby saw fit to forget that they had been envious of her standing with Sorrel and had quarrelled with her almost every day. They reiterated that poor Sorrel had lost her best friend, that the old lady had been like a mother to her, that she would miss her at every turn. Every scrap of kindliness and consideration of which those two selfish women were capable was lavished upon Sorrel, who was, of course, not mourning her relative at all. The falsity of the position made me at once angry and amused. And I asked myself, passionately, what other woman in creation, having taken a smuggler for a lover, would at his death have been enabled by circumstances to wear a black dress, lose her appetite, redden her eyes, and still be considered a respectable maiden, mourning an elderly relative's death?

And for what other woman would Tom Borthwick (arrested because he made no attempt to get away, but sat drinking himself silly and babbling like a fool in a public place) have stood up and sworn that she was innocent of the purposes of the *Sea-Gull* in her boathouse and the pack animals in her stable? Only Sorrel Kingaby could have both men and gods on her side like that.

So I thought, for a month, for six weeks, after that eventful evening. And then I began to wonder. And as day followed day my wonder grew; and my watchfulness; and my gradual conviction that there was, perhaps one thing even Sorrel Kingaby could neither charm, nor bribe, cajole, nor evade—old Mother Nature.

Then I was certain. It was not grief, either for Cousin Lou or for Dan Culver, which gave her, every now and again at an unguarded moment, that look of stark terror. Over and over I surprised it in her eyes, that captured, cornered look which, in any other person, might have roused pity in me. Nor would grief—and that some six weeks old—suddenly take the form of coming down belatedly to breakfast, at a moment when all the more substantial foods had been eaten, of refusing anything to eat except a slice of toasted bread, and then, at midday dinner, eating like a ploughboy. These were symptoms which I recognized, and I noted each one gloatingly. And yet, for all my gloating, I could not but admire the girl. She never missed a day at that office of hers. Twice she made the journey to Colchester and back in a day; and her general manner did not change at all.

The situation gave me food for much speculative thought. Of course, I was the only person who knew that she was not the virgin that she seemed; it would be a long time before anyone else in the house could possibly suspect anything. But the time would come when her state could not be hidden. Then what would

she do, and say? And what would the people of Bywater say? All those who had either admired or
condemned her unfeminine ways; who had either suspected or exonerated her over the contraband business.
All this I could know, just by waiting, and oh, how
exciting it would be.

Sometimes I did experience just one fear. She might
kill herself rather than face the shame and the scandal.
Where should we be then? The business and the house
would probably be sold and the proceeds divided
amongst the three girls. And they would, in time,
marry. Normal girls with portions usually did. So even
my hold on Dinah, a hold which I tightened in every
conceivable manner, would avail me little. But, since
I could not guard against Sorrel's suicide any more
than I could against her death from accident, or
natural causes, I did not worry unduly about it. All
the same, it was that thought, that I might be left, at
any moment, homeless, dependent again upon Jamie's
feeble exertions, which set my mind working in the
way it did.

For suddenly it seemed that Sorrel Kingaby was,
after all going to escape; was going to use her unique
position in order to bamboozle Nature herself.

The first hint came after a visit from Captain
Swann, Master of the *Mirabella*. Since his return, in
early autumn, just before I came back to Bywater, he
had made, as was customary, a short trip to Holland,
followed by a stay at Yarmouth for overhauling. In a
week or two the *Mirabella* was due for her run to the
East Indies, a voyage that would take many months.
He arrived about eight weeks after Miss Lousia's
death and supped alone, with Sorrel. After supper

they were closeted together for almost three hours. Next day, at the supper table, where every member of the household was always certainly and punctually present, unless prevented by sickness, Sorrel said, with an admirably casual air:

"My faith, I've been wishing to-day that I had someone I could send to Java. There's a tricky bit of business there, and really Captain Swann's brain stops short at navigation."

"I'll go," croaked Mrs Fennigard. "The climate might do my rheumatism good."

"How I wish you could, Aunt Carrie. Yours is just the kind of mind that is needed."

I watched carefully. I thought I knew what was coming. Sorrel loaded a forkful of food, conveyed it to her mouth, chewed and swallowed it, and then said: "I've a good mind to go myself."

Yes, I thought. That's the way of it. First—I've a good mind to go myself. Then—really it looks as if I shall *have* to go myself, and, finally, after the idea has grown familiar to everyone—I *am* going myself.

And the one person who might, both by virtue of her position and her smattering knowledge of the business, have asked the awkward question and lodged the effective protest was dead and buried. Not one of us round the table could do or say anything. If Sorrel had suddenly announced her departure on the *Mirabella* it would have served just as well as this gradual leading up to the decision.

Nevertheless, the stages which I had visualized on that evening were faithfully gone through. And within five days it had become an established fact that there was business in Java which could only be satisfactorily conducted by the head of the firm and that Miss Sorrel Kingaby, as courageous as she was unconventional, was going to sail in the *Mirabella* in order to attend to that business.

In Bywater there was still an idea that anywhere farther afield than Steeple Rising was "forrin parts"; and that the majority of places overseas were inhabited by cannibals. I think they visualised trade with such places being conducted solely through the strength and courage of men like Captain Swann, who presumably threw themselves ashore and snatched handfuls of things like cloves and peppercorns from under the noses of the protesting savages. In any case, during those few days the town was all agog with wonder and admiration at Sorrel's daring. We were asked in shops if it were true, the rumour; and such horrid prophecies were uttered that Phœbe, more than once, was driven to tears. It was difficult to explain to the child, or to the Bywater people with their childish minds, that there was, in Java, a branch of a sober and substantial Dutch firm, under the control of a gentleman named Voorlberg who sent presents to the head of the house of Kingaby and wrote letters in English that was punctilious if ungrammatical. His last gift, intended, of course, for Sorrel's father, had included a wonderful carved pipe with an amber mouthpiece, and I could remember her exhibiting it with merriment one day, and reading the funny little letter, while Miss Lou looked on disapprovingly, thinking, no doubt, that gift meant for a dead man should share the respect one accords the dead.

And I knew that, barring storm and accident, Sorrel, when she presented herself before Voorlberg, would be accorded a royal welcome and treated like a princess. Captain Swann would be sworn to secrecy, as well as held to it by the knowledge of which side his bread was buttered, and in due time Miss Kingaby would return, with the legend of her uniqueness reinforced, would be accorded the deference due to the intrepid traveller and given the increased affection which follows absence.

I turned the matter over in my mind until I could not bear it. The sight of all the innocents helping to prepare her for the voyage affected me as would the sight of a grave miscarriage of justice. And added to this disgust and irritation I bore the thought that something *might* happen to her. I did not believe in the cannibals, mention of whom had made Phœbe cry, but I did know that there were such things as storms and shipwrecks, privateers, strange diseases and snakebites, any of which she might encounter as well as having to face the risks of childbirth in very peculiar and unsuitable circumstances. We might, very easily, not see Sorrel again; and then Clarabel and I at least (and I was all *I* cared about) would find ourselves without a roof or a crust.

Something happened to my mind in those days, it seemed to fall into two halves like a neatly split nut. My thoughts never stopped, nor did they vary. On one side of the breach in my mind they dealt with all my long envy, my hatred, the sense of power lent me by my secret knowledge; on the other they dealt with fear and the future and the wonder how best to turn this situation to advantage.

And all the time the arrangements went forward—

smoothly—as Sorrel's arrangements always would. Cobbitt, of course was to have sole charge of the office and each month he was to make an allowance for household expenses which was to be controlled by Mrs Fennigard. Down to the very detail of replacing the children's clothes it was all mapped and planned. Sorrel hardly slept at all. I knew, for I was wakeful, too, wondering, worrying.

But at last, a bare two days before the *Mirabella* was due to sail, I made up my mind exactly what to do and say. I had not another moment to lose; and yet I thought I had, after all, chosen my occasion well, because it left Sorrel too little time to change her mind or plan any form of retaliation. I was waiting to ask her to speak to me after supper, in private, when she actually leaned forward and said with that cool politeness which can be worse than rudeness:

"Marian, would it be convenient for you to speak to me after supper? In the study." Once again I had the queer feeling that she could see clean through me.

There was a leaping fire of logs in the grate, a good supply of new candles, and on the table by the fire a coffee tray set for two. So, although she had consulted my convenience she had made her plan before asking me. Well, I had made mine, too.

She poured the cofee and set down, her feet on the fender, her skirt drawn up at the knee so that six or eight inches of leg and ankle, shapely but too thin for beauty, showed above her little black velvet shoes. The light was full on her face, and as I looked at her my last doubt vanished. Despite the capricious appetite and the grief and the recent over-working, her face had taken on a fuller, more mature look. And the fullness of her breast was no longer due entirely to the fluting of her gown above the girdle. There was a change in the eyes, too, indescribable in terms of expression, yet unmistakably. I thought back—ten weeks or a little more since Miss Lou's death. . . . Very soon, for anyone but lucky Sorrel Kingaby, the future would begin to present a problem.

"I wanted to speak to you about Dinah, Marian. It is a great comfort to me to know that you will be here, because she is very fond of you, and you can influence her, being young yourself, without making her rebellious. Do you think she is precocious?"

"No. After all, she is sixteen this year."

"Yes. She'll be grown up before I get back. And I am just a trifle worried. About young Groatan, you know."

That was a surprise, neither Dinah nor I had any notion that the little boy-and-girl affair between them, in which I played the part of sympathetic adviser and confidante, could possibly have come to Sorrel's notice. Before I could speak Sorrel went on, "You knew about it." But she did not say it accusingly.

"It's nothing," I said. "Mere calf-love on his side and flattered vanity on hers."

"Of course. The only thing is this—suppose, it develops, or something else of the same kind crops up, as it well may, I want you to hold yourself responsible, Marian. I've made every arrangement for the girls that I can possibly think of; I have even visualized the possibility of Dinah's marriage, and have gone into the question of a settlement with Mr Raikes. But I want you to see that she doesn't do anything—well, foolish —at a time when a girl most needs a mother. . . .

Make certain that what happens to Dinah is what you would wish, in time, to happen to your Clarabel. That's all. It may sound fussy, but she is attractive—she has you to thank for that, largely—and not oversensible. I do feel rather concerned about leaving her for so long just now. Still, if you will use your enormous influence, for *good* . . ." She emphasized the last word as though she suspected me of the capacity for doing otherwise. And suddenly the whole situation, her appeal to me, her concern for Dinah, this attempt to act the moralist, combined with what I knew, struck me as so exquisitely, ludicrously funny, that I laughed and laughed.

When at last I could stop I found Sorrel gazing at me steadily, gravely, and with doubt.

"Was that amusing?" she asked.

"In a minute I'll tell you just how amusing," I said. "You know, Sorrel, any other person to whom you confided your fears and anxieties about your sister might ask why, in the circumstances, you have decided to leave her, and the others, in the care of a senile old woman, a stupid stepmother and an ex-governess whom you don't really trust. I can spare you that question, because you see, I know the answer. I know why you are going on the *Mirabella*. Because you hope, by that means, to bear Dan Culver's child without anyone here being any the wiser. No, wait! Let me finish. It's your turn to listen now. It *is* a clever plan. No one without the knowledge that I happen to have could possibly see through it. Nobody would suspect the clever, wonderful, level-headed Miss Kingaby of being a smuggler's mistress, would they? A short time ago you mentioned my Clarabel. Her future is my concern, and I have already begun to give it thought. If you go away on Thursday, as you intend, and don't come back; or if you come back and take a fancy to turn us out, she and I would be beggars. Jamie Brooke, for all his Kingaby blood, is a poor sort of fellow upon whom I have no wish to be dependent. Now, if you put all those things together, and remember what I know and what I want, and act wisely, you can carry out your own plan, depending upon my everlasting silence. I'll even throw in the assurance that Dinah shall be watched as though she were my own."

I had kept my eyes on her face, and throughout my speech she had stared straight back at me, her green eyes set in the wide, helpless look with which a rabbit is said to regard a stoat. And although she had not changed colour, being already so pale, the contour of her face seemed to have altered before my eyes, growing hard, hollow, lined, until it might have been the death mask of an old, old woman, who had once been Sorrel Kingaby.

Something had touched her at last; and I had been there to see. In this one moment, while she stared at me, dumbstruck, I was avenged for all the rending envy that she had roused in me, for all the careless insulting kindnesses, for Jamie's inward disloyalty. Sheer joy rose in me; oh, more than joy! The kind of feeling that can come, I should think only once in a lifetime, the wild, dizzy mad zest of knowing that at last you have the whiphand, and that pride and power are helpless before you.

She gave me ample time to taste triumph before she said, between lips that moved stiffly, "And what price do you put on your silence?"

Although I had been prepared with my terms I had expected first to be met by protestation and reproach, even denial. I was a little startled by this matter-of-fact acceptance of my accusation; but I was ready. "First of all, an allowance for my lifetime. I'm not rapacious. Three hundred pounds a year will enable me to live where I choose, comfortably. That, and a thousand pounds to Clarabel upon her coming of age, or marrying, is, I hope you will agree, not exorbitant, especially in view of the fact that her father was your father's son."

She said, quite irrelevantly, I thought, "You've always hated me, haven't you, Marian?"

"This being our evening for truthful speaking," I said, "I will own that I have always thought you had too much for one woman."

"A situation that you are doing your best to remedy."

"That is one way of putting it. I think you must admit that I am offering you the one commodity you can hardly afford to refuse."

"Your silence?"

"Yes. Well, what is your answer? Will you see Mr Raikes to-morrow and have the settlement drawn up in legal fashion?"

"I will see him to-morrow," she said. "It means making a new will, as well."

She rose, slowly, and a little stiffly, smoothed down her skirt with an automatic action, and went to the desk on the far side of the room. From a locked drawer she took a sheet of stiff parchment paper and unfolded it. She studied the writing upon its inner side for a moment, and a hard little smile drew sharp lines at the corners of her mouth.

"Like most people," she said, "you overestimate my wealth and minimize my commitments. Three hundred pounds is more than I should spend on myself in five years. Still, that is neither here nor there. I had gone into the question very thoroughly and left you what I thought I could afford—but of course that is useless now." Her long thin fingers wrestled with the stiff paper for a moment, trying to tear it, but it resisted her stoutly, and, finally, crossing to the fire she bent down and dropped it into the heart of the fire. Watching the corners curl in the heat, she asked, in a conversational tone of voice:

"How did you know about Dan and me?"

I hesitated. I was not going to admit that night of watching; spying is an ugly word. Moreover, I had, within the last few seconds, felt my power ebbing away. As she had unlocked the drawer of the desk I had thought—Yes, after all has been said and done, the money *will* save her. She can buy my silence and her own immunity and emerge the winner, despite everything. And with the thought my hatred, momentarily appeased, had stirred again. I had not hurt her enough, yet. So now, after a moment's hesitation, I said, as though unwillingly:

"Need we discuss that?"

"It would interest me to know."

"Well then . . . he told me himself. You see, he and I . . ."

She shot me one glance and then, staring back at the fire, said:

"All right. You need not explain. He was like

the rest of you, no better, no worse." A strong rigor shook her and I saw her hands tighten spasmodically upon the mantelpiece. I was a little frightened. There must be a limit to what even she could bear . . . perhaps that last lie. And in her state . . . suppose something happened, a fit, a stroke, before that new will and the settlement were drawn. I half rose from my chair. "Can I get you anything?" I asked.

She said, in a quiet normal voice, "No thank you. Sit down, Marian, and listen while I tell you something." She propped one elbow on the mantelpiece and half turned towards me. "Perhaps for your own peace of mind, before you envy another person as you seem to have envied me, you should ask yourself what he has, or what she has, when you come to essential things. Consider me. What have I really had? After seven unhappy years, the possession of a business which was almost wrecked before I inherited it; and with it a house full of mouths and grasping hands. I suppose Jamie confided in you, too, so you know that my first love was, by a miracle of misfortune, my own half-brother, who used his knowledge to make a fool of me and get money for himself. The second man I cared for was, by your own showing, no better, a handsome vulgar fellow who traded in love as I trade in tea. The children were fond of me once because I saved them from Baildon. As they forget Baildon they turn from me. Apart from Lou, God rest her soul, has anyone ever bothered to ask whether I were tired, discouraged, in need of comfort? Not one. All along it has been Sorrel arrange this, settle that, provide the other thing. And now, when I have settled, arranged and provided to the best of my ability, you, whom I took in, you who have hated me while you shared all I had, come to me with the voice and face of an enemy, demanding blackmail. Ask yourself, am I so enviable?"

I could say nothing. Only I remembered Jamie's passionate denial of the knowledge imputed to him; I remembered my own recent lie. Men had, in truth, dealt with her less harshly than she thought. But women . . .

"I've tried," she went on in that same quiet voice which, nevertheless, had a ring of doom in it, as though she were addressing, not me, but Fate itself. And I suddenly remembered reading, long before, a definition of tragedy—Tragedy is the defeat of man by the gods. "I've tried. God knows where I made my mistakes. But, always excepting Lou, not one of the people about me has been faithful, or loyal, or even kind. No, they say, she has a shilling, so we will take half of it, and we will at the same time rob her of everything that makes for happiness; love, friendship, reputation. Yet there are men who have so much more and are not envied so cruelly. It seems to me that a woman may have only one thing of her own. . . ."

There was a silence during which she stared at the fire and I stared at her. This was an attempt, I thought, to talk me round, to get on my soft side, to ease the bargain. And, I thought, although I have never been in business, I can show you how to drive a bargain, my lady.

"Well," I said, "despite all this sorry talk you seem to me to have more than one thing of your own. What other woman in your position could hope to hide her shame? We all have our troubles, and you can get out of yours *providing* you help me out of mine. May I regard that as settled?"

"One thing of her own," she repeated, looking at the fire. Then suddenly she swung round to face me, and for the second time I was startled by the change in her. The stricken look had passed. The old, stubborn, battling expression which I knew and hated had taken its place.

"I'm afraid not," she said. She stared down at me, and her eyes were as cold and hard as green glass. She set her hands upon her thickening but still slender waist. "I may have been failed by my friends, but my enemies have served me well. You, Marian, have shown me in less than half an hour what all the thought in the world hadn't shown me. When I think of it . . . I was running away, hiding . . . at the mercy of every babbling tongue, every hungry eye. For the sake of respectability and the family name and the fear of gossip, and a hundred things that don't matter a snap of the fingers, I was going to throw away the one thing that might be mine. Which shall *be* mine! Since every hand and tongue and mind are against me, mine shall be against them. And as God's in heaven I'll breed a new man, fit to share what I intend to have. And I'll do it in the sight of all the tattling fools, without another thought. You shall be the one to go, Marian. To-morrow. Sam shall drive you as far as Baildon. What happens to you after is your concern. I shall stay here, where my son can be born in the house that will belong to him. And I shall have something of my own at last."

It seemed to me that there was a maniacal glitter in her eyes. She looked mad. She sounded mad. I wanted to say something: something that would bring her to her senses, but my mouth had gone dry. And when I thought of to-morrow my throat was closed by the fluttering of my heart. I did move my lips in some sort of protest, but no sound came. She nodded her head towards the door in contemptuous dismissal and, swinging round, seated herself at her desk. The squeak of her hard-driven quill followed me to the doorway, and after I had closed the door behind me I could still hear it for a moment. It was the only sound in all the silent house.

Epilogue

It was in 1937, just before the creeping shadow leapt forward to engulf the world, that I heard the name Kingaby for the first time. I heard it in a railway carriage, in which I was travelling to Bywater in order to spend a week-end with a friend who had taken a house there for the summer. The only other occupant of the carriage was a middle-aged, well-dressed woman with an intelligent and kindly face. We fell into conversation with an ease which would have dismayed those critics who deplore the reticence of the English race.

In the course of this conversation she mentioned that she was Headmistress of the Kingaby School for Girls, and that her holiday was being interrupted by the need to return to Bywater in order to meet some members of the Board of Education who were to inspect the premises prior to the taking over of the school as a Government concern.

"It's a great pity," she said, rather sadly, "it's such a very old foundation—for a girls' school, I mean, naturally—and has done some excellent work. But we could no longer afford to remain independent. Money value has depreciated since our Founder's day, and although we have tried various shifts we have been, quite reluctantly, driven to accept the Board as a last prop."

"Will it make so much difference?" I asked, aware of the regret in her voice.

"Not perhaps to my position. Indeed, the reverse: Burnham Scales and other delights. . . ." Her smile was wry. "I just don't like to see the old things passing.

Perhaps I am reactionary. Besides, I don't really think that the Government policy in education is satisfactory. . . ."

We gave one another our views upon this and sundry other subjects. The train drew in at the little station; we parted, and I forgot for some hours that I had heard the name Kingaby.

The church at Bywater had, besides its unusual round tower, leper squints and remains of pre-Cromwellian glass, some faint traces of wall paintings which had survived the application of Reformation whitewash. I spent the whole of a long hot sunny morning poking about in its cool, rather dusty shadows. When I emerged by the north door I chanced to glance to the side and saw, so near to the church wall that they seemed to be nestling between two buttresses, a number of tombs and headstones from which the name Kingaby leaped at me with what was, for the moment, puzzling familiarity. Then I remembered my acquaintance in the train and began to study the inscriptions with some interest.

They warranted little. There were none of the curious, amusing, or touching sentences which are so often the reward of a moment's deciphering; there were no texts, no detailed account of impossible virtues, no confessions of heavenly hopes. A reticent family, I thought, and singularly faithful to the name Josiah, which was here recorded as being borne by no less than six of them. At the end of the row, on a stone so low and plain that I thought it must have been a child's, was the bald inscription, "Sorrel Kingaby. Born A.D. 1781. Died A.D. 1865." A longish life, I thought idly, turning away, and one which covered an interesting period. This Kingaby, male or female, the strange name gave no indication, lived through the French Revolution, saw the introduction of the railway and the telegraph, witnessed perhaps greater changes in manners and customs and ways of living than any other eighty years could show. And with that trite thought I dismissed the Kingaby family for the second time, and went in search of lunch.

About a hundred yards from the church gate I came face to face with my train acquaintance, the headmistress. She greeted me cordially and, looking over my shoulder towards the church, asked, "Have you been looking at my Kingabys?"

"Incidentally."

"Well, yes, of course. To the impartial observer there are more interesting things. I tend to forget that. I've just got rid of my Committee, and was actually on my way to put this on the grave. During term time the girls see to it; but during the holidays it gets neglected, I'm afraid. Still . . . since I had to come back . . ." She glanced, rather shame-facedly I thought at the little potted rose she carried in her arms. It had six blooms, just at the perfect stage, and dark, glossy foliage.

"Are you busy?" she inquired.

"On the search for lunch," I confessed. "My friend likes to work on and ignore the meal."

"Come with me to dispose of this," she said impulsively. "And then come and lunch with me, if you will. I'd enjoy showing you the place."

"I should enjoy seeing it."

We turned back, and I watched while she set the lovely little tree against the plain head-stone and removed a length of straw, a spent match, and a dead dandelion head from the grave itself.

"She was an interesting woman," she said, as though in self-defence. "I've never had time to find out much about her—if it is there to find out—and in term time I hardly have leisure even for speculation. But I do sometimes wonder about her life and how it happened that as long ago as 1830 she had such sound, such modern ideas about girls' education."

I looked back to make sure of the date. "She set up the school in her lifetime, then?"

"Yes. In her fiftieth year. She had amassed by that time what was a big fortune for those days."

"Amassed. By what means?"

"Ordinary, legitimate trade. She inherited a business, worked at it just like a man, vastly increased it, and made a fortune. Oh, quite unusual, I assure you."

And still my laggard interest did not quicken. Miss Rennison, however, was undaunted; but, like the excellent teacher that I am sure she was, she did not flog the subject. She showed me over the building, pointing out the original Jacobean house which had been the Founder's home, and which had remained almost unaltered. It had been large enough to house the original school. That was architecturally a pity, for additions in 1830 might have been more sightly than those made as they were needed thirty, fifty and sixty-four years later.

During our inspection, and throughout the excellent meal, we talked on several subjects, with a tendency to revert to Miss Rennison's poor opinion of national education. "Sloppy," she said. "A fatal arrangement of responsibility without authority. So hopelessly undisciplined. They will not understand that you can spend all the money in the world, and all the effort, and goodwill—without discipline the whole thing is lost, a waste."

"Is the discipline harsh here?" I asked boldly. I had a vision of a hard-faced spinster, a business woman before her time, laying down rules which, at the risk of financial loss, must not be swerved from.

"Not at all. The easiest I have ever known. But sensible, sane. Oh, I see what you are thinking. No, they were my own ideas I was expressing. I can just imagine what it will be like hereafter, with a swarm of ex-elementary children ruining the garden, cheeking the staff and making the lavatories messy."

It was to take her mind off this grievance that I asked:

"What more do you know of this Sorrel Kingaby?"

"I told you, all too little. She conducted business in an office and warehouse which is now the gymnasium and cookery room. She had the most lavish ideas about diet and free time and taking walks. And there *was* a fund, it vanished before my time, for supplying pocket-money, and even for replacing faulty clothing. Imagine that . . . and then remember 'Jane Eyre.' And the ground rents of a row of shops in the Square were to go to a special thing called the Holiday Fund, so that any unfortunate who hadn't a home to go to could stay here and be taken to the threatre at Baildon, or a day trip to Colchester. Oh, she was very human, I assure you." She rose. "I'll show you her portrait. I locked it away at the end of term."

She took me into her own bedroom, a room at the top of the stairs in the old part of the house.

"I like to think that this would be her room," she said, with the same deprecating air, half earnest, half mocking at her own obsession. From a cupboard on one side of the fireplace she took a picture, small, two feet by two and a half, perhaps, in a narrow plain frame. She carried it to the light of the window.

"It's amateur work. Dated the year of Trafalgar . . . she'd be twenty-four."

It *was* amateur work; but whoever the amateur had been, he or she had had an eye for colour, and, which is rarer, for character. If there is such a contradictory quality as wistful pugnacity that little portrait had it. It showed a pale face, with sharp planes on cheek and brow, a childish arrangement of reddish curls, cold green eyes which looked prepared to see through any artifice, and, if necessary, stare out the devil himself, and—incongruous feature—above a chin like a stubborn baby's, a most beautiful, soft, full-curved, generous mouth. The whole head was gracefully set upon a thin neck that ran down to narrow square shoulders which, as soon as they were suggested, were lost in the dark background.

I said, not without surprise, "But she was very attractive." (I nearly added, "Not the sort to turn school-marm," but mercifully remembered myself in time.) "As pretty as that, well-to-do, in a time when men were plentiful. . . . I wonder she didn't marry."

"Too busy," said Miss Rennison, in a voice which told me a great deal about her at last. She held the picture against her chest for a moment and brooded. "As a matter of fact," she said, with the air of making a rather dangerous confession, "there is one old man in

Bywater who claims to know a great deal about her.
He's eighty or more, deaf as a beetle and very surly. I
tried to talk to him once, but he told me such a ram-
bling wild tale about illegitimate brothers, or sons, and
smugglers and aunts and governesses that I gave him
up as a bad job. A pity, because he might have been
a link. I think he did actually *see* her once, when he
was a child and she was a very old lady in a low carriage. The rest, of course, is gossip, or pure fabrica-
tion." Her voice hardened and she looked, almost lov-
ingly, at the little portrait before putting it back in the
cupboard and carefully locking the door. "Anyhow, I
may be silly; but I prefer to keep my illusions—or
rather to depend upon my own imagination instead of
old Middleditch's."

She spoke the name with rancour; I noted it with
care. But I said, soothingly, "After all, in a matter of
this kind one guess is as good as another, isn't it?"

She looked comforted, and smiled at me. "Exactly.
You know I *am* glad I met you. I have so enjoyed
showing you round and talking to you. One so seldom
finds a kindred spirit."

I thanked her for the pleasure, which, I assured her,
the visit had afforded me; but inwardly I denied the
expression "kindred spirit." Sorrel Kingaby's ideas
upon diet, healthful recreation, and suitable studies
for girls had left me entirely unmoved. But the tags
and shreds which dear Miss Rennison had obviously
so resented upon the old man's tongue had struck
an immediately responsive note in my quite different
mind. Already I was impatient to seek out the old
fellow and hear his story for myself. But I concealed

both my new interest and my impatience from the well-meaning idealist who would, I knew, deplore them both.

There were fourteen separate families of Middleditches in Bywater, and they boasted between them ten old men of seventy years or more. My weekend had already extended to five days before I had tracked down the one I wanted. He had the face of an elderly cherub, pink and white and placid, with a toothless mouth which gave him a wildly deceptive artless smile and a beguilingly childish lisp. He was, beneath this attractive exterior one of the rudest men I have ever encountered, and quite the greediest. He knew in an instant that he had something which I wanted, and he levied stern tribute in terms of strong black shag tobacco, a beverage known as 'alf-an-'alf, and a peculiarly virulent peppermint which could be scented at a hundred yards.

Sometimes he could remember nothing at all; at others he was stone deaf: now and again when a story was going well and my interest fiercely alight he would lapse into Essex speech, so individual and so plentifully sprinkled with outlandish words that I lost the thread of his narrative.

I listened to long, irrelevant stories, which, since they dealt with the memories of both his father and grandfather, covered the greater part of two centuries. But I held on, and every now and then the wide field of his verbiage would yield an ear worth the gleaning.

He was no Trader Horn, and I cannot pretend that these stories were mined from the old man's memories.

On only a few points was he quite clear and unshakably certain. He *had* seen Sorrel:

"Little nipper I wuz, 'bout as high as sixpennorth o' coppers. An' she worn't much bigger, little ole bit of a thing taking a airing in her carriage. I recollect my ole dad saying, 'There she goo, the ole faggot what flung a parful lot o' good chaps outa work when she shut up the business so's some bits o' gals could hev schoolin'.' Mighty bitter they wuz against her at the time. There worn't no wonder in Bywater then as to why her boy took off an' left her."

"But he'd gone long before she gave up the business," I said cautiously.

"Ar, so he had. And there wuz them as wuz sorry for her on that account. Me ole grandad what worked in her very own office usta say if it had bin one of his lads turned out so bad he'd a 'flayed him. But then, there wuz bad blood in him from the start. A smuggling dad and a brazen hussy for his mum, how'd they think he'd turn out? An' spoiled from the first breath he drew inta the bargain?"

"What happened to him?"

"Nobuddy knew. Come to no good, I bet. Me peppermints is done agin."

I took from my bag the awaited packet and apologized for the delay. Over his bulging cheek the old man's translucent blue eyes regarded me slyly.

"I bin wonderin'," he mumbled through the impediment, "whether you mightn' be some connection. Never see anybuddy so interested in them ole tales as you."

"No," I said. "I can trace my family straight back to the Civil Wars. There's no connection."

The peppermints were having a sweetening influence. He actually apologized! "No offence meant. I just bin wonderin'. That there school teacher I could understand. Like a lot o' others she bin using ole Sorrel's money. But why you bother about the ole tales puzzles me."

It puzzled me, too. For more than a week I had walked about in a kind of dream, peopled by men and women, long since dead—Jamie who ran away with the governess; the old lady who died on the night of the ambush; the smuggler whose son a respectable woman bore without shame or apology. Most of all, of course, I thought, speculated, and dreamed about Sorrel herself. And I wondered for a little while why the end of the story interested me so much less than the earlier part. I had experienced no disappointment when my question as to what happened to the son drew a blank, "Nobuddy knew." Then I realized that with his birth, and Sorrel's brazening it out, the story, for me, stopped. She would bring him up, and spoil him; he would disappoint her and go away; she would make a fortune and found her school; but her own development would be finished, the decisions would all have been made, the adventures survived, the final moulding cast.

And so out of bits and pieces I could gather, out of my own imaginings and speculations, I built up a picture and a story, combining perhaps as much of truth and of error as Miss Rennison's idea of a chaste educationist, or Middleditch's memory of an "ole faggot." After all, how much nearer, even with much documentary evidence, can we come to understanding any one of the myriad dead who have gone to their graves, carrying their real secrets, of motive and essence and personality, into the silence with them?